HOW I MET M
& other stories

At the same time I was conscious that my prospects of finding her were slim; the combined population of the five countries which divided us was 886 million, and it might be difficult to spot a matelot T-shirt in the throng. Nor did her message give more than the barest indication of her plans in India. She had told me that she intended whenever possible to avoid large cities, so I guessed that as soon as her bus reached Delhi she'd set off again south for Rajasthan. I spent the entire taxi journey back to Ankara, and the four-hour flight to Delhi the next day, second-guessing her route. Whenever I looked down at the ground from the aeroplane I became discouraged. Iran and then Pakistan spread out beneath us in massive folds of yellow and grey, and if you looked carefully you could just see the reflection of the sun glinting on the roofs of tiny cars and buses driving along interminable empty roads. Why would Anna not leave the bus at any one of the hundreds of hamlets I could see below me – or at a fort, she said she'd always wanted to see forts. And yet if she reached Delhi I felt it was possible, just possible, to predict her course.

Also by Nicholas Coleridge

Around the World in 78 Days
Shooting Stars
The Fashion Conspiracy

How I Met My Wife
& OTHER STORIES

NICHOLAS COLERIDGE

Mandarin

A Mandarin Paperback
HOW I MET MY WIFE & OTHER STORIES

First published in Great Britain 1991
by William Heinemann Ltd
This edition published 1992
by Mandarin Paperbacks
Michelin House, 81 Fulham Road, London SW3 6RB

Mandarin is an imprint of the Octopus Publishing Group,
a division of Reed International Books Limited

Copyright © Nicholas Coleridge 1991
The author has asserted his moral rights

A version of 'How I Met My Wife'
was first published in *Cosmopolitan* in 1986,
and a version of *The Spendthrift*
first appeared in *Company* in 1987.

A CIP catalogue record for this title
is available from the British Library
ISBN 0 7493 1224 6

Printed and bound in Great Britain
by Cox & Wyman Ltd, Reading, Berks

To Georgia

Contents

Introduction

It took me six years to write these fourteen short stories. Because I have always had a job working in the urgent world of magazines, they were mostly written on holiday, which partly explains why nine of them are set abroad. But looking back at my longhand manuscripts, I now notice a peculiar thing. Few of the stories were actually written in the foreign countries in which they are set. I see that I was writing 'The Man Who Loved Driving', a story set in Turkey, from the improbable vantage point of Jabalpur in Madhya Pradesh. 'The Big Game Hunters of Detroit', which mostly takes place near Jabalpur in Madhya Pradesh, was written in Tuscany. 'The Swaffham Madonna', set in Tuscany, was written while driving across Turkey.

'Lucky Beggars', which is a story about an English couple with small children on holiday in Sri Lanka, I wrote in Sri Lanka's maximum security jail in Colombo, where I had been hilariously imprisoned on suspicion of being an international Tamil terrorist spy. I am still grateful to the Governor of Colombo prison who ensured that I was undisturbed for hours at a time so that I could concentrate.

None of the stories in this collection is wholly true. Most are inventions; the two or three stories with their genesis in real events have been so elaborately distorted that any resemblance, as they say, between a character in the book and any living person is almost entirely coincidental. This is especially true of the story called 'How I Met My Wife', which happily had an altogether different ending in real life.

Various people gave me technical advice about this and that, which I sometimes ignored when it compromised the story. Anthony and Ewa Lewis tried to put me right on legal procedure. John Hatt and Melissa Colston were helpful on the subject of Indian tigers. Jake Brunner provided me with information about satellites. Napier Miles contributed a further twist to the story called 'Legal Tender'. Anthony Gardner and Ysenda Maxtone Graham read some early drafts. Linda Kelsey and Maggie Goodman published stories by me in their magazines which was wildly encouraging.

I am as ever enormously grateful to Leslie Gardner, my literary agent, and Helen Fraser and everybody else at William Heinemann. I would particularly like to thank Julia Elliott, who typed and retyped these stories so brilliantly until she virtually knew them by heart, and Georgia Coleridge for her unfailing enthusiasm and good ideas.

HOW I
MET MY WIFE

One summer's afternoon in 1984 I strolled into my old office in Carnaby Street. I had had lunch at an oyster bar, avoided poisoning and was feeling unusually reckless. Crouching behind my desk, where she was tidying a filing cabinet, was a most beautiful girl in a matelot T-shirt. She had perfect smooth white skin, enormous green eyes, and a wonderfully enthusiastic smile that made my heart leap. She explained that she was temping in the office for one day only, before flying to Turkey to go backpacking for six months. It was her year out before university. We talked about Turkey, a country I know well, and how she might head further east to India. I wrote out a list of books that she should take with her, and novelists she must read – Naipaul, Kipling, Rose Tremain – if she was to understand the countries at all. It took me a couple of days – by which time she was already in Istanbul – to realise that I badly wanted to see Anna again.

I thought about her constantly and experienced all the classic symptoms of being in love: stumbling across her Christian name in newspapers, imagining I saw her across restaurants, looking up when something happening in Turkey was mentioned on the evening news. To be surrounded by old friends became oppressive, to be alone morbid. I found it impossible to get a picture of her out of my mind, alone and adrift in Asia.

There followed a fortnight of detective work. From the personnel department at my office I discovered Anna's secretarial agency. From the agency I obtained her home address.

She lived with her parents in Fulham – not far from my own house, I discovered when I drove past. When I rang them they were in, and helpful, and told me what they knew of Anna's itinerary in Turkey. There was a poste restante address in Erzurum in eastern Turkey where they were writing to her, to await collection, but they didn't expect her to reach Erzurum for a couple of weeks. In an atlas I plotted her likely route. She had told me she was going to visit first the classical sites down the west coast – Troy, Ephesus, Pergamum, Priene – then the early Christian cave churches in Cappadocia. If she intended to reach Erzurum by the end of the month she must keep moving fast. She had told me she'd be taking the *Lonely Planet* guidebook to Turkey for its list of cheap, clean hotels – students and overlanders call it the Bible – and I bought a copy, and sat it next to the atlas and her mother's rough itinerary, and made a guess at where she was. If she'd arrived in Izmir on the 17th she would have visited Ephesus the next morning, the 18th, caught an evening bus to Denizli, stayed till the 20th ... and so on and so on. There were many variables. But eventually I settled on four possible towns, each with a choice of hotels, nine places in all. The next morning I discovered their telex numbers – those that had telex numbers, two didn't – from the Turkish tourist office in Hanover Street, and fired seven identical messages from my office into Cappadocia. The wording was nonchalant: 'Am likely to be in the area next week to research travel article. Any chance of a drink?'

As soon as I had sent them, I saw how slim – how preposterous – was the likelihood of Anna ever receiving one. But three days later a reply came back: 'Have just arrived and found your message. What a surprise. How on earth do you know where I'm staying? Will probably be here for four more days. Hope to see you if your work brings you here. Turkey is wonderful.'

I bought an air ticket and flew to Istanbul. A good thing about being a journalist is having a watertight excuse to go anywhere on a whim, without arousing suspicion, and offsetting the cost by writing a couple of articles. Istanbul is less than halfway to Cappadocia, so I took the overnight train to

Ankara and then a bus south-east past the lakes to Kayseri and then a rambunctious taxi to the hotel at Urgup. The journey from Ankara took twenty hours, but in a curious way it made little impression on me. I was incredibly calm. By now I could barely remember what Anna looked like, only that being with her was in some way vastly important, and so I sat in the taxi with my luggage at my feet and played clock patience on the back seat.

Anna's hotel was on the outskirts of the town, and consisted of two floors of rooms leading off open corridors above a pudding shop. There was a small reception area, none too clean, with a beige vinyl sofa on which were sitting three Dutch or German backpackers counting their money. The whole place smelt slightly of drains and cologne. Through a door behind the reception I could see an enormous grey telex machine – it was as big as a fridge – and it seemed nothing less than a miracle that my message could ever have got here. Sitting behind the desk was a misshapen Turk with a rheumy eye, who was intent on altering the plastic numbers on a special black plastic pinboard showing the exchange rate for traveller's cheques in various currencies.

'I am looking for an English girl called Anna who is staying here,' I said. 'Do you know which is her room number?' I longed for her to be in – the keys for half the rooms were dangling behind him from a wall of hooks.

The misshapen Turk raised his eyes to heaven and muttered '*Yok*' – no – and returned to his pinboard.

'Look,' I said, 'I know there's a girl called Anna staying here. English girl. I received a telex.' I rummaged for the precious message in my luggage. The Turk shrugged.

And then, protruding from a cubbyhole beneath his desk, I saw my name. Elation, my own name written in a girl's handwriting, a message for me here. I took it, unfolded it. It said: 'Dear Nicholas. I doubt you'll read this because you'll never find this hole of a hotel, but just in case, I'm afraid I've already left for India because I suddenly got the chance of a cheap bus ticket to Delhi (hooray!). I've always wanted to see Rajasthan etc. – forts, Taj Mahal, Lake Palace etc. Hope your article goes well. Love, Anna.'

3

Cappadocia to India takes five days by bus, and I could see from the date on Anna's letter that she'd left three days earlier. The nearest airport was Ankara, and if I took a taxi all the way I might make it in fourteen hours, and try to get a flight to India the following afternoon. It did not occur to me to abandon the chase, or even that my pursuit might irritate her. I had a fortnight to spare and enough money, and seeing Anna again had become a fixation. So long as there was a further clue, I would follow it up.

At the same time I was conscious that my prospects of finding her were slim; the combined population of the five countries which divided us was 886 million, and it might be difficult to spot a matelot T-shirt in the throng. Nor did her message give more than the barest indication of her plans in India. She had told me that she intended whenever possible to avoid large cities, so I guessed that as soon as her bus reached Delhi she'd set off again south for Rajasthan. I spent the entire taxi journey back to Ankara, and the four-hour flight to Delhi the next day, second-guessing her route. Whenever I looked down at the ground from the aeroplane I became discouraged. Iran and then Pakistan spread out beneath us in massive folds of yellow and grey, and if you looked carefully you could just see the reflection of the sun glinting on the roofs of tiny cars and buses driving along interminable empty roads. Why would Anna not leave the bus at any one of the hundreds of hamlets I could see below me – or at a fort, she said she'd always wanted to see forts. And yet if she reached Delhi I felt it was possible, just possible, to predict her course. On her first trip to India she'd surely head first for somewhere she'd heard of: Agra and the Taj Mahal seemed the likeliest, or Jaipur and the Amber Palace. Agra was the most probable, but I wouldn't go there for a simple reason. By the time I arrived in Delhi Anna would still have a day's start on me. Assuming she headed for Agra, she wouldn't spend more than two days there seeing the Taj and Fatehpur Sikri. Then she'd be sure to move west to Jaipur. If on the other hand she chose to go straight to Jaipur, she'd spend more time there, I reckoned, so I'd be able to catch her up. Catch her up or head her off. I became convinced Jaipur was Anna's destination.

My taxi from Delhi took four hours. I arrived hot and exasperated. I had not eaten or slept properly since leaving my flat in London sixty-two hours before. I took a room in the budget hotel most glowingly recommended by the *Lonely Planet* guide, and crashed out. By the time I awoke, according to the reception boy, Anna had checked in on another floor.

My presence, I saw at once, was going to be difficult to explain. The travel article excuse could not be used twice. Nobody, however little they knew about journalism, could swallow a double coincidence of such proportions. I realised I was in danger of looking uncool.

I crept downstairs for breakfast on the verandah and adopted a strategic position behind the *Hindustan Times*. The air was heavy with cinnamon and garam masala. I picked at toast spread with cherry jam and waited for Anna: not eagerly but with dread. My meeting with her at the office had been so short and inconsequential, it seemed nothing short of insane that I should be sitting on a bamboo chair in an hotel in Jaipur, seven thousand miles away, cowering behind a newspaper.

The Imperial is a bustling hotel. There are more than a hundred rooms and few people stay for longer than two nights. The other guests were for the most part Europeans: backpackers passing through. They had the pinched look of overlanders who had eaten poorly for a long time, and I hoped that Anna's expression had lost none of its freshness in the three weeks she'd been away.

My concern was unnecessary: I recognised her at once. Her smile was as open and warm as before. She sat down at the table next to mine, so that we were separated only by the width of a sheet of newsprint. I heard her order breakfast. 'Tea, mango juice, porridge and scrambled eggs for two.'

For two!

A gangling youth loped on to the verandah. 'Christ, Anna,' he said, 'what a hassle. I'd lost one of my socks at the bottom of our bed.'

'Well, at least we've arrived,' said Anna, 'and on our own at last. It really freaked me when that man almost turned up in Turkey. He pretended to be a real expert on travelling, but I bet he was secretly trying to pick me up.'

THE
MANCHU HORSE

When Ken Witts sold his contract office cleaning business and made a packet, he didn't see why he shouldn't experience some of life's little luxuries. But since he had spent his first fifty-six years becoming a rich man, and knew that the rich are habitually taken for a ride, he was determined to experience luxury on his own terms.

'There are two prices for everything in this world, my friend,' he enjoyed saying. 'There's the price you're asked, and the price you're prepared to pay. All I ask for is the second price.'

Nineteen times out of twenty he got it, too. He was a relentless bargainer, and seldom went anywhere without putting up a special proposition. He insisted on discounts in places where it never occurred to others to ask for one. Most people are too squeamish or too proud to negotiate the price of a suite in an hotel. Ken Witts wasn't. As soon as he'd seen a suite he liked (and he was diligent about viewing every available one) he sought out the general manager.

'Now listen here, my friend,' he would say, 'I think we can do business together, you and I. You have a suite on the sixth floor of your hotel that's unoccupied, and I have a good mind to take it for a week. The only problem is the price. Your helpful little lady at reception tells me the room is £210 a night not including breakfast, which sounds steep to me. Now I'm prepared to give you £140 a night, cash. Do we have a deal?'

Sometimes the general manager would reply sarcastically, 'I

regret we don't barter at the Palace, sir. The price of our suites is exactly as you were advised.'

Then Witts would become angry. 'Don't get starchy with me, sonny,' he'd say. 'Everything's negotiable in this world. They told me at the front desk you've got eight vacant suites. What are you telling me? That you're turning down nine hundred quid for nothing? That you want me to stay at the Regal up the road? Is that what you're saying?'

It was remarkable how compelling this logic seemed to be, and how often Ken Witts got his way.

'Providing you don't mention it to any of our other guests, sir, I think we might be able to accommodate you at the rate you propose.'

'That's fine by me, friend,' replied Ken Witts, 'providing you throw in the breakfast.'

The funny thing was, that when he finally got the suite he wanted, he didn't really enjoy it much. He had little taste, and no feeling for creature comforts. Huge marble bathrooms gave him no pleasure, and if you asked him to describe his bedroom he wouldn't have a clue what colour his bedcover or the curtains were, or whether there was an elegant piece of furniture. Once the bellboy had shown him how to work the bath taps, and where the mini-bar fridge was hidden, Witts sprawled on his bed and watched television. He had never married, and had no girlfriend to accompany him on these hotel visits. Indeed, one of his favourite arguments for a discount was that, as a single man in a suite, he deserved a substantial kickback, since he used only one bath towel, half the coathangers and only one side of the bed.

Ken Witts was a big man, with a stomach grown fat from years of delegation in office cleaning. His complexion was florid, he had a full head of wavy grey hair and unexpectedly elegant hands. His posture was good, and in a suit (the price for which he haggled over shamelessly with his tailor) he could look distinguished. If you asked him what attracted him to stay in grand hotels, he replied, 'Well, I owe it to myself, I've worked hard to make my money.' But what really thrilled him were the huge sums he was able to chisel off. Although the cost of suites at five-star hotels started very high, his discount often exceeded the entire cost of staying at a smaller place. It tickled him that the people who ran these exclusive places were every bit as susceptible to a fair bargain as anyone else.

For three years he bartered his way around Britain. There was hardly an hotel in Piccadilly or Park Lane that didn't succumb to his cheapskate propositions, and the country hotels were, if anything, even less reluctant. Witts lost count of the weekends he spent in Georgian manor houses outside Bath and mock-Tudor ones in Berkshire without ever paying more than two-thirds of the official tariff. He bargained his way around the Highlands of Scotland (now there was a challenge; some of those castle owners really earned his respect) and then the health clubs and spas.

Restaurants presented a different challenge. The mark-up on wine is invariably high, and it was a simple matter to choose a good bottle of burgundy from the wine list at eighty pounds and offer fifty for it, providing the negotiation took place well in advance of dinner. With food, Witts would take the restaurant manager to one side and say, 'I see you have monkfish on the menu tonight, friend . . .' and it was a rare night that a couple of pounds couldn't somehow be filleted from the price.

You might reasonably wonder why these smart establishments were so accommodating. By the time Ken Witts had completed the bargaining, there was little or no profit left for them in his patronage. Largely, I suspect, it was the novelty of the situation that made them succumb. Managers of such places have many qualities, but few are trained to cope with someone like Ken Witts. If they tried to resist him, his arguments became more and more detailed and specious. He quoted the cost of the raw materials, and in this he knew what he was talking about. If he chose a *langoustine* salad, restaurant managers were reminded of the wholesale price of shellfish, lettuce, brown bread and lemons, as a means of demonstrating how little it was really costing them. Witts never made much allowance for the reputation and overheads of a place. In his opinion a *langoustine* salad was a *langoustine* salad, whether you ate it at the Ritz or at a seaside café.

'It's exactly the same principle as contract cleaning,' he said.

'Keep your labour costs low, buy your materials below wholesale, and pass on part of the saving to the customer to undercut the competition. Basic business practice. It's no different just because you're in the luxury hotel biz.' It was sharp cost consciousness that had made Ken Witts's fortune. In the thirty years he was building his company, it was his boast that nowhere were cleaners more badly paid. He had a fleet of old buses that collected his workers at five in the morning from pick-up points all over London – Caribbean women from Lambeth, Poles from Ealing, Tamils from Southall – and dropped them at the merchant bank and insurance companies he had contracts to clean. His turnover of staff was exceptionally high, but this was no disadvantage. There were always new immigrants prepared to put up with his paltry wages, until they found something better.

It so happened that, one bank holiday weekend, Ken Witts was staying at an expensive Elizabethan hotel just outside Pershore in Worcestershire. He was well pleased with himself, having achieved a big discount on a big bedroom overlooking the lawn, never an easy thing over a bank holiday in high season. So generally benign did he feel that when he was approached by a fellow guest in the morning room he smiled encouragingly at him.

After a few uninteresting pleasantries, the fellow guest said, 'Mind if I ask you something? What's your bedroom like?'

'Large,' replied Ken Witts rather smugly.

'Ours is a rabbit hutch. My wife went mad when she saw it. It's nothing like the one they put in their brochure.'

'So what are you doing about it?' asked Witts. Situations like this were always a trial for him. His instinctive reaction was to take up cudgels on the stranger's behalf, escort him to the manager's office and secure a whopping compensation with misery money on top. But his better judgement said, 'No, there's nothing in this for you, Kenneth Witts.' He knew that if everybody went round bagging discounts, niggling away at the proper price, then his own special negotiations could only become tougher.

'What did I do?' said the fellow guest, whose name was Martin Pendle. 'I went straight to the manager, that's what I did, and I told him to shift us to another room. Don't worry, I took the brochure along with me, and I said, "Give us this room, please, the one you photographed, with the window seat and the garden view and the tapestry settee."'

'And what did he say?' asked Ken Witts, perturbed.

'He said no,' said Martin Pendle. 'He said that room was already taken.'

Ken Witts relaxed. The room in the brochure was his; he had expressly requested it.

'So I said to the manager, "Where are you going to put us, then? Barbara's refusing to unpack in our present room and is asking to go home." Well, he looked thoroughly uncomfortable at this, and kept saying how unfortunate it all was, and that being a bank holiday weekend the hotel is full, and there are no other bedrooms in the whole place. Well, that was not good enough, and I told him so. "What do you wish us to do then, sir?" asks the manager. "Would you like me to refund your deposit and you can stay somewhere else?" I said, "What, on a bank holiday when everywhere else is full up too, and we can't go home because we've nothing to eat and the shops are shut for the holiday? I'm not accepting that," I said. "What I want's a discount, and a large one too."'

Ken Witts did not like the sound of this. He didn't like it one bit. He clenched and unclenched his fingers inside his pockets. If there were any further discounts to be had at the Pershore Park Hotel, they should properly be coming his way. Witts was as taut as a Bengal tiger that has just caught wind of a rival sloping on to his territory.

'And did you get your large discount?' he asked as nonchalantly as he could manage.

'Not easily,' replied Pendle. 'The manager kept going back to his first offer, that if we didn't like the room we should go home with our deposit refunded. I'm telling you, that really made me hit the roof. I threatened to take him to court for misrepresentation in his brochure, and reminded him what a field day the local newspaper would have over that. Eventually he proposed a twenty-five per cent rebate on the room.'

'And you took it, my friend?'

'No way,' said Pendle. 'I told him exactly what he could do

with his twenty-five per cent. It was bloody derisory. I told him I'd spent more than that just getting here, what with a full tank of petrol and wear and tear on the car.'

Ken Witts looked at Pendle with a new respect. Depreciation on your car, indeed. That was a line he'd never even thought of. He'd have to watch Pendle.

'By now,' said Martin Pendle, 'we'd been arguing for an hour and a half and the dinner gong was sounding. So I says to the manager, "You're never going to get anyone else for that room now," and I demanded a straight fifty per cent.'

'And what happened?'

'I got it. And fifty per cent off the food too. Just as I meant to when I went in there.'

Ken Witts felt queasy, and steadied himself against the arm of a sofa. Fifty per cent on a bank holiday weekend. It was a remarkable achievement, for which he felt an insane jealousy. *Fifty per cent.* He himself had only achieved forty. The extra ten per cent was a slur on his professionalism. Unable to make even a pretence at further civility, he went up to his room. The lunch gong sounded but he could not bring himself to eat. The idea of sitting in the same dining room as Martin and Barbara Pendle, and knowing that every mouthful of camembert soufflé and quail stuffed with apricots was costing them ten per cent less than it was costing him, put Ken Witts into a black mood. All afternoon he sulked in his bedroom. He dared not look out of the window, in case Martin and Barbara were playing discounted croquet on the lawn or eating a discounted cream tea. He could take no further pleasure in the Pershore Park Hotel. In the evening he asked for his dinner to be brought upstairs to him on a tray, and he watched television.

By the next morning, Ken Witts's peevishness had subsided into grudging admiration, and he resolved to do some industrial espionage. There was something cunning about Pendle, and Witts suspected that the idea of a discount had occurred to him long before he and Barbara were shown their small room. 'Pendle's done this before,' he said to himself. 'There's real technique there.'

Ken Witts found Pendle alone at a table overlooking the

clock golf course, where he was enjoying the sort of hearty full English breakfast that is only cheap at half the price.

'I've been thinking about that refund you got on your room,' said Witts in his most avuncular manner, 'and I've got to say I hand it to you. I'd never have the bottle to bargain like that.'

'That's because you haven't lived out East,' said Martin Pendle. 'You learn to haggle for everything out there, it's expected of you. In fact the Chinese in the shops are quite disappointed if you don't. You ought to see the Hong Kong shopkeepers when they get the bit between their teeth. You can spend days agreeing a price.'

Ken Witts had never been to Hong Kong, and he felt a warm surge of greed inside him, which started in his stomach and quickly moved to the tips of his fingers and toes. He had a strong premonition that Pendle was going to tell him something that would profoundly change his life in some way. He felt like the early explorers must have done, on first being told about the New World of America, and all the fresh challenges it presented.

'It's in the art galleries you really have to haggle,' went on Pendle. 'They call them art emporiums out there – enormous places some of them, behind Connaught Road in Central. You've never seen so much stuff: paintings on silk, blue china, some of it valuable, some not; glazed rice bowls, ivory carvings, enamel trays. As soon as a tourist steps through the door it's a hundred per cent on everything. You'd be mad to pay more than half the asking price, but people do, you know, you'd be amazed. Barbara and I were out there for six years with Cabot's, the rubber firm, and we spent days in some of those places, striking a deal on this or that.'

'And you always beat them down to half eventually?'

'As often as not. Fifty per cent off. Fifty-five per cent. Fifty-five's what we aimed for.'

Martin Pendle meticulously spread a fourth slice of toast with lime marmalade. It was easy to imagine him in Hong Kong, pummelling away at the price day after day, refusing to close the deal until every last Hong Kong dollar, every last scrap of fat on the meat, had been worn away.

'Not that the young Chinese salesmen are a patch on their grandfathers,' said Martin Pendle. 'Now those old boys really did know how to haggle. Crafty as sin, and prepared to invest real time in a sale. The young ones are all for turnover, but the old guys would spend weeks negotiating on a single piece. They didn't care whether they sold it or not, you see, or anyway pretended they didn't. So they'd fight you over every dollar. I've heard of guys who went back to the same shop every afternoon for a month, and on their last day in Hong Kong they'd say, "OK, this is my final price, do you want it or don't you?" And then the cunning old Chinamen would say, "It isn't enough, I'll not sell below such-and-such a price." And of course the poor guy's exasperated by then and doesn't know what to do, because his flight leaves that evening and he's spent all that time trying to buy the vase or whatever. So he caves in, and pays the Chinaman exactly what he asked.'

'But that old school have retired now, you say?'

'All except one,' said Pendle, 'and he's the wiliest old bird of them all. When I think of the hours I wasted with Sam Lee Fu; it was like beating your head against the Great Wall of China even to get ten per cent.'

'Ten per cent doesn't sound your style, my friend.'

'But it was high at Sam Lee Fu's. I'm telling you, that man is a legend in Hong Kong. He must be slightly psychic or something, because he always knows exactly how much you want a particular piece. He's a mind-reader. None of the old bargaining tactics work on Sam. For instance it's no good putting up a "blind"; you know, pretending you're keen on a certain painting, when you're actually keen on another one, and changing horses mid-deal. Sam sees through that at once. To do business with that man is a revelation. Some of the Hong Kong millionaires send their sons along to haggle with him, because it's the quickest way of learning how to strike a hard bargain.'

Throughout this conversation Ken Witts's breath came in short, thick pants. His heart beat like a metronome, and his tongue became wet with avarice. Of course he knew at once that he must pit himself against Sam Lee Fu. For a year he had felt mildly dissatisfied with his life, and the explanation, he saw now, was lack of challenge. Britain was soft. People were pathetically willing to sell their products short. Ken Witts only had to ask for a rebate and they were tripping over each other to give him whatever he wanted. There was no pride left, and no belief that anything had intrinsic value. Witts thought big corporations might be to blame. Nobody in Britain was trading their own, personal property any longer. Everything belonged to chains, globally branded. What did it matter to the manager of the Palace Hotel whether Ken Witts paid this price or that price, providing volume was maintained? But to a man like Sam Lee Fu it mattered. When he knocked ten per cent off the price, it was ten per cent of his own money, not some anonymous stockholder's dividend.

'What does he sell, this Sam Lee Fu?' asked Ken Witts. 'Does he have a speciality?'

'He sells everything,' said Pendle, 'but the best stuff is kept in the little alcove in Sam's own office. Paintings on silk, very old and rare some of them. Two big folders of them.'

'Pricey?'

'Well, there's the rub. There's no fixed price. You've got to agree a price with Sam. But yes, some are very pricey indeed. You're talking 140,000 Hong Kong dollars minimum, £10,000 sterling. But there are paintings in the folders for ten times that. The asking price, that is.'

ii

Ken Witts would dearly have loved to fly to Hong Kong the very next day, but he was shrewd enough to bide his time. He knew nothing about paintings on silk. If he sparred with Sam Lee Fu now, he wouldn't last one round. Even if he achieved a respectable reduction in percentage terms, he wouldn't be certain whether or not he had a bargain. Sam could start the negotiation at four times the proper price, and Ken Witts would sit there, green as a girl guide, courting humiliation.

He was acutely conscious that his joust with Sam was the great contest of his career. He had come up against some tough birds before; there was a company secretary at a particular insurance firm who had questioned his quote for binliners, and a facilities manager at a bank who had actually tried to negotiate the annual cleaning contract review below the rate of inflation. But these were minnows next to Sam Lee Fu. The trouncing Witts had suffered from Martin Pendle at the Pershore Park Hotel still rankled badly; and if Pendle could only squeeze a ten per cent discount out of Sam, what chance did he, Kenneth Witts, have? In the back of his mind, Witts very likely saw his encounter with the Chinaman as a grudge-match against Martin Pendle too. If he could obtain fifteen, even twenty per cent from Sam on a painting that really was worth the money, it would more than compensate for Pendle's extra ten per cent room rebate.

He went into training with as much dedication as a heavyweight boxer preparing for a title fight in Las Vegas. Nothing was to be left to chance. Ken Witts gave himself four months before going to Hong Kong, during which time he determined to learn everything that could possibly be useful for his bout with Sam Lee Fu. He obtained a ticket to the British Library, and under its vast dome studied scholarly books on Chinese silk painting, until he could distinguish at a glance the Sung from the Ming period, and decode basic calligraphy and seals. He attended sales of Chinese art at Christie's and Sotheby's, and found pretexts to seek advice from experts in their oriental painting and textile departments. He learnt about pigments in Chinese inks, and the sexual habits of the silkworm. He learnt how a modern copy of an old design can be artificially aged by submerging it in green tea, and how to recognise the tell-tale tidemarks. Realising that it might be helpful to speak the language (lest Sam Lee Fu should make some revealing remark to an assistant during the negotiations) Witts bought Linguaphone tapes for his car, and grappled with elementary Mandarin and Cantonese. He acquainted himself with Chinese folklore, and the ancient art of reading character from the face. At lunchtime he ate in Chinese restaurants, where he tried to discover how a Chinaman looks when he is telling a white lie. 'Is the fish fresh?' he would ask every Monday, carefully watching the waiter's eyes. In the evening he conducted controlled experiments with Chinese liqueurs and plum wine, until he knew exactly which ones made him drowsy and acquiescent, and which aided clear thinking.

At the same time he did not neglect his bartering muscles. He flexed them daily until they were like steel. He haggled with butchers over the price of sausages. He haggled in fruit shops for bags of cherries. He haggled at news kiosks for his evening paper. Every week he felt his technique becoming surer.

When the four months of training were up, Ken Witts did not feel dissatisfied. His expertise in Chinese silk painting had developed quite remarkably, and he doubted whether there were many non-professionals who knew more than he did. An indication of his progress was that he could now open any Christie's catalogue of oriental art, cover the auctioneer's estimate of its value printed underneath each painting, and guess the amount to the nearest twenty pounds. He was as ready as he would ever be to enter the ring with Sam Lee Fu.

iii

He flew first class to Hong Kong, having negotiated, through a bucket shop, a discount so dramatic that his seat cost him less than the full fare in economy. Normally he kept such triumphs to himself, but as the plane soared above Frankfurt and the air hostesses circled with champagne he couldn't resist asking his neighbour what he'd paid for his seat.

The neighbour consulted his ticket. 'Here we go,' he said, '£3,120 return.'

'Daylight robbery,' said Witts. 'I paid £460.' And the pleasure he took in his own cleverness lasted all the way to Kai Tak Airport.

He struck a deal at the Mandarin Hotel, then made straight for Sam Lee Fu's gallery in Des Voeux Road. It was an enormous glass-fronted emporium, with a giant pair of jade dogs on either side of the entrance, and an array of merchandise for tourists filling the front room. There were displays of tea sets and facsimiles of ancient scrolls, and boxes of ivory chopsticks in the worst possible taste, which came with gilded chopstick-rests on which your name could be engraved. There were many horrible models of Chinese junks, and pads of paper for taking telephone messages printed with auspicious Chinese mottoes. A beautiful young Chinese girl inquired whether he needed any assistance, and Ken Witts asked to be taken to the owner.

Sam Lee Fu was tall for a Chinaman, and there was something ambassadorial in his bearing. His manner was studiedly courteous, but there was a faint disdain and aloofness about it that must have deterred countless people from bargaining too vigorously. He was a grand figure in his grey silk suit and embossed grey silk tie. The sole oriental note in his dress was a pair of soft Chinese slippers, monogrammed in gold thread with his initials. His grey hair was brushed straight back from his temples, and dressed with a sickly-smelling unguent. His eyes, which were his only feature that betrayed his great age, were puffy and deep-set. He rose from behind his desk when Ken Witts was ushered before him, and introduced himself with elaborate reserve.

Ken Witts, keen to avoid revealing his mission for as long as possible, declared his admiration for the huge range of merchandise, and implied that he might be interested in purchasing a glazed rice bowl. All the time that he was speaking, Sam Lee Fu regarded him blankly. Around his lips played a barely perceptible smile, whether of amusement or superciliousness it was impossible to say. Ken Witts found it disturbing.

'But your real interest, I surmise, is in something rarer than a rice bowl,' said Sam Lee Fu at last.

Ken Witts started for a second before regaining his composure.

'To tell the truth, friend,' he said bumptiously, 'I'm a long way from making up my mind what to buy.'

'Perhaps,' said Sam Lee Fu, 'you would like to look at some old paintings on silk, while you think about your rice bowls.'

'You've got old paintings?' said Witts, extremely startled but trying to convey the same nonchalance with which he had questioned Martin Pendle about tactics at the Pershore Park Hotel.

'I have old paintings,' said Sam Lee Fu.

He unlocked a cabinet from which he produced a pair of

folders tied with crimson ribbon. These he laid before Ken Witts on a low table, motioning him to sit down in an armchair. Sam Lee Fu then settled himself on the opposite side of the table, on a bamboo stool.

He loosened the ribbon on the first portfolio, and opened it flat on the table. Inside were thirty or forty paintings, leafed between tissue paper, and Sam Lee Fu displayed them one by one, moving them without commentary from one side of the folder to the other. At each painting he paused for about twenty seconds for Ken Witts to appraise it.

Witts could see at once that the paintings were of the highest quality. There was Sui calligraphy with the most delicate brush strokes. There were Tang landscapes so fine that only once or twice a year did work of such quality turn up in the auction houses. There were sixteenth-century Ching paintings of junks in the harbour at Lantau, and Ming dynasty sketches of bamboo groves. There were gods and demons and emperors, and a marvellously subtle Yuan brown-ink sketch of the Peak.

When any painting particularly caught his eye, Witts restrained himself from betraying the slightest glimmer of interest. It was important at this stage that Sam Lee Fu should have no inkling of which pictures excited him. And yet Witts had the impression that those paintings he secretly admired were displayed for a slightly longer time than the others.

Only once did Sam Lee Fu speak.

'This is a good piece, six hundred and fifty years old, Yuan dynasty,' he said of a picture of demons.

Ken Witts admired it for a moment, before noticing a faint glaze of tannin in the fold of the silk. The painting was ten, fifteen years old at most, and artificially aged with tea. Sam Lee Fu acknowledged Witts's unspoken detection with a tiny bow of his head, and moved on to the next painting.

The moment Ken Witts saw the Manchu horse he knew he must buy it. It wasn't the oldest painting or the best preserved, but it had a quality about it. It was very spare. The artist had used barely a dozen brush strokes to create the whole beast. And yet it was full of personality. Like so many early seventeenth-century Manchu sketches, it was surprisingly contemporary in its lines. The horse was rearing on its hind legs, and on its back was the merest suggestion of a saddle, achieved with a single flourish of the brush. The ink was very black and viscous, made with a mixture of soot and resinous gum. Ken Witts had no doubts about its authenticity or its value on the open market. He had seen a similar but coarser piece auctioned at Christie's less than a month before, and it had sold for £32,000 plus buyer's commission. All these thoughts passed through Ken Witts's mind in a few seconds, and he made a point, when the horse was displayed before him, of hurrying Sam Lee Fu on to the next piece, as though impatient to see something better. When he had carefully inspected all the paintings in both folders, he asked Sam Lee Fu to take him through them again. This time he weeded out those pictures that were of no interest to him, until he had pared down his choice to a dozen. When the Manchu horse appeared for the second time, he made a little play of dithering over whether or not to retain it, before electing to keep it in the running as an outsider.

Ken Witts had by now spent three and a half hours in the gallery and, heavily jet-lagged, he was exhausted.

'Tomorrow, friend,' he said, 'I'll be back at the same time. Keep my choices reserved.'

Sam Lee Fu bowed his head, and began carefully to retie the ribbons around the folders. When Ken Witts had gone, he clapped his hands and an assistant joined him from behind a screen.

'Well, Kwan,' said Sam Lee Fu. 'You were watching Mr Witts?'

'All the time,' replied Kwan.

'And?'

'From his expression, I think he likes best the bamboo grove and the junks in Lantau harbour.'

'I believe it is the Manchu-period horse he wants,' said Sam Lee Fu. 'It is only a feeling, but we will see. I think we will enjoy some bargaining tomorrow.'

Ken Witts was not displeased with his first day's work. The Manchu horse was a painting worthy of the enterprise, and he had been impressed by Sam Lee Fu. The man was shrewd, and Witts would have to proceed with the utmost caution. Thus far, he was sure, Sam Lee Fu had not the slightest idea where his preference lay. Witts chuckled happily to himself as he ate his breakfast. Out of the window he could see the Star Ferry, slowly crossing the bay between Hong Kong Island and Kowloon pier, every inch of its deck crowded with Chinese on their way to work. Slightly to the west he could see the Outlying Islands Ferry Terminals for Lantau and Macau, surrounded by little stalls selling dried fish and noodles, and on the Kowloon side were the mass of offices and tenement buildings, their roofs a tangle of advertisements for international banks and quick-service tailors. Witts passed the morning with the *South China Morning Post*, ate lunch in the coffee shop, then strolled around the block to Des Voeux Road.

Sam Lee Fu bowed at his return and offered him a cup of tea.

Witts accepted, while reminding himself that a cup of tea costs nothing at all in relation to a painting, and that he mustn't allow such small kindnesses (which are in any case a cynical part of the softening-up process) to affect his judgement.

The dozen paintings he had reserved were spread out on the low table, and Witts studied each one for a long time, peering at them from close up and from far away. Sam Lee Fu once again watched him with an amused detachment that irritated him.

Two hours went by, and the beautiful young Chinese girl whom he'd seen in the shop on the first day came in with a bottle of brandy, soda and two glasses.

'You will take small brandy?' asked Sam Lee Fu.

'Very weak,' said Ken Witts.

'A man who looks too intently at objects of desire may lose his wonder,' said Sam Lee Fu.

'Is that Confucius?'

'My own,' replied Sam Lee Fu.

'I think,' he went on after a bit, 'that you begin to arrive at your choice.'

'Slowly, slowly,' said Witts. 'There are a lot of paintings I like in Hong Kong.'

'There is no rush. The pictures are old. It takes time to discover which one is yours.'

Sam Lee Fu appeared to mellow with brandy and spoke of his grandchildren. 'For me there is no pleasure so great as teaching my grandson to fly his kite.'

Ken Witts closed his ears and concentrated on his next move for acquiring the Manchu horse. All this talk about grandsons flying kites was another old softening-up technique, a shameless appeal to sentiment. Ken Witts wouldn't have been surprised to learn that Sam Lee Fu had no grandchildren at all.

In due course Ken Witts decided the time had come to broach the subject of money.

'There are two pictures I like more than the others,' he said. 'Could you give me a price on them?'

He pointed to the Ming sketch of a bamboo grove, and the seascape of junks in Lantau harbour.

Sam Lee Fu studied them, and gave a troubled intake of breath. 'Both very good pieces,' he said. 'You have excellent taste, Mr Witts, I congratulate you on it.' He then named prices for both pictures, which sounded to Ken Witts about one and a half times their worth.

He sat silently for a moment as though assimilating what he'd heard. Then he said casually, 'And the Manchu horse? What, by way of comparison, is the price of that?'

Now Sam Lee Fu knew for certain which painting Ken Witts wanted to buy.

'The horse?' he said. 'I'm sorry to disappoint you, Mr Witts, but that piece is not for sale. I am at fault. It should not have been in the folder at all.'

'Why the hell not?'

'It has certain sentimental associations for me. The painting was collected by my grandfather and came to me when he died. I am sorry,' he said, removing the horse from the table, 'but that one you cannot have. Buy the bamboo grove or the Lantau junks by all means. Both are excellent pieces.'

Ken Witts now made a very stupid error, which he was to

regret as soon as he'd spoken. He persisted in asking about the horse.

'But if it *was* for sale?'

'Yes?'

'If it was, what would it cost?'

'That is a difficult question to answer,' replied Sam Lee Fu. 'I have never, of course, given any thought to the matter of price. And then there would be the sentimental value to consider too. All these things would have to be considered.'

'But as a rough guide?'

'A rough guide? Seventy thousand pounds sterling. That is the figure that comes to mind. But as I say, I haven't thought about it, since the painting is not for sale.'

iv

Ken Witts was furious with himself. He had been outmanoeuvred completely. Sam Lee Fu must have guessed all along that it was the Manchu horse he wanted, or why else would he have invented that nonsense about his grandfather and pretended the picture wasn't for sale? All his own ruses to put the Chinaman off the scent had failed abysmally. Sam Lee Fu must have seen straight through them. No wonder he looked at him so superciliously when he praised the other pictures as blinds. Witts cursed his stupidity a hundred times. So convinced had he been of his own cleverness that he hadn't even advanced any of his special arguments. He had made nothing of the poor quality of the silk, or the very slight discolouration of the border. He hadn't mentioned seeing better examples of Manchu horses in London auctions. All he'd done, in fact, was allow Sam Lee Fu to see how badly he wanted the painting, and galvanised him into pricing it at an absurd £70,000. To get it down to a fair price of £30,000 might take five years, if it could be done at all.

Ken Witts had half a mind to catch the first flight home. He had been so thoroughly outclassed that he doubted anything could now be salvaged. A tourist, wandering in off the street, could have obtained a better first price than he had. All evening he stamped crossly around the Mandarin. There is a small arcade of shops on the mezzanine floor of the hotel, and Ken Witts glared at the shopkeepers as he passed by, because they reminded him of his failure.

The next morning, feeling stifled by Hong Kong, he decided to take the hovercraft over to Lantau, which he hoped would clear his head. It did no such thing. All the way there, and all the way back, as he bumped across the South China Sea, he brooded about Sam Lee Fu. There were several tall Chinamen on the hovercraft, and each time Ken Witts caught sight of one he blanched. The man was beginning to haunt him.

That afternoon, by an extraordinary feat of will, he managed to restrain himself from visiting Sam Lee Fu's shop. Instead, he kicked his heels in his hotel bedroom and watched cable television. The anguish this restraint caused him was considerable, but he knew that only by a heroic pretence of indifference could he re-enter the ring. Little by little a new strategy was beginning to form in his mind. If Sam Lee Fu thought it expedient to pretend he wasn't interested in selling, then he, Kenneth Witts, would pretend he wasn't interested in buying.

On the afternoon of his fourth day in Hong Kong, Ken Witts once again made the short walk to Des Voeux Road. He found Sam Lee Fu drinking tea in his office.

'You did not come and see me yesterday, Mr Witts,' he said.

'I've come to say goodbye,' said Witts coolly. 'I'm off home in a few days, and might not have a chance to see you again.'

Sam Lee Fu regarded him beadily. 'I am sorry that the horse painting you wanted was unavailable for sale. I trust that hasn't hastened your return to UK.'

'The horse? Oh no, I've found another Manchu-period horse in one of the other galleries, so my journey has been successful.'

'You have already bought this other painting?'

'Not yet, but we have nearly agreed a price. You Chinese like to haggle a bit, don't you?'

'There is room in most prices for a little discussion,' agreed Sam Lee Fu stiffly. 'Often such things are possible.'

Ken Witts felt a surge of optimism, but managed to look unimpressed.

'Well, Sam,' he said, 'it was good meeting you. If I'm in Hong Kong again I will look you up.'

The Chinaman smiled. 'I hope that before you leave, Mr Witts, you will do me the honour of having dinner with me this evening.'

'Alas, friend,' said Witts, 'this evening I can't manage. I'm already having dinner with the man who is selling me the horse. But thanks for your offer, I appreciate it.' Then he shook Sam Lee Fu warmly by the hand, and made his way back to the hotel.

Sam Lee Fu clapped his hands for Kwan.

'Kwan, you will follow Mr Witts to the Mandarin, and keep him under surveillance. See whose house he goes to.'

Kwan shrugged, and slipped out.

Throughout the fifth day Sam Lee Fu waited for Ken Witts to return to his gallery. He had developed a measure of admiration for Mr Witts. By Chinese standards, of course, he lacked sophistication. But he knew a good deal about Chinese painting, and Sam Lee Fu preferred to sell his better pieces to people who could appreciate their worth. When Witts returned he would let him buy the horse, but the price would be high. He had enjoyed his ploy about buying a different horse; the man had more imagination than he'd given him credit for. But it was naive of Witts to think he'd fall for it. Kwan had waited all evening in the lobby of the Mandarin, and Witts had never left the hotel. So much then for his dinner with this other, fictitious gallery owner. Sam Lee Fu laughed. Oh yes, Mr Witts would return.

But Ken Witts did not return. By the evening of the fifth day Sam Lee Fu was puzzled, and by the sixth morning he was anxious. Why didn't Witts come? He knew he wanted the painting, and Kwan's vigil in the lobby disproved the existence of any rival dealer. At noon Sam Lee Fu rang the reception at the Mandarin, and was told that Mr Witts was still in residence, and had given no instructions about checking out. 'Good,' thought Sam Lee Fu, 'there is still time. This afternoon he will come.'

But still Ken Witts did not come. He had resolved to stay away from the shop for forty-eight hours, and the strain this imposed was taking its toll. Filling the day was terrible for him. He took a taxi to Stanley Market, but had no stomach for haggling over plastic buckets or wicker baskets. He rode the tram up to the Peak, but derived little pleasure from it. So he returned to the Mandarin and watched more television. The time passed very slowly.

On the evening of the sixth day, Sam Lee Fu took a step that he had never taken before with a foreigner. No doubt he had grave reservations, for it involved loss of face, but eventually, his patience exhausted and his curiosity needled, he telephoned Witts at his hotel.

'Mr Witts? It is Sam Lee Fu here. I am ringing to ask you, how was your dinner with the other gallery man?'

Ken Witts could feel the innuendo down the line.

'Fine,' he replied, 'just fine. The Mandarin does a good dinner, even when it's room service.'

'So you didn't eat at the dealer's house?'

'Oh no,' said Witts, 'we ate up here in my room. You wouldn't catch me out in Hong Kong after dark.'

Sam Lee Fu was momentarily nonplussed. It hadn't occurred to him that the dealer might have gone to Witts's room, and he cursed his lack of foresight.

'And your discussions proceeded satisfactorily, I trust? You have by now purchased your painting?'

'Not quite,' said Witts. 'There is no rush. The picture is old and these things take time, as you told me yourself.'

'Well, Mr Witts,' said Sam Lee Fu. 'I think you might be interested to know that circumstances have changed regarding the horse painting in my own gallery. If you wish to buy it, it is possible.'

'What's that?' exclaimed Ken Witts. 'Your heirloom from your grandfather is on the market? Are you sure you can bring yourself to part with it? Well, I'll tell you what,' he went on, 'I'll come and take another look at it tomorrow afternoon, to see how it compares with the other one. But one thing I've got to tell you – the price you mentioned is way over the top. If your horse really is for sale, I'll not pay a penny more than £12,000 sterling for it.'

Ken Witts and Sam Lee Fu greeted each other like old friends, or rather like tycoons who have scrapped for so long, not always cleanly, that they derive pleasure only with others of their kind. The horse painting was displayed in the middle of Sam Lee Fu's desk, and he clapped his hands and called for tea. It was obvious that, with the subterfuge behind them, Sam Lee Fu was looking forward to a good, hard haggle.

The beautiful Chinese girl, whom Sam Lee Fu addressed as Su-su, arrived with the tea and a plate of sweet rice crackers. When Ken Witts had tasted these, and pronounced them good, Sam Lee Fu said, 'I have some good news for you, Mr Witts. The price of this painting is reduced by £10,000 to £60,000 sterling.'

'Then I am sorry, sonny, but I am obviously wasting your time. When I told you yesterday on the telephone that I wouldn't pay more than £12,000, I meant what I said.'

The parameters of negotiations firmly established, the two men embarked on their gruelling wrangle. For four hours they chided and cajoled each other, put up feints and indulged in the most outrageous flattery. Several times Ken Witts threatened to break off negotiations and retire to the Mandarin. More than once Sam Lee Fu pronounced Witts unworthy of his grandfather's horse. No appeal to the emotions was too low to be brought into play.

'You know,' said Witts, 'it may sound funny this, but one buys paintings for the strangest reasons. What really attracted me to this horse in the first place was the thought of showing it to my grandson. He's nine years old now, and nuts about riding. For me there's no pleasure so great as teaching my grandson to canter.'

Sam Lee Fu stared doubtfully at Witts. He didn't look like a grandfather, and Sam Lee Fu wouldn't have been surprised to learn that he had no family at all. But he wasn't determined enough about closing his ears, and found himself easing the price by a further £10,000. Consequently, by close of hostilities on the seventh day, Ken Witts had increased his offer for the horse to £18,000, and Sam Lee Fu had dropped his price to £50,000. That evening Ken Witts celebrated by himself with a bottle of expensive but discounted champagne. It had been a highly satisfactory day's work. Already he had secured a 28.5 per cent discount, almost three times more than the inept Martin Pendle had ever achieved.

On the eighth day, the haggling proceeded gently, and the gap was narrowed from both ends by another £5,000. On the ninth Ken Witts, knowing that the Chinese enjoy cognac above anything, presented Sam Lee Fu with an excellent bottle of Hennessy XO, and poured him triple measures until the price fell to £40,000. On the same evening Sam Lee Fu suggested they continue over dinner in a dim-sum house, and Ken Witts allowed himself to be nudged up to £25,000.

On the tenth morning the negotiation moved into a new, hypothetical phase.

'Just supposing,' said Ken Witts, 'and I'm speaking entirely without prejudice here, that I was fool enough to go up to £30,000, I assume I could pay by American Express card?'

'You could pay by whichever means you chose,' replied Sam Lee Fu, 'though naturally, in the case of American Express, I would expect you to pay their service charge. You know they levy a six per cent fee on all transactions, which on £30,000 is £1,800. So your total bill would be £31,800.'

'That's outrageous,' said Ken Witts. 'Now I really have heard everything. Let me tell you, settling your account with American Express is your lookout, not mine.'

'There you are mistaken,' replied Sam Lee Fu. 'In Hong Kong, often such things are possible.'

By the eleventh afternoon the figure of £30,000 had acquired a certain solidity, and the means of payment exercised all their ingenuity. Sam Lee Fu, horrified by the concessions on price he had already made, was unmovable on the credit card levy.

'All right,' said Ken Witts at last, 'I'll tell you what. I will pay in cash, but I want another five hundred off the price.'

'Out of the question,' snapped Sam Lee Fu.

'Why?' asked Witts. 'If I pay in cash, there'll be no record and no tax to pay, as you well know, you crafty bugger.'

'Thirty thousand in cash,' insisted Sam Lee Fu. 'Thirty thousand is final. It is an excellent price, and I will not go below it. But if we can agree, I have a special present for you, Mr Witts. I have admired your stamina, and you need someone to help you celebrate your purchase and unwind.' Sam Lee Fu clapped his hands. 'Su-su,' he called, and the beautiful young tea girl joined them in the office. She was wearing a che-sun of delicate yellow silk, which set off her soft white skin and lustrous black hair. She looked innocent and sweet-natured.

'Su-su,' explained Sam Lee Fu with real tenderness, 'is the daughter of my sister. She is my favourite niece.' Su-su looked down modestly. 'When we have completed our deal, Su-su will come to visit you at your hotel. I think she will make you very happy.'

'For £500 she'd need to,' said Ken Witts. 'I could get a good short-time girl round here for twenty quid. I'm sure she's a lovely lass, your niece, but not worth £500 by a long chalk.'

At this, Sam Lee Fu went very quiet, and seemed to lose all interest in the negotiation. But after a while he said, 'OK, I accept your terms of £30,000 sterling in cash. I am an old man, Mr Witts, but never have I bargained with such an adversary as you before. You have beaten me very low on the horse painting, but I congratulate you. And Su-su will come to you as a gift, as a sign of my esteem.'

Ken Witts cared more for discounts than love, but he was nevertheless not insensible to the compliment of Sam Lee Fu's gift of his niece, which he accepted with a clumsy Chinese bow. Then he made his way to the Hong Kong and Shanghai Bank where, by prior arrangement with his own bank in London, a facility had been made available for the withdrawal of a large amount of cash. He returned to the gallery with a stash of notes, which Sam Lee Fu counted, while Ken Witts watched Su-su carefully wrap the painting, first between tissue paper, then in stiff cardboard, and finally in layer upon layer of red and yellow crepe. Each layer was elaborately tied with ribbon, and the corners held down with gaudy gummed stickers painted with good luck messages. The package was then slipped into a brown paper bag which Ken Witts clutched tightly to himself all the way back to the Mandarin, then hid behind a row of bottles in the mini-bar fridge in his room.

He did not much look forward to Su-su's visit. If truth be told, he was rather nervous, and would have been happier gloating over his triumph alone. But when the girl arrived at his room, he opened the door to her in a towelling dressing gown, and was not ungratified by the warmth of her affections. Afterwards, Ken Witts shared a half-bottle of champagne with Su-su, and allowed her to gently massage his back and neck. Then he fell asleep.

The following evening, having nothing further to detain him in Hong Kong, Ken Witts took the return flight to Britain. It was really only then, stretched out in his seat with a flute of champagne, that he could fully savour his victory. He had come up against the best in the world on foreign terrain, and had emerged as top dog. The first thing he would do when he got home was write to the Pershore Park Hotel and obtain Martin Pendle's address. Then he would send him a postcard ostensibly thanking him for his advice about Sam Lee Fu, but letting him know all about his fifty-seven per cent discount.

It was only as the aeroplane began its descent into Heathrow that Ken Witts remembered import duty. It was a shocking realisation. If Her Majesty's Customs and Excise were now to start piling on their taxes, he might just as well have not bought the painting in Hong Kong at all. There was only one possible course of action, and that was to brazen it out, and head straight for the green channel for people with nothing to declare.

Ken Witts was a distinguished-looking man in his way, and it was possibly this that prompted the customs men to detain him for a spot check (for it is always the least likely, most respectable people they pick upon, while drug runners and currency fraudsters are waved cheerily on their way). Ken Witts tried to look unconcerned as his luggage was rifled, but luck was against him, and a customs officer was soon asking him exactly what the beautifully wrapped red and yellow crepe parcel contained.

'Oh that,' he said. 'Only a silly Chinese picture of a horse, not cigarettes or eau-de-Cologne or anything.'

'I'm afraid, sir,' said the customs officer, 'that I must ask you to unwrap it.'

'Not seriously, friend?' said Ken Witts. 'The young lady in the shop spent hours wrapping it, and you can't really ask me to rip it open. It's a present you know, for my wife, who's nuts about horses.'

'I'm awfully sorry, sir,' said the customs officer, 'but I must insist.'

Ken Witts unwrapped the parcel as slowly as possible, pausing at every new layer of stickers and ribbon in case the officer would relent. But he didn't relent, and when they reached the level of stiff cardboard, he knew the game was up. He removed the tissue paper.

'This reminds me of that game we used to play as kids,' said the customs officer. 'Pass-the-Parcel. Except that there's no present in the middle of it.'

Ken Witts couldn't believe it, and scrabbled through the billowing mound of crepe for any trace of the Manchu horse. But it was nowhere, nowhere at all.

'Well, one thing's for sure, sir,' said the officer. 'If there's nothing inside, we can't tax you on it. So you're free to go.'

Ken Witts glared at him, and nodded gloomily. But then he laughed.

'It doesn't matter,' he said. 'It really doesn't matter at all. I never liked that horse much anyway. And at least I got the best price he's ever given. A fifty-seven per cent discount. That's what I call a real bargain.'

THE MAN WHO LOVED DRIVING

I admit that I was surprised to receive one morning a postcard inviting me to drinks to celebrate the engagement of Margaret Ashe; not surprised that I had been invited (Margaret was a friend of ten years' standing), but surprised she was to be married at all. I knew nothing of her fiancé. His name, she informed me on the postcard, was Malcolm Hunt. 'Come and inspect Malcolm (Hunt),' was how she put it.

I had last seen Margaret two or three months earlier, and she had made no mention of a boyfriend. On the contrary, she made a joke out of not having one. Her search for a boyfriend was never far from her mind.

'How are you?' I would ask.

'Still on the shelf,' she would reply, raising her eyes in a resigned way. 'Though not for lack of trying.'

Lately a trace of bitterness had crept into her conversation which I found uncomfortable. Margaret's quest for the perfect man, which began as a joke, had taken on a desperate edge. Ten years had passed and no suitor had appeared. At eighteen she had been popular, even sought after. But, as sometimes will happen, the boys who courted Margaret one by one met other girlfriends, until she found herself increasingly alone. I got the impression that she was not often asked out in the evening. Her flat, which was small and consisted mostly of corridors, was in a conversion off the Wandsworth Bridge Road, and I noticed that if ever a television programme came up in our conversation Margaret was an expert on the plot. Her jobs, which she frequently changed, were by her own description dull and routine; one month she would work as a receptionist for a doctor's practice, the next as a temporary secretary in the Foreign Office pool. Whenever she started a new job she would ring her friends, ostensibly to pass on her new daytime telephone number, but perhaps also as a means of staying in touch. If this was Margaret's intention then, in my own case, it certainly worked. Whenever she rang we made some plan to meet for a drink or a pizza, and Margaret would bemoan the dearth of suitable men.

If I give the impression that I find Margaret dull then I do her an injustice. I enjoyed her company. To see her was entertaining and, until her recent bitterness, undemanding. She would kick off her shoes, tuck her legs under her on the sofa, and joke about the tedium and various injustices of her job. Almost always some office dragon had taken against her for a tiny breach of office protocol, and Margaret amusingly described the victimisation she endured. She drank gin by the tumbler, and the revenges she planned against her employers grew as she became indignant with alcohol. When she laughed her face was very pretty, and I was sorry that she did not have a boyfriend to follow these office sagas in daily instalments.

'Do you think I should change jobs?' she would invariably ask.

'It certainly sounds like it.'

'OK, you've decided me, I'll sack myself on Friday.'

And then she would accept another large gin.

'What I'd really like,' she would say, 'is a good holiday. Pity there's nobody fanciable to go with.'

When I arrived at Margaret's engagement party there was already a small crowd of guests assembled. You could not, however, describe it as being in full swing, because there was nothing remotely swinging about the eight or ten people standing around the fireplace. Their melancholy presence served only to emphasise the dull social life from which Margaret's engagement was presumably releasing her. The sitting room, with its morose rubber plant, was at the best of times a drab setting. That night Margaret had arranged several bottles of white wine and a cereal bowl filled with Hula-Hoops on side tables. Arranged around an insipid pool of blue cheese in a Pyrex dish were slices of raw carrot and florets of cauliflower.

Margaret seemed ill at ease at her engagement party, and I thought I detected, at the arrival of each new guest, a slight displeasure that they were able to make the occasion at all.

'I hope you are going to introduce me to Malcolm,' I said, pouring myself a drink. 'I've only come to see him, you know.'

'You won't like him,' Margaret replied. She was always pessimistic about people getting on.

'How do you know? I expect him to be terrific if you've decided to get married to him.'

'He is.'

Margaret smiled and led me across the room. Malcolm Hunt was twenty-nine, three days younger than Margaret. 'Which means I can boss you around, doesn't it, darling?' she said teasingly.

'How do you do,' he said in a flat, atonal voice. It was the kind of voice – running from sentence to sentence without topographical interest – that is characteristic only of the academic or unashamedly stupid. He was of medium height and build, but with prodigiously stocky shoulders which strained the cut of his jacket. His hair was full and fair, his colouring almost albino, and above his pink puffy lips grew a meagre blond moustache. But what I noticed about him most were his shoes: black leather brogues, so highly polished they shone like Perspex.

'Were you – are you – a soldier?' I asked.

'No,' replied Malcolm Hunt flatly. 'Why do you ask?'

'Your shoes. They're so gleaming, I thought . . .'

'It's for the showroom,' he replied. 'I keep them that way for the showroom. I sell cars. High-performance Italian cars. Some Ferraris, but we've a second licence to sell DeTollinis. People buying cars straight from the assembly line have a right to expect clean shoes.'

As it happened I knew Malcolm Hunt's showroom well, because it was set at the end of Clabon Mews, a shortcut on my morning drive to the office. It was newly built and I had been surprised, when it shot up four years before, that it had ever got planning permission. The walls were of magnifying mirror glass and there was a chrome awning, more suited to a Sheraton hotel than a cobbled London mews, which overhung the street. Sometimes, as I drove by, wonderful cars were being shifted in and out of the showroom (often by a special hydraulic lift, which lowered them into a basement), and, now that I thought of it, I was fairly sure I had registered Malcolm as one of the several young salesmen backing them up.

When I mentioned to Malcolm that I passed his showroom each morning, he showed extraordinary delight at this frankly unsensational news.

'Do you?' he said, his face alight with enthusiasm. 'You should come for a test drive one day, when you next change your wheels. We keep the full range.'

And that was the extent of my first exchange with Margaret Ashe's husband-to-be.

ii

I couldn't go to Margaret and Malcolm's wedding because I was already committed to staying with old friends in Istanbul. They had rented a flat near the Edirnekapi gate and, since they both worked during the day, I was mostly left to amuse myself. Each morning I took a taxi along the Fevzi Pasa Caddesi to Topkapi Square, and from there made my sight-seeing expeditions by foot. Istanbul is not an easy city for tourists. To find less well known treasures requires concentration as you forge your way through the traffic from mosque to mosque. The Saturday of Margaret's wedding came and went, but it belonged so utterly to a different part of my life that I didn't give it a thought.

Late one afternoon I was strolling past the Topkapi, half searching for a taxi back to the flat, when two familiar figures appeared on the pavement from the postern gate of the Ayasofya. To see them in such unlikely surroundings was so startling that I blinked in disbelief. And yet there was no mistaking them: Margaret in the denim skirt she wore so often in London, Malcolm in a sports jacket, white shorts, ankle socks and a gleaming pair of conker-brown brogues.

They did not see me approaching for some time, such was the press of tourists and street hawkers, and I thought they looked uncomfortable in Istanbul. Sensing their inexperience, the street traders were savage. Pistachio nut vendors, kelim and cold drink merchants, shoeshine boys, children selling postcards and tasselled bathmats of the Galata bridge – all converged on the English honeymooners. Malcolm's puffy lips pursed in irritation as he attempted to dismiss them. One small shoeshine boy, heroically adhesive, was trailing them the length of the street, pointing from his wooden brush box to Malcolm's already brilliant shoes and back again to the brush box, insistent there should be no misunderstanding over what was on offer.

I thought how strange it was that, of all the places in the world to choose for their honeymoon, they should have plumped for Istanbul. In my conversations with Margaret she had never expressed the remotest interest in visiting the East; indeed, her holiday destinations were wholly sybaritic. I could list a dozen places where they would have been happier. And yet, here in Topkapi Square, hotly pursued by a retinue of pistachio vendors, were Margaret and her DeTollini salesman.

'Margaret!'

Their surprise at seeing me in Istanbul was second only to mine at seeing them.

'When did you get here?' I asked.

'Yesterday,' said Margaret.

'But it seems longer,' said Malcolm.

They were staying in the Hilton Hotel at Cumhuriyet; not an hotel I would have recommended myself, and I said I wished that I'd known they were coming, since I could have found them a room somewhere more evocative.

'It doesn't matter,' said Malcolm, 'we're only here until tomorrow morning. Then we're off driving.'

We had tea in a café and Margaret brought me up to date. The wedding ceremony and reception had clearly gone off according to plan, and then they had taken the evening flight to Istanbul. That was yesterday, and they had spent today warding off street tradesmen in the heat.

'And tomorrow you're driving where?' I asked.

'Everywhere,' said Margaret. 'It sounds like everywhere anyway. I don't know the exact names of the places, Malcolm's been planning the route for weeks, but the great news is the car. That really is amazing. Explain about the car, Malcolm, you're the expert on that.'

Malcolm, whose reaction both to me and to the city of Istanbul in general had so far been distinctly lukewarm, suddenly cheered up.

'It's great news,' he said. 'We'd always planned to drive through Turkey for our honeymoon, and I'd rented a car through Hertz. Quite a decent machine but nothing special, they don't keep high-performance models in Turkey apparently; it was a Ford Sierra with four-wheel drive and power steering. Fairly basic accessories. No fuel consumption monitor and the sun roof was manual. But they assured me it was reliable. One of the boys at the showroom was with Hertz before joining us, and he telexed head office on our behalf.

'Anyway,' he went on excitedly, 'at our wedding reception we were given a wonderful surprise, weren't we, darling?'

'Wonderful,' said Margaret. Was it my imagination, or was there a faint weariness in her enthusiasm? 'A wonderful surprise.'

'You see, the boys in the showroom, they'd all clubbed together for our wedding present, and they'd had a brand new DeTollini 550 Spyder driven out here by Freddy – he's the garage mechanic, a great character, Freddy – and he'd driven this car, straight off the assembly line, right through France, Germany, Yugoslavia, Bulgaria, Christ knows where else, all the way out here to Istanbul, and it's ours to borrow for two weeks. Then Freddy's flying out to Istanbul again – it's all part of the present – to drive the car back to London.'

'What an original idea,' I said.

'Christ yes. This is one of the first 550s to come on to the UK market. It's got computerised graphic steering, self-locking laser door-locks, and automatic overdrive. You probably saw the write-up in *Autocar*. The tyres are a quarter of a centimetre wider than the 450 and incorporate the NASA research on molecular stress so the cornering control is precision.'

'Where are you planning to drive exactly?'

'I can show you easily enough,' said Malcolm. From his jacket pocket he produced a large-scale motoring map of Turkey which he spread out on the café table, carefully weighting its corners with glasses of tea and ashtrays. Many of the trunk roads had been marked with fluorescent highlighters. 'We'll take the E80 from Istanbul to Izmit for a start,' he said, tracing the route with his finger, 'and then bear south on the excellent route 650 from Sakarya to Kutahya.'

'There are supposed to be amazing mountains,' said Margaret.

'Thank God for the overdrive,' said Malcolm. 'After that it's pretty much Burdur, Antalya . . .'

'Where there's a good museum,' put in Margaret, 'and lovely-sounding ruins at a place called Aspendos.'

'. . . Mersin, north to Kayseri, Sivas, then east to Malatya, Erzurum and Van.'

I confess I was astonished by Malcolm's route. It ringed the whole of Turkey. The distances, even on a straight road, were incredible, three thousand kilometres at least. Twisting and turning over the mountains, and stopping to see the classical sites on the way, would take eight or ten weeks.

'Heavens,' I exclaimed, 'are you sure you can do all this in a fortnight? I don't mean to interfere, but if I were you I'd choose to see one area of Turkey in more detail. You realise you'll never be off the road if you go to all those places?'

Malcolm glared at me. 'Actually, this whole route has been very carefully worked out,' he said. 'I'm sure you mean well, but until you've experienced the horsepower of these new DeTollini engines you really can't appreciate the possibilities.'

'It does go awfully fast,' said Margaret; 'it's going to be so romantic.'

'I'm sure it will be,' I said hastily, 'and I look forward to hearing all about it when you get back.' I scribbled down my address in Istanbul. 'You must come and have a drink. I expect you'll need one by then.'

Early morning is the best time of day in Istanbul. Sunset over the Bosphorus is all very well, but there always seems to be a film of diesel in the atmosphere, which in the early morning has dissolved, leaving the air pure and luminous. My hosts headed for their offices rather early, so I had the flat to myself. I put on a dressing gown and carried my breakfast on to the balcony. Between the new apartment blocks you could just make out the minaret of the Kariye museum, and it was fun to watch the shopkeepers in the street below opening their shutters for the day. One morning, five or six days after Margaret and Malcolm had set off in the DeTollini, I was annoyed to hear a faint tapping on the front door. I had just settled myself with a glass of tea and, knowing no Turkish, was tempted to ignore whoever it was rather than become embroiled in a frustrating exchange. The tapping continued still faintly, and I think it was the pathetic softness of the knocking which eventually persuaded me to go to the door. The concrete stairs leading up to the flats were open to the world, and in my opinion (though I did not, out of politeness, mention it to my hosts) rather dangerous. They gave you the impression, when you first opened the door, that your visitor was about to fall backwards into space.

When I opened it that morning, however, my visitor fell straight forward of her own volition. She must have been leaning against the door, and as soon as the bolt was drawn she stumbled and collapsed in a heap on the hall floor. It was Margaret and she was deathly white, her eyes ringed with grey from lack of sleep. Her hair was crusted with dust, the denim skirt smeared with motor oil. The change in her, in so few days, was hard to believe. Her cheeks, normally rounded, were sunken as if she had eaten nothing at all, and there was in her expression a look of terror that was chilling.

I led her on to the balcony where there were comfortable chairs, and poured her a glass of tea. I assumed there had been a car accident.

'Is Malcolm OK?' I asked softly.

'I don't know,' said Margaret. She was very distracted, and I hesitated to press her.

'What happened?' I asked at last.

'We've split up,' she replied. 'I mean, I've left him.'

My astonishment must have shown in my face, because Margaret went on defiantly. 'You won't change my mind, you know,' she said (as if I was about to try). 'I couldn't stand it, I just couldn't stand it. No, don't try to talk me into that, because I won't go back, really I won't.'

'How did you get here?' I asked quickly.

'By bus, coach – you know those horrible buses they have with tapes playing all night long.'

'From where?'

'Somewhere called Mersin, I think it was called.'

'*Mersin?*' Mersin is an industrial town on the far eastern Mediterranean coast, not far from the Turkish border with Syria. 'You've come all that way on a coach? It must have taken thirty hours.'

'About that,' she said. 'Slightly longer, in fact, because I had to change buses and ran out of money. A Turkish man gave me some and then sat next to me on the bus, talking, and I didn't dare go to sleep.'

'I think you should have a bath and then sleep now,' I suggested.

'I'd like a bath,' she said. 'But I couldn't sleep, I'm too exhausted for that.'

Margaret had a bath, while I found her some clean clothes and a tumbler of gin and tonic which I thought would help her rest later on. She looked better with the dust out of her hair, but still terribly weak. She stretched out on the sofa and I persuaded her to eat some melon. Then she dozed while I read my book, and later, saying she felt stronger, she drank the gin. As Margaret sat on the sofa with her feet tucked under her and a glass in her hand, I was reminded of our old gin-induced conversations in my London flat.

'You must think me awfully stupid,' she said suddenly. 'For years I've been boring you about finding the perfect man, and just when I thought I'd found him, I leave him.'

And then she began to cry; at first in soft, choking sobs, which developed into wild howls of despair that were terrible to hear. All the misery suppressed on the long coach was now released. She wept uncontrollably. She shook, and buried her head in a cushion. From what I could hear through the sobbing she seemed to be rehearsing a justification for never returning to Malcolm; sometimes to her friends, sometimes to her mother. 'If you'd *been* there you'd understand,' she kept saying over and over. 'If you'd been there in the car.'

After an hour of this, worn out with hysterics, Margaret dozed again, and when she awoke she was deadly calm. We moved outside on to the balcony and for a while sat in silence. Then, hesitantly at first, she began to explain what had happened to her in the five days since we'd said goodbye in Topkapi Square.

After some false starts she told the story well. She wasn't imaginative, but was meticulous about detail. She would have made an excellent witness in court.

They had set off from the Hilton in high spirits, the De-Tollini gleaming in the sunshine, its sleek mustard-coloured bodywork attracting a crowd of admirers at every traffic light. No car like it had ever been seen in Turkey. Malcolm basked in the glory of being its driver. He had never felt quite so proud as he was during those first few miles on the outskirts of Istanbul. Margaret loved it too. She was deliriously happy. The passenger seat was specially designed by an osteopath for comfortable driving over long distances, and she was fascinated by the array of knobs and switches on the dashboard. The glove compartment, used for the first time, seemed like a walk-in wardrobe as Margaret carefully placed her guidebook and sunglasses inside. Malcolm had never been so attractive to her as he was at that moment. 'Behind the steering wheel,' said Margaret, blushing a little, 'he was so masterful.' His driving was superb. He could exactly judge the width between two moving vehicles, and his instinct for braking distances was uncanny. When he accelerated through the gears (he insisted, of course, on a non-automatic car) he was like a pianist playing an arpeggio. In all the three months she had been driven by him in London, round and about the Wandsworth Bridge Road, Margaret had never once heard the engine straining in the wrong gear. And when he took her out into the countryside he drove incredibly fast and yet she never felt frightened, and this feeling of being in danger and yet in very safe hands excited her and made her feel like singing. Malcolm drove with only one hand on the steering wheel, but his grip was firm.

The motorway from Istanbul to Izmit is dismal. It passes half-finished apartment blocks, cement factories, gravel pits and mounds of dust. Almost all the vehicles on it are enormous lorries thundering past on their way to Ankara, hooting and flashing their headlights and swerving from lane to lane, gusting black clouds of diesel from their exhausts. People who know about these things say that the hundred kilometres to Izmit is one of the three most dangerous highways in the world (the others are approach roads to Tehran and Mexico City). It scared Margaret rather, but Malcolm was exhilarated. Whenever there was a gap between lorries, he lunged for it, changing from fourth down to third and up into fourth again with a single fluid action of his wrist. When he overtook, his eyes narrowed and a slight dampness appeared on his moustache.

'You will be careful, won't you?' said Margaret. 'I can hardly bear to look.'

'When in Turkey you've got to drive like a Turk,' replied Malcolm. 'They play by different rules over here. You either do it their way or lose out.'

Margaret studied her guidebook.

'Malcolm,' she said, 'as far as I can see the best place to stop for the night is near Kutahya. There's a nice-sounding hotel and they've got hot springs. Listen to this: "The sulphur springs, deliciously warm and inviting, well up through mineral-rich rocks. Geothermal water is beneficial for stomach, liver and eye complaints. Both drinking and bathing are highly recommended, and the springs are a lively meeting place for the local populace." Oh, Malcolm darling, do let's stop near there and see them.'

'Schedule permitting, of course,' said Malcolm. 'But I'm determined to put a good few miles between us and Istanbul today. We can't afford to slip behind.'

All day long they drove without stopping along the great highway that forges due south through the Turkish mid-west.

For hours on end the scenery was flat, but after that the road began to climb through grey and purple mountains, incredibly beautiful with their deep gorges and sheer rock faces, and then climbed even higher, so that the road they had driven along an hour before was nothing more than a pencil line in the valley below. Other traffic was plentiful and unpredictable. Lorries groaned their way up mountain roads at ten kilometres an hour, before careering down the other side. Ford and Bedford trucks, weighed down with gas canisters or cucumbers, accelerated towards them on the wrong side of the road. Austins and Fatihs, hooting wildly, threatened to force them over the edge of the cliff. Overtaking was mayhem. Drivers sped past on blind corners where an oncoming lorry would mean death. Coaches pulled out without warning to overtake them, at the precise moment they were passing a farm vehicle themselves, so they scraped past three abreast. Small children stepped out into the road without looking, and dogs scampered across it, not always successfully (Margaret saw four dead dogs on the first day alone). Malcolm relished the journey. With each new hazard he enjoyed it more. He did not talk now, but drove in absolute silence, his eyes fixed to the road like a man in an amusement arcade playing the Crazy Motorist machine.

His driving became bolder.

'For God's sake,' shouted Margaret once or twice, 'that lorry's *too close*, darling.'

'Keep calm,' Malcolm would reply, 'I'm accelerating out of trouble.'

On corners he was reckless. Taking his lead from the Turks, he hit the pedal and trusted to luck. Several times the car threatened to plunge into the gorge, but each time Malcolm managed by some miracle to hold the road.

'Malcolm, I do wish you wouldn't *do* that, it scares me,' cried Margaret.

Malcolm smiled distantly; his mind was fully occupied with how to pass the huge red Otosan truck that was making him reduce speed as it laboured towards the brow of the hill.

They did not stop for lunch, and it was six o'clock by the time they reached Kutahya.

'Hooray, hooray,' said Margaret. 'Here we are in Kutahya. You've driven brilliantly, darling. Let's go and explore the hot springs.'

'Afraid not, darling. I hadn't reckoned on the mountains being quite so steep, so we've lost ground. We must strike straight on for Afyon, though I'd be happier if we made Burdur tonight.'

It is a hundred kilometres from Kutahya to Afyon, and by the time they arrived it was getting dark. As they drove into the market square the sun was disappearing behind the town hall with its heroic bronze statue of Kemal Atatürk.

'Let's find an hotel quickly,' said Margaret. 'I'm exhausted by all that driving.' She laid her hand on top of Malcolm's on the handbrake. 'You must be tired too, darling. Let's have a lovely celebration supper for getting so far.'

But Malcolm was engrossed in his map.

'I estimate we've covered 360 kilometres since Istanbul,' he said, 'which isn't bad. But I did set Burdur as the target for the first day and I want to stick to it. So it looks like we're about to have our first taste of night driving in Turkey.'

'You don't mean it,' said Margaret. 'Come on, do let's find an hotel and have a walk round this town. We haven't seen anything all day except the back of lorries.'

But Malcolm was already moving on. 'These headlights are going to be an experience,' he said. 'They give a broad beam up to thirty yards when they're dipped, but undipped they're like searchlights. I'm told they're quite blinding, so look out everybody, here I come.'

Margaret was cross. She was tired and longed for a drink. She also felt humiliated that her own wishes were of so little account to her husband. This was their honeymoon, their joint honeymoon, and it angered her that Malcolm was apparently the only person who could take decisions. But the countryside was pitch black, and all Malcolm's attention was taken up with the headlights. They did not disappoint him. Their flexibility was amazing. The intensity of light could actually be altered by the driver so that, for instance, the dipped headlights could be set mellow while the undipped ones glared viciously. Malcolm relished them. If an oncoming lorry behaved selfishly and strayed towards the middle of the road, Malcolm blitzed it with the full beam. It was so strong that it lit up the entire cabin and you could see the lorry driver shielding his eyes in pain.

'That'll teach him,' said Malcolm. 'He won't do that again.'

They drove for two, then three more hours. Progress by night was frustrating, since only the slowest lorries were still on the road, and Malcolm was obliged to take dreadful risks to pass them. Margaret tried to doze, but every few minutes she was jolted upright in her seat as Malcolm jammed on the brakes. They had driven for eleven hours and her head spun with tiredness. She felt sick too from lack of food. Too exhausted now to protest, she leaned against the passenger door dreaming of bed.

'I say, Margaret,' said Malcolm at last, 'I'm pretty shattered. It's still quite a long way to Burdur and I don't think we can make it tonight after all. Let's stop somewhere. Have a look in the guidebook for an hotel, will you?'

Margaret looked, but she knew already that it was hopeless. They were miles from any town, and the villages were rough places with nowhere to stay.

'There must be somewhere,' said Malcolm. 'People have to stay somewhere.'

'They do. In the big towns. If you'd read the guide you'd know that. That's why I asked you to stop for the night at the last place . . .'

'Well, if you're convinced there's nowhere,' said Malcolm, 'then there's only one thing for it and that's to kip in the car.' He swerved off the road on to the verge and wrenched up the handbrake. 'We'll probably be more comfortable anyway than at a local fleapit – at least we won't get bitten to death by bedbugs. In fact,' he said as more and more advantages of sleeping in the DeTollini rushed into his head, 'when you think about it, this car is probably the most luxurious hotel in the whole of Turkey. You've got a bedside radio, cassette machine, vanity mirror, cigarette lighter . . . you've got to admit it's not bad.'

The passenger seats reclined like aeroplane ones, and pretty soon Malcolm and Margaret were stretched out side by side, like strangers on a wide-bodied jet, separated by the hand-brake and gear stick.

'I'm turning the heater off,' said Malcolm, 'or the battery will go flat during the night. Sleep well, darling.'

But Margaret did not sleep well. Anyone who has tried to sleep all night in a car, even in a DeTollini 550 Spyder with reclining aeroplane seats, knows that it is never comfortable. Her neck quickly became stiff, and there was nowhere to put her elbows, and without the heater it became bitterly cold. Her husband's muffled snoring, far from reassuring Margaret, only maddened her. It was so unfair that he could sleep and she could not. And, though she knew this was silly and illogical, she was also rather frightened. Every twenty minutes or so a lorry would grind towards them and, in the stillness of the night, Margaret could hear its approach from miles away. And then the lorry would come nearer and nearer, its engine getting louder and louder, until Margaret was sure that it was going to crash straight into the back of the car, and she braced herself for the impact, and didn't dare relax again until it had definitely passed by. Or else she fancied she had heard the lorry slow down as it got closer (wasn't the engine softer now than before?) and that it was going to draw up alongside them, and then God knows what might happen in the back of beyond. Malcolm kept saying that the laser door-locks couldn't even be wrenched open with a crowbar, only unlocked with the key, but it was small comfort in the dead of night.

It began to get light and still she hadn't slept. Her arms were numb and she sat up and rubbed them and looked outside. The dawn was very grey and she could see that they were parked by a clump of gorse, and that somewhere in the distance were mountains. Malcolm was fast asleep. His complexion, in the grey light, was pallid. Not long after this Margaret finally dozed off.

When she awoke, the car was moving.

'Morning, lazybones,' said Malcolm.

'Where are we?'

'Twenty kilometres from Burdur. I didn't wake you, but I wanted to get on. We've been driving for an hour already. I thought we might do another hour or two and then stop for breakfast. It's still early. It's only ten past seven.'

The night in the car had left Margaret feeling dirty and anxious for a bath and clean clothes, and she was pathetically encouraged by Malcolm's promise of breakfast.

'Maybe there'll be somewhere we can have a shower, too,' she said. 'I hate sleeping in cars. Promise me we won't make that mistake again, darling.'

'But you slept like a log, Margaret.'

'Actually I hardly slept a wink.'

'You looked asleep to me,' and he laughed in an annoying way.

They stopped for breakfast at a roadside café attached to a garage. While Malcolm filled the car with petrol, Margaret chose feta cheese, tomatoes, cucumber and fried aubergines from a glass refrigerated counter. They sat at a little wooden table by the side of the road and, as the sun came up, Margaret began to feel warm again.

'You know,' she said, flicking through the guidebook, 'there's a famous bridge not far from here. It's Seljuk. Or at least the brickwork is Seljuk, the foundations might be older. Shall we go and see it?'

'It's a nice idea,' said Malcolm, 'but we really do have to move on. I don't know whether you've noticed, but some of these lorries driving past the restaurant now, we overtook earlier this morning. That yellow truck, for instance, the yellow Bedford, we passed an hour ago. And now it's getting ahead again. If we keep letting that happen, we might as well have not bothered to overtake it in the first place. I mean, it's a great idea in theory to see your old bridge, but just consider how many lorries will get ahead of us in two or three hours. We'd be right back to where we were yesterday afternoon. Which would completely cancel out the advantage of sleeping in the car.'

All day they drove. If anything Malcolm was more silent, more absorbed and more exhilarated than before. Margaret stared out of the window as though in a trance. Sometimes they passed through villages, and children waved at the sports car in excitement. Margaret waved feebly back, feeling like a princess being whisked away into exile, with no control over her own destiny. Sometimes they passed signposts pointing off the road to tiny mountain villages, but she no longer bothered even to suggest a detour to visit them. At lunchtime they stopped for a few minutes for Malcolm to check the water and Margaret to buy tomatoes, which they ate in the car. In the early afternoon they passed a lake. Some time later Margaret noticed a ruined fortress halfway up a mountain. There was nothing about it in her guidebook. It would have been fun to explore.

Malcolm became bolder. By now he was truly the master of his car. Its obedience was absolute. When he needed an extra burst of speed coming out of a corner, he got it. When he needed to slow from ninety down to fifteen in twenty seconds he did it in ten. The roads between Burdur and Antalya are among the best in Asia and it was a joy to drive on them. There was less traffic than before, and the distances they were covering were huge. Malcolm found he could average 140 kilometres an hour, which is difficult to achieve even on the West German autobahns. If only Margaret didn't sabotage the schedule with her constant red herrings, then there was every chance of adhering to the itinerary.

From Antalya they headed east along the coast road, past Side and Alanya and the great industrial plants on the highway to Mersin. After Alanya the scenery becomes flat and uneventful, and the villages fewer, and their scarcity made it all the more frustrating to Margaret when they passed through them without slowing down. It is the custom in Turkey to display the name of each village and its population (Nefus: 2,412) on a blue sign at its approach, and she found herself wondering what the villagers she would never meet were actually like. Hundreds of thousands of people seemed to flash past them and yet, she brooded, they had barely seen, let alone spoken to, a Turk since leaving Istanbul.

On one thing she was determined, and that was that they should spend the night in an hotel. As dusk fell she became more insistent, and when Malcolm still showed no sign of stopping, she pleaded.

'You and your precious hotel,' said Malcolm. 'Why on

earth come all the way to Turkey just to stay in an hotel? There are hotels everywhere. I'd rather see the countryside. Look out of the window if you want to see Turkey.'

But at nine o'clock he relented, and they drew up on the outskirts of a town called Nervin where a small hotel, the Izmit Pansyion, stood next to a garage. It was not somewhere that Margaret would have chosen to stop. The hotel, even from the outside, looked squalid: half a dozen bedrooms opening off a narrow verandah above a restaurant. But at least it was an excuse to get out of the car, and Malcolm said he felt safer if the DeTollini was parked where he could see it. They carried their suitcases from the boot through the restaurant, and followed the owner upstairs to their room. The wooden door was padlocked and, when the Turk had struggled with the key, he pulled it open and led them inside. The room was dark and very dirty. A pair of truckle beds stood head to head, each with a heavily stained mattress. Folded on the end of each bed was a single sheet and a blanket. The only other furniture was a rickety wooden table covered with a plastic tablecloth. On the window sill was a pink plastic comb and an empty bottle of Pepsi-Cola.

When the Turk had gone downstairs Malcolm surveyed the room in disgust. 'I can't think why you want to stay here, Margaret. It's revolting. Have you seen the mattresses? Look at those repulsive brown stains.'

'It wasn't my idea to stay here, actually,' said Margaret. She too was sickened by the room, and was furious that she was now to be held responsible for its shortcomings. 'The reason we've ended up here is because you wouldn't stop. There were plenty of good hotels in Antalya.'

'Well, you can sleep here if you want, but not me. I'm going to sleep in the car. It'll be far more comfortable.'

'Please don't, Malcolm. Please don't,' cried Margaret. 'You can't sleep in the car on our honeymoon.'

'I'm afraid I must,' replied Malcolm. 'Some of the men downstairs in the restaurant were eyeing it in rather a suspicious way. They won't get inside, of course, but they could scratch the paintwork.'

Margaret opened her suitcase and started to unpack. The

squalor of the bedroom made her modest trousseau look magnificent. She took out several cotton dresses, still crisply ironed, and laid them across Malcolm's bed, wondering whether she would ever now get an opportunity to wear them. The piles of skirts and blouses, reminding her of her high spirits when she packed them, mocked and depressed her.

They went down to the restaurant for supper. The place was full of men watching television. On the wall in the corner was a black and white set broadcasting a cabaret show with Western girls, who danced about behind a Turkish singer. The girls wore long sequined dresses with splits up to their hips, and this embarrrassed Margaret, because she could feel the eyes of the Turks in the restaurant moving from the screen to her and back again. They ordered kebabs, but the griminess of the place had taken away Margaret's appetite.

'You don't mean it about sleeping in the car again, do you?' she asked. 'Do say you were only joking, because I'm a bit frightened by all these men.'

'Nonsense,' said Malcolm through a mouthful of kebab. 'You'll be perfectly safe. And if you feel scared, come down to the car. I'll be parked right outside.'

Margaret did feel scared, but she did not move to the car. Outside on the verandah she could hear movements, and coughing, and suspecting that people were sleeping there she dared not open her door. Instead she wrapped herself in two blankets, over all her clothes, half longing for morning and half wishing it would never come.

Not long after dawn she crept downstairs and found Malcolm already hard at work. His feet protruded from underneath the car, and by his side was an array of tools.

'I'm changing the oil,' he called to her. 'It's advisable to drain it completely with a DeTollini every two thousand miles. And I want to tighten the exhaust.'

'I need the guidebook from the glove compartment,' said Margaret. 'Do you know where the car keys are?'

'Here,' said Malcolm. 'But for God's sake don't leave them inside.'

Margaret retrieved her book and settled on a bench outside the restaurant. She watched Malcolm ease himself deeper under the big end of the DeTollini, so that only his brown brogues and white ankle socks protruded. All morning she had felt very calm. She no longer felt angry with Malcolm, only surprise at herself that she should be sitting here, in this remote village in Turkey, with a man, with a husband, for whom she felt nothing but indifference.

Malcolm called out, 'Margaret, can you pass me the third smallest spanner?' and she slid it dutifully towards him.

As she returned to her bench, Margaret noticed a commotion on the edge of the car park. Several Turks were loading suitcases and sacks on to the roof of a dolmus, and the sign on the front of this local bus said MERSIN. Margaret hurried towards it, determined.

'Mersin?' she asked. 'You are going to Mersin?'

'Mersin,' nodded the driver.

Margaret climbed aboard.

'And from there,' I said, 'you caught another bus to Istanbul?'

'More or less,' said Margaret. 'The dolmus took ages to set off, and all the time I expected Malcolm to appear at the window. I was willing him not to catch me. I could see his shoes sticking out from under the car, and every time he moved an inch I froze. But of course he was so absorbed with the exhaust pipe he never gave me a thought.'

'Let me pour you some more gin,' I said, 'because now that I've heard your amazing escape, there's one thing I've just got to ask you. I hope you won't think me nosy, but I can't resist. Why exactly did you marry Malcolm in the first place? What on earth was it about him that you found attractive?'

Margaret smiled. 'That,' she said, 'is easy. I loved him for his enthusiasm. You've no idea what it's like to be surrounded, day after day, by apathetic people. The people I worked with never enjoyed what they did, and most of my friends are the same. I suppose I was too. Being surrounded by apathetic people all the time is infectious. I felt I was only half alive most of the time, sleepwalking through life, isn't that the expression? And then I ran into Malcolm. His enthusiasm for cars made me feel great – not that cars had anything to do with it. He could have collected stamps. But I loved that keenness.

It was infectious. He snapped me out of my depression. I thought I could put up with all the car talk, because he drove me to new places. He made me forget about my crummy jobs. That's why I fell for Malcolm.'

'And what happens now?' I asked. 'Does Malcolm know you're here? I have an uneasy feeling he's about to burst through the door in pursuit. He could drive much faster than your bus.'

'Oh no,' said Margaret. 'There's no danger of that. I know exactly where Malcolm is, exactly where.'

And then, delving into her bag, she produced a black leather keyring, from which dangled the smartest car keys I'd ever seen.

'A DeTollini 550 Spyder,' said Margaret, 'is laser-locking. And quite impossible to open without these.'

THE BIG
GAME HUNTERS
OF DETROIT

i

On Graydon P. Farb's fifty-fifth birthday he announced his retirement.

'I've worked hard enough for two lifetimes,' he told his friend Franklin J. Morgan. 'On Monday morning I'm putting my affairs in the hands of a good stockbroker. And from then on I'm going to do nothing except hunt, so you'll have to look to your laurels, Franklin J.'

Morgan chuckled. 'Graydon,' he said, 'you can go hunting from now until your hundredth birthday; but if you think you're going to bag yourself a mountain lion, then you're going to die a mighty disappointed man.'

Graydon Farb laughed at his old friend's barb, but he wasn't laughing inside. Both men were mad keen hunters, and they were extremely competitive. For forty years they had spent every vacation together on hunting trips, and the walls of their neighbouring houses in Detroit were lined with the trophies they had collected. Their displays of antlers and stuffed heads were remarkably similar, so visitors could hardly tell them apart. In both houses there were moose heads, with their large overhanging snouts, and elk and caribou mounted on wooden shields with engraved metal tags underneath them saying exactly where and when they'd been shot. Both hunters had bighorn sheep and bison and raccoons. They had red and grey foxes, Arctic foxes (in both their blue and their white coats), wolverines and several rusty-faced coyotes. They had grizzly bears and Alaskan brown bears and even a Canadian polar bear, which Graydon P. Farb's black maid thought had a soulful face and dusted tenderly.

But their most prized trophies were their big cats. Of all the adventures they'd embarked on together, it was the trips to hunt jaguar, lynx, ocelot and mountain lion they most enjoyed; when they camped out for a fortnight at a stretch, all alone with the best guide money could buy, high up in the Rockies waiting for a jaguar, or crouched in swampland in ambush for a lynx.

But there was one tiny difference between the two collections. Franklin J. Morgan had a mountain lion, and Graydon P. Farb did not.

Morgan's mountain lion hung in pride of place on the wall behind his chair in his den, where no guest could possibly avoid seeing it. It had a big tawny face, greenish gold eyes and thirty teeth, the sharpness of which Franklin Morgan had asked the taxidermist to accentuate. Not only had its head been mounted, but its four paws too, with their eighteen vicious claws, and its long swishy tail with its dark brown tip was coiled like a lassoo beneath its head. Mountain lions, which are sometimes known as pumas or cougars or even panthers, have become scarce in North America, and the few that remain conceal themselves in the deepest forests and the murkiest swamps, so it is understandable that a mad keen hunter like Franklin Morgan should have taken such pride in his trophy. But the thing that pleased him most of all, the thing that really satisfied him about his mountain lion, was that Graydon Farb didn't have one too.

Every Saturday evening, when they weren't away on hunting trips, the two old friends had dinner together in Detroit. One Saturday Franklin would go over to Graydon Farb's house on Lake Shore Drive, and the next Saturday Graydon was invited back to Franklin Morgan's house on Lake Shore Farms. Graydon Farb dreaded each return dinner, because it meant sitting for two long hours right opposite the mountain lion. He suspected that Franklin made these dinners in the den last extra long on purpose, with especially complicated food, to increase his discomfort. And always, towards the end of the meal, Franklin Morgan never resisted rubbing in his triumph.

'You know, Graydon,' he would say with horribly false modesty, 'that damned cougar must have been the wiliest cat I ever had the privilege to hunt. If it hadn't been for a large slice of old-fashioned luck, I don't reckon I would ever have shot him at all.' And then Franklin would tell his story, which Graydon had heard a hundred times before, and which served no other purpose than to show him in a good light, and to remind his guest that his own collection was incomplete.

'One of these days, Graydon,' he would go on, 'you should go shoot a mountain lion yourself. Because I'm telling you there's no pleasure that quite equals taking out that wily old cat.'

And then Graydon Farb would sit at the table, fuming with annoyance, and half wishing that the stuffed cougar would leap off the wall and bite his old friend's head off.

Both men looked remarkably alike, which was perhaps not so surprising since they had lived such similar lives. They were tall and lantern-jawed and prosperous and fit and stubborn. On the weekdays they wore suits, but at weekends they dressed as hunters in L. L. Bean duck boots and lumberjack shirts. Neither had married, because no potential wife could bring herself to move in among so many dead mammals. In any case they were both selfish. They had inherited family money which they had increased by skilful investment, and since they had nobody in the world to support but themselves, they had grown even more self-centred. So they lived in their big houses in the best part of Detroit, looked after by their maids, and wondered only whether their next trip should be up to Alaska to hunt timber wolf or back to the Rockies for bobcat.

Now on the night that Graydon Farb announced his retirement from supervising his own stocks, it had indeed been his secret intention to shoot a mountain lion. His plan was to rent a cabin close to the swamps, hire himself the best trackers, and stay there for as long as it took. Three months, six months, a year, it didn't matter how many wet nights he had to endure, because in time a cougar would come along, and then – bang, bang – Franklin would have nothing left to brag about. But Franklin's crack that he couldn't bag a mountain lion if he lived to be a hundred riled Graydon. For forty years the two men had joshed each other over which of them was the better shot. They each had stories about the other missing pots at close range, and this kind of light-hearted rivalry between old buddies made up much of their conversation. But in recent years Graydon Farb had become unsure whether Franklin Morgan really meant well with his jokes. They had taken on a nasty tone, and were often hurtful and snubbing. Graydon laughed them off, but he was left with the impression that Franklin really did consider himself the better shot. And since this was palpably untrue, it riled him all the more.

It was less than a week after the dinner that an amazing notion came to Graydon P. Farb.

He was composing letters to trackers when the brainwave hit him. Instead of hunting a mountain lion, he would use his retirement to hunt something even more ambitious. He would hunt an animal so rare and grand that, when he brought it home to Detroit, Franklin J. would curl up with envy. And he knew at once what this special animal should be. A tiger! He was going to shoot a tiger!

After all, he reasoned, why shouldn't he? Tigers are, he knew, a protected species in danger of becoming extinct. But recently their numbers have picked up a bit, and a single, solitary tiger was hardly likely to make much difference. And of all the big game in the world, the tiger is the quarry that carries the most prestige. Next to a tiger, a mountain lion is nowhere, he laughed, not in the same league. If he could shoot a tiger, nobody would have the slightest further interest in poor Franklin Morgan's mountain lion, with its mangy brown tail coiled like a garden hose.

And then Graydon Farb had his second brainwave. He wouldn't have his tiger's head mounted on the wall. He would have the beast stuffed whole, its entire body, just as it was at the moment he squeezed the trigger. And he knew exactly where he would keep his tiger too: right next to the visitor's chair in his dining room. So that every other Saturday night, when Franklin Morgan came over, the great cat would be prowling at his right hand, just by his wine glass, never allowing him for one minute to forget.

The next morning, as soon as Graydon P. Farb woke up, he remembered his ambitious plan and became excited all over again. But when his euphoria had subsided a little, he began to realise that it is no easy task to shoot a tiger, and that if he was to succeed he would have to plan every single step of the operation with the utmost care. It would probably take many years, and if he hurried the plan, or there were any slip-ups, he would certainly end up in prison for many years more. But the more he thought about it, the more exhilarated he felt. 'After all,' he said to himself, 'calculated risks are nothing new to me. All my life I've risked my money on this scheme or that, having weighed up the bears and the bulls, and have always come out ahead. And now that I am retired, I have all the time I need, and all the money too, to devote to making a killing.'

A rather surprising fact about Graydon P. Farb and Franklin J. Morgan was that, of all the hunting trips they had made together, not one had ever taken place outside the United States of America or Canada. They were strongly patriotic (which is kinder than saying xenophobic), and they took the view that a good American moose or bobcat was worth shooting every bit as much as a Kenyan antelope or a Rhodesian zebra. The truth was that, at the age of fifty-five, Graydon Farb knew next to nothing about foreign animals, and was far from sure where in the world tigers are to be found.

So after breakfast he drove downtown to the big Barnes & Noble bookstore, and bought himself every book on wild animals they had in stock. A sign of quite how ignorant Graydon Farb really was is that the first thing he did when he got home was to flick through a picture book called *The Children's Compendium of Animals in Africa*. Inside he found pages of beautiful colour photographs of elephants, zebras and lions drinking at waterholes, but not a single picture of a tiger. It seemed very odd, and when he searched for it in the index, thinking he must have missed the page, the tiger still was not mentioned. Only later, when he consulted another book, did he learn to his amazement that there are no tigers at all in Africa, and never have been; they are only to be found in India, Malaysia, Burma and Sri Lanka.

One of the reasons why Graydon Farb was so rich was that he learnt from his mistakes, and was meticulously organised. For the next six weeks he read and made notes on every tiger book he could lay his hands on. He decided that the Indian tiger was the most practical kind for him to hunt, partly because English is widely spoken in India and he realised that he would want guides and would need to be able to communicate with them, and also because there are more tigers in India than anywhere else. Almost all of them, he read, live in huge national parks dotted all over the country, in the foothills of the Himalayas or in certain remote parts of Rajasthan, Madhya Pradesh and Uttar Pradesh. But he read too that the national parks are well guarded, and numerous rangers are employed to deter poachers. Good tiger skins are valuable, and in a poor country like India there are always desperate men prepared to run risks for a good profit. But the penalties for poachers are stern, and Graydon Farb broke out in a sweat whenever he thought of spending twenty or more years in an Indian jail.

ii

When Graydon Farb arrived in Bombay, he booked a suite in the Taj Hotel under a false name. The pseudonym he chose was Zebediah Fairley, which was the name of the brother of his maid at Lake Shore Drive, and he had procured a credit card under this pseudonym for the trip. He had also obtained a false American passport, at huge expense, in the name of Zebediah Fairley, but instead of the·old man's photograph inside there was a picture of Graydon Farb in a lumberjack shirt. There was good reason for this subterfuge. In case his tiger hunt went wrong, he needed a secure false identity which would prevent him from being traced, and at the same time he had to be able to pay for his trip. Indian currency regulations for foreigners are strict, and it is forbidden to pay your bill in a good hotel except in foreign currency, in other words with traveller's cheques or by credit card. And when Graydon cashed a traveller's cheque in a bank, he knew that his passport number and details would be carefully recorded. He had no desire to leave a trail of information behind him which could be traced by the police. The charge card bills he ran up in India would be sent to Zebediah Fairley in Detroit, who would bring them round to his sister at Lake Shore Drive, who would in turn settle them with cash through the mail. In the unlikely event of Zebediah ever being questioned about his payments in India, he would say in all honesty that he'd never left Detroit in his entire life, and had never owned a charge card either.

After he'd had a bath and a rest, and eaten a snack in the hotel coffee shop, Graydon Farb took a yellow taxi to the Indian Board of Trade. It took him a very long time to find the correct department, and then he had to join a queue that curled back and forth along a wide, dark corridor. Several people were fast asleep on the floor, wrapped up in scraps of blanket, and trays of tea glasses were passed precariously above the queue and delivered to offices on either side of the corridor. Inside, Graydon could see dozens of clerks sitting on high wooden stools, and everywhere there were towers of yellowing papers and box files.

All the time he was jostled and overtaken by messengers in white shirts and dhotis, and Graydon seriously doubted that he'd ever reach the front. After three and three-quarter hours he worked his way into the room itself, and caught the eye of a particular clerk.

'The name's Zebediah Fairley,' said Graydon Farb, 'and I come from Detroit in the United States of America. And where I come from you can't buy any mangoes, leastways not your succulent Indian mangoes. So what I want to do is export mangoes through Bombay International Airport and sell them back home.'

The clerk at the Board of Trade was a quick-witted man, and he at once suggested another idea.

'Sir, why go to the expense of air-freighting your mangoes?' he asked. 'Sending them by sea is the best way. People are packing the fruit unripened and allowing it to ripen on the voyage.'

For a moment Graydon Farb was nonplussed. The reason he could not export by sea was that tiger flesh, unlike mangoes, would not ripen on a long voyage: it would decompose.

'But freighting the mangoes by air is part of the marketing exercise,' he explained to the incredulous clerk. 'We're going to make a special thing of it: "Sun-ripened mangoes from market to icebox in twenty-four hours".'

The clerk seemed bemused but satisfied by this reply, and issued Mr Zebediah Fairley with the sheafs of papers and declarations and applications for bank guarantees and customs and excise registrations that he would need to become an exporter through Bombay International Airport.

Graydon Farb's second excursion took him out to the airport, or rather to the crowded area of warehouses and freight companies outside the airport gates. His mission was to find an export agent who dealt in airtight metal crates. After numerous false trails he was eventually led to Mr Ram Singh of the Lakshmi Import-Export Company, who had exactly what Graydon Farb needed.

'The name's Zebediah Fairley,' said Graydon, 'and I come from Detroit in the United States of America.' Once again he told his story about mangoes, explaining that if he stored them in airtight metal crates their quality would not be impaired during the flight.

It is not likely that Ram Singh believed his story. Probably he suspected that Zebediah Fairley was a drugs smuggler. But the important thing was that he sold him six airtight metal crates, and agreed to store them in his warehouse until such time as they were needed.

When Graydon Farb got back to his hotel he was well satisfied with his morning's work. He felt that delicious, glowing feeling that activity so often induces, even when you know you have taken only the first few steps of a long and arduous journey.

'You know something, Graydon P.?' he said to himself. 'You really are one helluva bright guy.'

He thought of Franklin Morgan – it was the middle of the night in Detroit – and his mountain lion staring glassy-eyed and doleful from his dining room wall. What a thoroughly second-rate animal the mountain lion was! It lacked even the distinction of being endangered. Why, any hunter who cared to, could wriggle on his belly in the swamp, and given enough time a mountain lion would stroll into his sights. Whereas the tiger was a rare aristocrat, hunted for centuries by maharajahs and nawabs and viceroys. All this and more went through Graydon Farb's happy mind as he took his siesta at the Taj Hotel. Whoever heard of the Maharajah of Oudh or Ghenghiz Khan or any other great game hunter demeaning himself to go after a mountain lion? And what characters in literature had adventures with mountain lions on a par with Mowgli or Little Black Sambo? No, the superiority of the tiger could not be questioned. Only if he bagged the yeti itself, chuckled Graydon Farb, could he trump himself on his tiger.

But this far, he acknowledged, when his ebullience ebbed, had been the easy bit. He had two more Herculean tasks to undertake in Bombay. Not only must he purchase a rifle capable of slaying a full-grown tiger; he must hire guides prepared to smuggle him into a game sanctuary and transport a tiger's carcass back to Bombay.

The following morning Graydon Farb went to the classified advertising desk of the *Times of India* and placed two small advertisements in the next day's edition.

One said: 'Rich American collector will pay top prices for sporting guns, any date, make or action. British, European, Indian and Rajput shotguns all considered. Strictly foreign-currency payments only. Apply Zebediah Fairley, c/o Nataraj Hotel, Marine Drive.'

The second advertisement said: 'Guides with knowledge of all wildlife and game required for delicate business matter. No references necessary, but discretion essential. Apply in person between 2 and 4 p.m. tomorrow to Room 20, Epsom Hotel, N. M. Joshi Marg.'

On his way back from the *Times* office, he called in first at the Nataraj Hotel and, having primed the front-desk receptionist with an impressive tip, asked him to take messages from any applicants. In two days, he said, he would return for them, when another tip would be forthcoming. He looked round the lobby of the hotel and was pleased with his choice. The Nataraj was a top-class establishment, quiet and respectable, but in no sense a meeting place like the Taj or the Oberoi. That suited him well. If his advertisement drew the response that he hoped it would, the Nataraj would exactly fit the bill.

From the Nataraj he took a taxi back towards the Taj, but when he was halfway there he asked the driver to divert to the Epsom instead; there was no point in letting the doorman of the Nataraj know that he was calling at such a different class of hotel. This was Graydon Farb's second visit to the Epsom. He had spotted it from a taxi a couple of days earlier, two floors of filthy rooms above a welding shop, overlooking the main railway line to the Victoria Terminus. There was no telephone, which was why he must now return in person, to reconfirm his reservation for Room 20. The owner of the Epsom, primed on Graydon Farb's earlier visit with ten American dollars, leapt up from his mattress bed on the floor behind the reception desk.

'Mr Fairley, so good to see you,' he said. 'But your reservation is for tomorrow. Your wish now is to stay two nights?'

Graydon Farb shuddered. The idea of spending any night at all in this cholera-infested dormitory made him nauseous.

'Only tomorrow,' he said. 'And for a business meeting only. Only doing business in the room, not sleeping.'

The Epsom hotelier's eyes narrowed cunningly. 'How much business you do in the room, Mr Fairley?'

'I don't know yet,' replied Farb. 'I'll need it for two or three hours at most. But it's difficult to guess the numbers. If there's a lot of visitors, they'll have to form a line down here in your lobby.'

'But the police, Mr Fairley,' objected the hotelier. 'They will close my hotel if I permit immorality. And what is the hurry, why have so many girls one after the other? You should take your time.'

'There won't be any girls,' said Farb, 'or anything else for that matter, not like that.' He removed another ten-dollar note from his wallet, folded it in half, and impaled it on a sharp brass spike intended for messages on the reception desk. 'I am interviewing men for a business deal I'm involved with.

And what I'll need from you is an afternoon's privacy, you got me?'

'Oh yes, Mr Fairley,' the hotelier replied, slyly removing the note from the spike. 'The Epsom has very good reputations for after-lunch business.'

When Graydon Farb returned to the Nitaraj two days later, he found three messages awaiting him. Two were from dealers who had left their cards. These he dismissed. He knew of both places already, and had no intention of buying from a licensed gun dealer. He would be asked to produce a shotgun licence of his own, which he did not have, and his purchase would anyway identify him as thoroughly as if he'd imported his own favourite shooter from Detroit.

The third reply was more promising: a cream-coloured envelope sealed with black wax and a coat of arms of cobras and a mongoose. The letter inside gave as its address the Racquets and Gymkhana Club of Bombay. It said: 'I noticed your advertisement in the *Times* this morning, and having a number of sporting guns I no longer need, I would be delighted to meet you. Please send a message to me at my club suggesting a time and meeting place. My plans are reasonably fluid in the coming week. I would be obliged too if you could confirm that, should our negotiations conclude to our mutual satisfaction, payment will be made in foreign currency, and that the transaction will remain a private matter between ourselves. Yours sincerely, Chandra Ellora.' Underneath his signature he had written in capitals, no doubt for the sake of clarity, RAJA OF ELLORA.

Graydon Farb could have hollered with delight. His advertisement could not have drawn a more likely-sounding response, and he larded himself with praise since praise was due. 'You know something, Graydon P.?' he said. 'You really are one helluva smart guy.'

The condition about insisting on paying top prices with foreign currency was a master stroke. No Indian would consider selling anything for rupees, as he well knew, and it was this intentional touch of naiveté that must have prompted Chandra Ellora's note. He replied at once, suggesting a drink in the bar of the Nitaraj that very evening, and sending a boy to the Racquets and Gymkhana Club with instructions to await a reply.

Chandra Ellora, when he arrived at the Nitaraj an hour or so later than the time agreed, was a man in his early thirties with oiled back hair and wire-framed glasses with exceptionally thick round lenses which lent him a bug-eyed aspect. Graydon Farb heaved himself out of his leather armchair and vigorously pumped his visitor's hand.

'Do I call you Raja or Mr Ellora or what?' he drawled.

'My dear fellow,' replied Chandra Ellora. 'Do call me "Shortcake", everyone does. It goes back to school, you know – my nickname.'

He wore a fawn suit, perfectly pressed, a white shirt with pearly studs, and a blinding orange tie from Hermès with a stirrup motif. But what you noticed chiefly were his rings: on each finger of his left hand and was a different gold signet ring glinting dully amidst the Perspex and chrome of the Nitaraj bar.

'I see you're a collector of jewellery,' said Graydon Farb.

'Oh, my signet rings, you mean?' said Shortcake Ellora languidly. 'They're a perfect piece of nonsense, aren't they? An affectation I picked up at Mayo College. When we were ten or eleven years old we all started wearing our old family signet rings and, you know, the habit just stuck.'

'They look like valuable heirlooms to me,' said Graydon Farb.

'Not valuable,' said Shortcake Ellora. 'If they'd been remotely valuable, the old Begum, my grandmother, would have taken them with her to Paris and squirrelled them away somewhere. They're purely sentimental. And it's rather amusing to see the different coats of arms for each of our estates. Ellora – the cobras and mongoose – I think I used to seal my letter to you. But the Bharatpur and Tiptur seals are fun too with their pig-sticking.'

'Do you still have all those estates in your family?'

'Absolutely,' said Shortcake. 'They're quite valueless. In fact it costs us rather a lot of money each year to keep them up. But the bearers have worked for the family for God knows how many generations, so we can't throw them out. They cheat us like the blazes, of course, on their keep, but there again we don't pay them anything, so I suppose they must. And it means we have to spend two or three weeks in each place every year, picnicking, or they become awfully slack.'

'Just picnicking?' asked Graydon Farb in a tone that suggested no worse fate than picnicking ever befell man. 'Don't you get any hunting?'

'Awfully seldom,' said Shortcake Ellora. 'My grandfather was an absolutely mad keen gun and pretty well cleared the whole estate of game at Bharatpur. When he died he left only the snakes behind him.'

'Disappointing for you.'

'So few of the ruling families run shoots now. "Bull's-eye" Bhubaneswar might have some rough shooting at Bhubaneswar, I'm not certain.'

'Which is why you might be prepared to sell me a gun,' asked Graydon Farb ingenuously.

'Why not? If there's nothing to shoot, there's no great value in keeping a gunroom. Grandfather used to order them from Holland & Holland twenty at a time. The hunting lodge at Tiptur is stacked with gun cases, most of them never opened except for cleaning. All bought in the late thirties.'

Remembering that he was posing as a collector of guns, Graydon Farb questioned him excitedly about all the different pieces at Tiptur: the old flintlocks with their elaborately engraved stocks used by Shortcake's great-grandfather, the .577 Express rifle ('as recommended by Sir Samuel Baker, who shot with us actually more than once at Ellora'), the heavier German Männlicher rifles with their recoil heelplates, and the Holland & Hollands untouched in their baize-lined cases.

'What I'd like to do, if this doesn't inconvenience you,' said Graydon Farb, 'is to visit with you someday soon at your home and see all the guns for myself. But in the meantime, I sure would like to buy one of your .577 Express rifles, if you'll sell me one.'

Shortcake Ellora removed a small leather pocketbook from inside his jacket.

'If I put it up for sale at Sotheby's, the estimate on a .577 Express would, I'm told, be five to six thousand dollars. If you're paying cash, shall we agree on four thousand? I'll send a boy from the club to collect it, if that suits you, and I'll have a bearer deliver the gun before the end of the week. He can come up to Bombay with it on the train.'

'And you guarantee it still works, this rifle? I only collect firearms that are in good working order.'

'I'm sure it does,' said Shortcake Ellora. 'Robust as anything. After all, they were made to be trundled about on elephants, for hunting tiger. And they can't have had much wear, greased-up in their cases. But I'll tell you what, I'll send round a box or two of bullets with the gun, and you can blast away on the hotel roof. If it doesn't work, send it back to me.'

The ground floor of the Epsom Hotel reminded Graydon Farb of a bus station, since the forty or so men waiting there were mostly sitting on red bundles of their possessions. 'In case they are required for work this instant time,' said the hotelier. The bundles contained clothes and cutlery, everything they needed.

It was obvious to Graydon Farb that few of the applicants were remotely suitable for his purposes. They were too old and haggard, unshaven in a grey bristly way, with spindly legs and an air that could only be described as woebegone. Several, he suspected, were friends of the hotelier; they did not seem like readers of classified advertisements. Nor did many look as though they had much knowledge of wildlife or game. He doubted that they had left Bombay in their lives.

The truckle beds in Room 20 were scraped back against the walls, and a rickety table set up as a desk. On this Graydon Farb arranged his notebook, and asked for the applicants to be sent to him one by one. Within an hour he had dismissed thirty-five of them and asked six to remain.

For the second round of interviews his questions were more searching, and also more leading. He asked them which game sanctuaries they had visited, whether they had worked there, how recently, and how keen was their concern for wildlife. Two said proudly that they were supporters of the Worldwide Fund for Nature, and these he immediately sent home.

One man, older than the others, had been employed as a

bearer by a nawab living north of Calcutta, and had travelled into the Sundarbans, he said, on tiger hunts.

'The tigers in Sundarbans were being man-eaters, ten or eleven feet in length from nose to tail,' he said. 'Some tiger was killing thirty, forty peoples before being shot. Old peoples, young childrens, everyone he was eating until his timely end.'

Graydon Farb was impressed.

'And your job was what exactly on the tiger hunts? Tracking them, or were you loading?' he asked.

'Oh, neither of those things. Much too dangerous. My job, it was opening the bottles for the aftertime. For the refreshments. I was an uncorker by profession, sahib.'

Another applicant Graydon Farb rejected for being too slow. His brain seemed porous.

This left two candidates – Ali and Unmesh – both thirtyish and friends. They had arrived together and been interviewed consecutively, Ali waiting for Unmesh outside the door of the room. There was something essentially untrustworthy about them, which he liked: their reluctance to look him straight in the eye, their inconsistencies over how long they had spent as rangers at several different sanctuaries, whether or not they had actually been rangers at all. But their familiarity with game parks was not in doubt. Graydon had studied the guidebooks to every sanctuary, and their knowledge of the size of the herds of chital, and the numbers of barasingha and tiger, was accurate. And yet their manner was that of poachers not gamekeepers. When he asked them for references, Unmesh protested, 'But you said no references necessary in your advertisement.' And when he asked them for their full names and their address in Bombay, Ali said it would be simpler to leave messages for him at the hotel.

There were two other factors about Ali and Unmesh that commended them: their religion and their poverty. They were both Muslims, which Graydon felt was preferable to being Hindu or Buddhist. Graydon Farb was no theologian, but he knew that Hindus are fatalistic and adopt wild animals as gods. And strict Buddhists will not dig their vegetable patches in case they slice a worm with a spade. He could not afford any nonsense. He did not want his tiger transforming into a deity at the very moment he was squeezing the trigger, or any scruples about killing living things to come between him and his trophy. Ali and Unmesh, he guessed, had even fewer scruples because they were poor. And because they were poor the money he would offer them – two thousand dollars each – was going to bind them to him with the devotion of a bearer to his maharajah.

But Graydon P. Farb didn't say any of this to the men. Instead he told them to meet him tomorrow at noon, in the same room, since he wanted to talk to them some more.

When he returned to the Epsom he found Ali and Unmesh waiting for him: Ali, the taller of the two, spiky-haired with popping eyes and an incipient pot belly; Unmesh diminutive and wild, with broken teeth and bright orange gums. Both were wearing exactly the same clothes as the day before, stained linen trousers and check shirts. In all likelihood they had been kipping since yesterday on truckle beds outside Graydon Farb's interview room.

As soon as he was alone with them, Farb became combative.

'There's no point denying it, you fellers, I know all about you,' he said. Then he brought his fist down on the table with a loud crack. 'You weren't rangers, either of you, were you?' he shouted. 'Admit it, tell me I'm not mistaken. I know all about you.'

Ali and Unmesh stared at the floor without saying anything.

Graydon Farb hit the table for a second time, so hard that the legs buckled under the impact.

'Answer me!' he shouted. 'You were never rangers, were you? Never! I know what you were, you were poachers. *Poachers!*'

Unmesh shifted uncomfortably in his chair.

'You!' bawled Farb in his ear. 'How many tiger skins have you sold, you skunk? Ten? Twenty? And you,' he continued, turning his attention to Ali, 'how many tigers have you slaughtered?'

'Don't worry,' Farb went on after a while, 'I'm not the police. And I'm not going to tell them either. Not if you confess to me how many tiger skins you've poached.'

Still the men sat silently, refusing to answer.

Graydon Farb opened his wallet and removed two fifty-dollar bills. He placed them on the table in front of them.

'Tell me you've poached tigers and this is yours.'

The men sat motionless, watching the money, watching each other. A minute passed. And then, by some telepathic signal that seemed to travel between them, both men reached out their hands and closed them around the banknotes.

Graydon Farb smiled, stood up and shook both men by the hand. Ali and Unmesh watched him nervously, still half expecting the room to fill with policemen.

'Relax,' said Graydon Farb. 'Relax, fellers. You like tea?'

He unlocked the door of the room, walked to the head of the stairs and bellowed. Then he returned to the room and waited for the milky chi to be brought.

When they were alone again, Graydon Farb embarked on a line of questioning that would last late into the evening. He wanted to know about every single tiger that Ali and Unmesh had ever tracked or shot. He demanded precise dates, locations and sizes of the animals. He asked exactly how they had entered the wildlife sanctuaries, whether they'd come close to being caught, whether the rangers were ever bribable, and the length of time it took between entering the reserve and securing a kill. As the men were reassured that Graydon Farb was not police, they became franker. They told him about the commissions they had received from Bombay skin merchants, and how the heads and skins of the tigers were smuggled by boat from Bombay or Cochin across the Arabian Sea and up the Red Sea to Saudi Arabia and, they thought, on to the Gulf States. Sometimes, Graydon Farb noticed, Ali and Unmesh contradicted each other, and on these occasions he was careful about establishing accuracy. And again and again he returned to the same questions: which game reserve is the easiest to infiltrate, and where could a tiger most easily be shot?

At nine o'clock he sent out for thalis and beer, and the table with its buckled legs was set up for supper. When they had finished eating, Graydon Farb pushed back his chair and fixed Ali and Unmesh with a hooded, conspiratorial stare.

'So what you're telling me, fellers, is that the Kanha game

park in Madhya Pradesh is the one you consider the easiest to move around in?'

He looked thoughtful for a moment, produced his wallet again and began to count fifty-dollar bills on to the table between the remnants of the food.

'Five hundred . . . five fifty . . . six hundred,' he intoned. 'One thousand and fifty . . . one thousand one hundred . . .' and on and on until two thousand US dollars were in a pile in front of him.

Then he said, 'One thousand dollars for each man if you take me into Kanha. And if you find me a tiger to shoot, there's another thousand bucks. Are you on?'

Ali and Unmesh grinned.

'No problem,' said Ali. 'You want to go now, sahib?'

'Not now,' said Graydon Farb. 'And you two aren't going anywhere either, you understand? For the next six days you'll stay close to this room where I can contact you. I don't want you loose-talking with anyone. When you want something to eat you'll order it from the kitchens downstairs and have it sent to the room. Have you got that?'

Ali and Unmesh nodded as they divided the dollar bills.

'Every morning at eleven o'clock I will come here to the hotel to talk with you,' said Graydon Farb. 'And you'd better make damn sure you listen closely. Before we go to Kanha there's one helluva lot to arrange.'

And then Graydon Farb left the squalor of the Epsom for the cool of the Taj Hotel. He was well pleased with himself, because he was one helluva brilliant guy.

iii

The six-hundred-mile journey to Jabalpur, the staging post for Kanha, took them two full days by road, and Graydon Farb thought he might never survive it. Unmesh and Ali took turns driving. The jeep that Graydon had brought at such a premium lurched from side to side, weighed down with tents, bed rolls and tarpaulins, and the bulging sacks of provisions that Ali and Unmesh had insisted on packing. Pans and cauldrons rattled in the back, wedged between coils of rope and canvas bags. Graydon Farb had no idea what half the stuff was they'd found to bring along. But he had the consolation that they were at least making progress. And wedged on the floor, next to his seat, was a .577 Express, as good a rifle as he could possibly hope for. The recoil, it was true, was more abrupt than modern rifles, and the hammer a bit clumsy, but Graydon had established that it was in perfect working order. And for sheer accuracy, virtually nothing has been developed in the last hundred years to better the .577 Express. Shortcake Ellora had been as good as his word, and the rifle had been delivered to the Nitaraj and the deal concluded. 'And the guy doesn't even know my real name,' laughed Graydon Farb to himself. 'Zebediah Fairley, my ass!'

Security remained uppermost in his mind. He had considered flying to Jabalpur – an hour's hop – and hiring a jeep there, but the only agency that offered jeep hire insisted on supplying their own drivers. Safer, thought Graydon Farb, to avoid Jabalpur altogether. It is a large town – the regional centre, with a strategic railway station – but, he reasoned, virtually impossible to drive through without attracting attention in a loaded jeep. And hotels were another risk. To stay at an expensive one meant registering, with all his passport details, and it was preferable as a double precaution if Zebediah Fairley was unassociated with Madhya Pradesh. Staying in a native hotel – a prosperous, lantern-jawed American – he would be almost more conspicuous. So he resolved to camp unobtrusively off the road, until they reached the jungle.

Kanha National Park is not only one of the largest wildlife sanctuaries in India, but also among the oldest; as early as 1910 it was cordoned off as a tiger shoot for the Viceroy, with hunting lodges and an airstrip. And it was one of the first to become a conservation area too as, almost valley by valley, the park expanded until two thousand square kilometres were protected. The horseshoe-shaped Kanha Valley is bounded by the two spurs of the Mekal Ridge, which forms the southern rim of the park. To the east is the Halon Valley, where herds of chital and blackbuck graze; to the west, the tangly forested Banjar Valley – the jungle – where tourists bounce around in jeeps photographing tigers.

All this Graydon Farb learnt from his guidebooks, and from the small-scale map of Madhya Pradesh that he juggled with such difficulty in the passenger seat.

The important decision was where exactly they should enter the park. If they had been tourists they would have made for the main gates at Kisli or Mukhi, where the tourist bungalows are, and where guides join the jeeps to point out the animals. These guides talk to each other by short-wave radio, so that news of a sighting of a leopard – or a tiger – is relayed from vehicle to vehicle.

Ali and Unmesh favoured penetrating Kanha from the north, and Graydon Farb could see the logic in this. There are fewer roads in the north and no official point of entry. Nor are tourist jeeps permitted to drive there: the north of the park is set aside entirely for animals. And yet, although they are not marked on the tourist map, there is an extensive network of grass tracks, infrequently used.

'How many rangers are driving around here?' asked Graydon Farb.

Unmesh reckoned one, sometimes two jeeps. 'Two jeeps *maximum*,' he said. 'For driving two ways to the overnight lodge.'

This, explained Unmesh, was a wooden stockade – scarcely more than a bivouac – where a couple of forest rangers would park for the night and listen. And in the mornings they examined the grass tracks for tyre marks, and the jungle for signs of tree clearances or poaching. And, of course, if they heard a shot, they would radio for help from the control lodge at Kanha.

But the beauty of the northern boundary was its combination of accessibility and remoteness. If they based themselves five or so miles north of the overnight lodge, only a few miles into the park, they could probably camp for several days without being detected. And it was, said Ali, excellent tiger country; if luck was with them, they should have no trouble at all in tracking one.

So they skirted Jabalpur, took the main road south-east to Mandla and there, instead of heading for Kisli, continued on the main road running north of the park. When they reached the town of Bichia they left the road, followed a rougher asphalt road for ten miles, then doubled back on tracks for six or seven miles in the direction of Ronda and the overnight lodge. As soon as they left the asphalt road their progress became frustratingly slow. Ali and Unmesh were continually out of the jeep clearing brushwood and fallen tree trunks from the track. Or else the wheels began to spin over wetlands and the jeep must be partially unloaded and pushed. Because these paths were rarely used, they were badly overgrown; at times it became dark as they drove beneath a canopy of vegetation, before emerging again in a grassy glade or a meadow. There were two tributaries of the river Nilo to be forded, and Graydon Farb knew he would have become hopelessly lost if it wasn't for his guides. He had always seen himself as a great picker of people, so he took boundless satisfaction in his choice. 'You know something, Graydon P.?' he said to himself. 'You really are one helluvan exceptional guy.'

As they drove deeper and deeper into the jungle, the wildlife became profuse. Sambas and chital ran hither and thither, and peafowl flapped and floundered in their path. Twice they needed to retrace their route for a stretch to avoid swamps, and another time, thinking they heard the distant grind of an approaching vehicle, they swung the jeep off the track and behind a clump of sindur bushes.

By now they were five miles into the park and they began to search for place to pitch camp.

Unmesh climbed barefoot out of the jeep, held back the branches on the side of the track so they could pass, and then carefully repaired the flattened vegetation behind them. Slowly the jeep edged through the brushwood until they were a hundred yards off the track, where Ali began to reverse and turn the vehicle backwards and forwards to clear a space wide enough to pitch tents. It was dusk and, aside from the langur monkeys calling in the trees above them, the jungle took on a new stillness. It became cold too, but Graydon Farb forbade the lighting of a fire. Instead they ate cold chapattis and peeled oranges, after which Graydon Farb gave his guides the benefit of some of his longest hunting stories from the Rockies and Alaska.

'And what is the plan tomorrow, fellers?' he asked before he turned in.

'Early starting tomorrow,' said Ali. 'From five o'clock to seven o'clock we are hunting tigers. Morning times and evening times the best times for hunting him.'

As he lay in his tent waiting for Ali's five o'clock call, Graydon Farb doubted that he had ever been so excited. Here he was, in the middle of the jungle, his .577 Express at his side, waiting for a tiger. And the entire credit for being here was his own. His ingenuity thrilled him. If there was a solitary note of regret about this trip it was only that Franklin J. Morgan wasn't able to see him at this moment. Not join him here, of course – just see him. Graydon Farb chuckled. The sight would probably kill him, poor old stay-at-home Franklin.

Dawn at Kanha is unbelievably cold, and the hunting party that left camp on foot had a polar air about them: Graydon zipped into a thermal waistcoat, Ali and Unmesh shivering in sack-coloured shawls like refugees from some natural disaster. The ground underfoot was wet with dew, and the trees dripped sticky globules of dew and sap on to their heads. But the men felt exhilarated when, barely fifty yards from their tents, Unmesh pointed out paw marks in the mud.

'Tigress,' said Unmesh.

Graydon Farb squatted on his haunches to examine them. 'How fresh are they?' he asked.

'Maybe one hour,' said Unmesh.

Then he pointed out the slight slide marks on the tracks, in the direction the tigress was going. 'This meaning she moves fast,' said Unmesh. 'But we follow.'

The tracks followed the banks of a stream for a hundred yards, then sheered off into a swamp where they became lost in a clump of roots. The three men stood in frozen silence, listening. Unmesh knelt by the tracks for a minute, and examined trees for clues to the tigress's direction. Graydon Farb had slipped the safety catch of his rifle, poised to shoot at the first sight of his quarry.

'Listen,' hissed Ali.

Graydon Farb listened but could hear nothing.

'No birds,' said Ali. 'And no monkey call. Maybe the silence means tiger is close by.'

Graydon Farb massaged the trigger of his rifle. The silence of the swamp was eerie. And the dawn sun, as it began to filter through the canopy of vegetation on the edge of the swamp, gave the scene a bleached-out, almost wintery aspect.

But after two or three minutes – it seemed longer – the birds resumed their singing, and lapwings and curlews flitted again between the trees.

Unmesh, who all the time had kept his head half-cocked close to the path, stood up.

'Tigress too far away now,' he said. 'It is better we are returning to camp.'

'So early?' protested Graydon. But he did not insist on carrying on, since he was exhilarated by his close call and pleased with Unmesh for picking up the tigress's tracks.

'Evening time we look again,' said Ali.

And so they spent the day resting near the jeep, taking it in turns to sleep and to keep watch for forest rangers.

Their evening hunt was less eventful. No tracks were picked up this time, though Unmesh was able to show Graydon Farb a clearing where a tiger had dragged his kill – there were remnants of chital – and where he had sprayed the ground with urine, a strong musky smell.

'Is it the same tiger as before?' asked Graydon.

'Different tiger,' said Unmesh. 'Before it was tigress. This time man tiger. Bigger.'

Graydon Farb brandished his rifle excitedly. He wanted his tiger to be enormous. He wanted it to fill half his dining room on Lake Shore Drive. And he knew exactly how he'd have the beast stuffed too: mounted on a rocky plinth, just like they do it at the Natural History Museum in New York, one paw raised, ready to pounce. Mr Bennack, his tame taxidermist in Detroit, would know what to do. He would do anything, that feller, providing you looked after him; he didn't mind what he stuffed, legal or not, if you paid him enough. Graydon Farb

77

guessed that, in any case, old Dick Bennack would give anything to stuff a tiger. Sure as hell he would – it would be the crowning glory of his career.

There was still no sign of a forest ranger, and Graydon Farb felt optimistic as he ate his second supper in the jungle. The confidence of his guides was contagious. 'Tomorrow morning we will find tiger,' Ali had said. 'Starting earlier time – four o'clock.'

Graydon Farb slept soundly, dreaming of orange coats and zig-zag black stripes. But at a quarter past three he was shaken awake by Ali.

'Quickly, come,' he hissed. 'We have found tiger. Quickly, quickly.'

Graydon Farb pulled on his boots – he slept in his clothes – and grabbed his rifle. 'It's early,' he said.

'Unmesh heard the tiger growling,' said Ali. 'It is not far away. Unmesh is watching it. Quickly, quickly.'

Graydon Farb followed Ali into the darkness, stumbling over branches and brushwood as he went. Ali had a torch, but its beam was paltry in the vastness of the jungle. They followed the banks of the same stream where they'd found paw marks the previous day, but further this time, to a different patch of swamp. And then in front of him on the path Graydon could make out the silhouette of Unmesh, his arm raised behind him, signalling them to stand still. Then Unmesh motioned him to raise the rifle and directed its barrels towards a tangle of reeds.

'Wait,' whispered Unmesh. In his right hand he was holding a hefty stick, and dangling from his belt was a rubber torch, bigger and more effective-looking than Ali's, which he unbuckled.

'When you see the tiger, shoot suddenly,' he said. 'The torch is bringing light.' And then he swung the beam into the depths of the reeds, where Graydon could see the tiger, green eyes gleaming fiercely, its vast head raised to charge them. He released both barrels consecutively, the first shot pounding into the animal's forehead, an inch above the left eye, the second bullet cracking into its shoulder. So accurate was he that the tiger fell instantly to the ground, only the noise of its huge body crashing down in the undergrowth breaking the quiet of the jungle.

Graydon was all for rushing forward to inspect his trophy, but Unmesh restrained him.

'Maybe tiger is not dead yet,' he said. 'Better if we wait some minutes.'

So they waited on the path, their eyes fixed on the clump of reeds where the tiger had fallen – Graydon Farb cursing impatiently, since the silence of the beast confirmed he had shot it stone dead. Meanwhile Ali ran back to the jeep to fetch the tarpaulin bag Graydon had brought to transport his trophy back to Bombay.

Ali and Unmesh spread the heavy bag on the ground, then carried it forward to the reeds, Graydon providing covering fire from the path in case the tiger really was playing dead and charged them. But when they were on top of the tiger they signalled that all was well – the beast was truly dead – and crammed its carcass into the bag.

'Don't hurry it, fellers,' said Graydon when he saw the tiger's haunches disappearing inside the tarpaulin.

'Actually, sir, I think we must hurry,' replied Ali. 'The shots might have been heard by forest rangers. We should leave this place quickly.'

Graydon saw the logic in this. After all, he had the rest of his life to admire his tiger, and he could tell from the immense size of the bag that it was full-grown. An eight-footer at the very least, perhaps even a nine-footer, he thought, as he helped force the beast's tail – already cold and stiff – into the bag and secured the metal fasteners. Then Ali and Unmesh suspended the bag from a stout pole which they carried on their shoulders back to the jeep. Graydon Farb swaggered behind them in perfect spirits. Not many hunters these days could say they'd shot a tiger on their second day in the Indian jungle.

They struck camp at once, retraced their route to the asphalt road, roared through Bichia and on to Mandla. At Mandla they stopped for the first time since leaving the park, filled the jeep with petrol and bought blocks of ice to lay across the tarpaulin bag. Until Graydon Farb had his trophy safe in an airtight metal crate, he wasn't taking any chances; a dead animal could decompose in weather like this in a matter of hours. They bought fresh ice on the outskirts of Jabalpur, and twice more in the main road to Bombay, but still Farb was apprehensive. So when they reached Bombay they made straight for the airport and the Lakshmi Import-Export Company where, as good as his word, Ram Singh's six metal crates were stacked ready in the warehouse.

Graydon Farb waited until they were alone, then heaved the tarpaulin bag out of the back of the jeep and into a crate. The other crates they half-filled with the camping equipment, to equalise the weight with the crate containing the tiger, and then they filled them to the brim with mangoes bought from the fruit stalls outside the airport gates. An Air India flight left Bombay for London the following morning, and from Heathrow the crates would be transferred to the Pan Am flight to Detroit. Graydon Farb presented his export papers from the Board of Trade at the customs and excise desk, where they were pronounced 'in order' and stamped. In less than two days, thought Graydon Farb triumphantly, my tiger is coming home to Lake Shore Drive.

And so it was. The great metal crates were heaved into the hall and their lids unscrewed, filling the place with a rich scent of ripe mango. But the tarpaulin bag, so far as Farb could see, had not been tampered with and smelt fine.

Graydon Farb ordered a van to take the bag round to Dick Bennack's studio, where he would meet the taxidermist in an hour's time. But first he drove himself over to Lake Shore Farms.

He found Franklin J. Morgan in his den, polishing the stock of his favourite duck-shooting gun.

'Hi, stranger,' said Franklin, putting the shotgun aside. 'I'd pretty near given you up for dead.'

Graydon Farb noticed a reserve about his welcome.

'No need to look so poker-faced, old friend,' he said 'I haven't got a mountain lion if that's what's bugging you.'

Morgan brightened. 'They're mighty wily, those cougars,' said Morgan. 'As I've always said, if it wasn't for a slice of good old-fashioned luck, I don't reckon I would ever have bagged one myself.'

Graydon smiled. Franklin J. Morgan's smugness was going to last for another twenty minutes at most.

'But I did get myself one trophy I guess will interest you,' said Graydon. 'It's over at Dick Bennack's place right now. You want to drive over to look see?'

Franklin Morgan agreed in a condescending way, so they both got in Graydon's car to head across town.

Graydon drove with suppressed excitement. He could hardly wait for Dick Bennack's congratulations. Old Dick Bennack sure knew a great trophy when he saw one.

But Dick Bennack's manner was not congratulatory at all.

'What is this you've sent over to me, Graydon? Is it some kind of a joke?'

'Quite the reverse, Dick,' said Graydon Farb proudly. 'It's the real thing. I shot him myself in India. Dick,' he added, 'I want that tiger stuffed fancier than anything you've ever done before.'

Dick Bennack laughed. 'Great joke, Graydon,' he said. 'I never had you down as a practical joker. But seriously, where *did* you get hold of this darned thing? The straw began spilling right out of it as soon as I slit his belly. It must be sixty years old at least. The way they've done it, I reckon this tiger was stuffed in about 1925.'

THE PERFECT PAIR

A True Story

Nobody was at all surprised when Katie Mulholland and Alex Mustoe announced their engagement. They had been inseparable for more than four years, clearly loved each other, and were of the perfect age to get married, Katie being twenty-six and Alexander four years older. Each time they went away on holiday together – to Sardinia, Tobago or skiing in Zermatt – their friends predicted, 'Katie and Alex will come back engaged this time.' And eventually they did, which gave everyone the double satisfaction of being proved right, as well as boundless and genuine delight for the couple.

Katie and Alexander were in every respect a perfect pair. Both were blond, amiable and pleasant-looking. Alexander had a wide face, tightly curled hair and an engaging grin. Although he never said anything remotely memorable, or expressed any opinion that differed from those of his friends, he was charming, good-humoured and relaxed. During the day he worked as a financial analyst for a firm of City stockbrokers, but he seldom mentioned it. His real pleasure in life, one felt, came from his holidays, his friends and from Katie.

Katie Mulholland was, beyond a doubt, an ideal match for Alexander Mustoe. She was that rare thing, a genuine English rose, small and slender and sweet-natured with perfect fair skin, blue eyes and a pointed little nose like a miniature dog. Her blonde hair, which sometimes she tied back with a black velvet bow, was thick and straight. Like Alexander, there was nothing introspective about her. She had learnt to regild picture frames and set up a little business in a workshop in Pimlico, which she shared with two other girls and a busy telephone. Unless they were hectic, she rang Alex every afternoon to make plans for the evening. 'Katie's what I call a really *nice* girl,' her friends' mothers would say. 'One day she's going to make a wonderful bride.'

Alex Mustoe had a flat in a mews in South Kensington, opposite Christie's in the Brompton Road, and it was here that he and Katie did most of their entertaining. Katie's flat in Dawes Road, which she shared with her sister, was rather small, so she prepared the food for their dinner parties in her little kitchen and then drove it over to Alex's. They were disciplined hosts and invited people for dinner once a fortnight. When they were invited anywhere, they always paid back. Katie cooked the first course and the main course, and Alex always made one of his specialities: bread and butter pudding or Greek yoghurt with a spoonful of cherry jam. Once a year, in June, Alexander gave a drinks party to which he invited the same people. The list hardly varied from one year to the next. It didn't bother him: these were his friends.

Hanging in the bathroom of Alex's flat were two enormous, framed collages that Katie had made from old holiday photographs. The faces of their numerous friends smiled out at them. John and Mark and Alice and Tiggy in Ischia; Philip water-skiing in Corfu; Annie painting her toenails on the caique; Vicky off piste. Katie and Alex liked to go on holiday in a group of friends, especially if Willie Buchanan was in charge. Willie was Alex's oldest friend and a great team leader, so they were always pleased when he rang to say he'd booked a chalet for a week in Courchevel or taken a villa sleeping ten with a tennis court in Portugal. His handsome dark face was all over the collage. When Katie and Alex got engaged it was obvious that Willie would be best man.

On the grass verge outside the church, and all along the village street, cars were parking and doors slamming. Girls were adjusting their hats, and men who had driven down from London in their waistcoats were pulling on their tailcoats. It was ten minutes to three and the bells of St Michael's Church were pealing loudly. John and Mark and Alice and Tiggy had been lunching at the Red Lion on the village green and now hurried towards the church to bag a decent pew. Vicky was brushing flecks off Philip's shoulders. Annie was wrapping her wedding present in the back seat of a car. From every direction men in morning coats and women in summer dresses were converging on the church, pushing their way past the little crowd of villagers who had gathered at the church gate to see the bride. Elderly aunts and grandparents of Katie's were greeting each other under the Norman porch, and a large party of Mustoe cousins, who were staying for the wedding at a local hotel, arrived in convoy clutching their invitations.

Mr Richard and Lady Rosemary Mulholland
request the pleasure of your company
at the marriage of their daughter
Katharine Louise
to
Mr Alexander James Mustoe
at
The Church of St Michael and All Angels
Upper Eastingford, Gloucestershire
and afterwards at
Eastingford Knoll

When Katie and Alexander had come to draw up their lists for wedding invitations, they realised to their dismay that they'd need to ask almost three hundred people; they had so many friends, and their parents had insisted on so many relations and friends of their own. They would be hard pressed to fit everyone in the church, and the ushers had been instructed to pack them in tight.

'Ten to a pew, not less than ten,' Richard Mulholland had told them. 'Otherwise half the congregation will be left standing outside in the churchyard.'

His wife, Lady Rosemary, had planned the whole day with precision. It had been an enormous effort, but she had loved doing it, she told everyone. Katie was her oldest child and the first to get married. And Rosemary had taken to Alexander Mustoe as soon as she met him; she liked his straightforward good manners and obvious honesty and consideration for her. He'd been charming throughout the wedding preparations too, ringing her regularly from his office to discuss this detail or that, and showing such enthusiasm for her choice of flowers and the marquee they'd put up for the reception at Eastingford Knoll.

Now the bridesmaids were forming up in the porch: four little girls in white dresses with yellow sashes and ballet shoes. Each was clutching a posy of buttercups and daisies, which matched the yellow and white theme of the flowers in the church, and around their necks were the little seed pearl necklaces that Alexander had given them yesterday, at the rehearsal, as bridesmaids' presents. 'What sweet bridesmaids,' every single person said as they went into the church. 'How lovely it is to be at a proper country wedding.'

Inside the church, the village organist doodled inconsequentially with his stops in, while a phalanx of tall, athletic ushers squeezed more and more guests into the pews, like guards on the Tokyo underground.

Lurking in the front pew, looking nervous as bridegrooms do, was Alexander. And beside him, looking sleek and confident in his morning coat, as best men do, was Willie.

At two minutes past three there was a flurry of activity at the back of the church, and the dazzle of flashbulbs that announced the arrival of the bride. And then the organist struck up with 'Praise my soul, the King of heaven' and Katie began her solemn procession down the aisle – small, slender, sweet-natured Katie, who had never looked quite so lovely as she did at that moment, with just that hint of smugness in her face, that brides have, as she held on to her father's arm, and her four pretty bridesmaids scuttled along in her wake, holding on to her train. The congregation sang lustily, slow to chide and quick to praise, and whispered to each other how beautiful Katie looked.

And so the wedding proceeded: Katie making her vows in a surprisingly strong voice for such a slight girl, which made her older relations swell with pride. Willie Buchanan – taller and sleeker than ever – produced the wedding ring on cue, which was duly blessed, and Alexander James and Katharine Louise were pronounced man and wife. The vicar of St Michael's, who had known Katie since she was ten or eleven and had prepared her for confirmation, gave a short, old-fashioned address in which he mysteriously likened Alexander to the captain of a village cricket team and Katie to the opening batsman and wicket keeper combined. Psalms were sung, then 'Love divine, all loves excelling', the wedding party disappeared into the vestry to sign the register, and finally Alexander and Katie reappeared to the strains of 'Jerusalem' and processed back down the aisle, smiling and waving at John and Mark and Alice and Tiggy as they swept by.

At Eastingford Knoll nothing that is conventional at a traditional wedding reception had been neglected. Guests arrived at the front door of the house, were directed through the Mulhollands' drawing room and out through French windows into a pink and white striped marquee on the lawn. The grass had been covered by yards of coconut matting, and ranged along the billowing walls of the tent were round tables decorated with baskets of pink and white roses. A score of ladies from the village handed round glasses of champagne, triangles of bread with smoked salmon, asparagus rolled in brown bread, and rather delicious sausages on sticks with Dijon mustard. The pretty little bridesmaids soon kicked off their shoes and ran around the tent playing tag and shrieking. Elderly, stubble-cheeked men in tailcoats swayed up to Katie saying, 'You don't know me, but I'm an old, old cousin of your husband's. Alexander's certainly a lucky chap, and I wonder whether I might take the liberty of kissing the bride?'

At the far end of the tent was a small raised dais – a couple of feet high – on top of which was a three-tiered wedding cake, thick with royal icing and garlanded with orange blossom and white freesias. Here stood Alex and Katie – Katie radiant as she stood beside her still-nervous husband – to cut the cake with Richard Mulholland's Brigade of Guards sword. And here too they were joined by Katie's favourite godfather and sleek Willie Buchanan, to make their speeches on behalf of the bride and groom.

First, as is the custom, spoke genial old Gerry McNeill. A farmer and lifelong friend of the Mulhollands, he had not a brain in his head nor a mean bone in his body.

'How proud I feel,' he said, 'to stand here today and propose the health of my dear goddaughter, who I have no hesita-

tion in saying is quite the loveliest-looking girl in the tent today.'
There was a roar of agreement from the crowd of friends
and relations pressed around the dais, as genial old Gerry
McNeill turned affectionately towards his goddaughter.

Gerry McNeill did not eschew any cliché in his long, warm,
touching and stupid speech. Katie, he recalled, he had seen
in her bath when she was two years old, and he thought
Alexander a lucky chap to have the same opportunity today.
He remembered Katie coming to stay with him when she must
have been nine or ten years old, and how competitive she had
been at the game of ludo, and how he trusted she was now a
little more sanguine about such things or Alexander was in for
some choppy moments. He remembered her too as a Brownie,
as a Pony Club member, as a naughty but endearing schoolgirl
and, most recently, as a gilder of picture frames. 'May Katie
and Alexander's life together be itself gilded with happiness,'
he concluded, as he urged the sea of morning coats and hats to
toast the health of the bride and groom. 'May their happiness
be as golden as the paint in Katie's workshop.'

Once again a great cheer went up from the crowd, as three
hundred glasses were raised to wish the couple well.

And only now, as he stepped forward to the microphone,
did the grey and strained look of the bridegroom begin to
register with the crowd. I had vaguely noticed his tension
during Gerry McNeill's speech – indeed, throughout the day –
but such were the high spirits of the bride, and the widespread
feeling of goodwill, that it had been easy to overlook it.

But one could not now ignore his gaunt expression; there
was a tautness about Alexander's mouth, and an emptiness
about his eyes that was chilling. And though he mustered a
smile as he took his place at the microphone, there was no joy
in it.

'Er, ladies and gentlemen, I'd first of all like to propose a
toast to our bridesmaids,' said Alexander dryly, looking down
at the four pretty little girls in yellow sashes clustered around
the cake. 'If I wasn't already married to the most wonderful
girl in the world, I'm sure I'd like to be married to one of our
gorgeous bridesmaids today ... Davina, Janie, Lucy and
Jemima. Ladies and gentlemen – the bridesmaids.'

'The bridesmaids,' responded the crowd, and took another deep sip of champagne.

'So many people,' went on Alexander, 'have taken such trouble to make today a success that I hardly know where to begin. The vicar, of course, the Reverend Philip Goode, and Mrs Phipps and Mrs McGuire who arranged the stunning flowers in the church, and Mrs, er' – he momentarily consulted the piece of card in his hand – 'Mrs Spence, who produced the delicious food here at the reception. Thank you all very much indeed for all of this. And more than anyone, of course, I want to thank Katie's mother, Rosemary, who has been the brilliant general behind the scenes and really has organised everything so meticulously today. If Lady Rosemary was at the helm, England really would have nothing to fear!' At which joke the crowd laughed jovially, and a little cheer went up for Rosemary Mulholland and her sterling powers of organisation.

Now that he was underway, Alexander spoke more confidently, and it was only the deathly-white pallor of his skin, and a certain deadness about his eyes, that gave one the slightest cause for concern.

'And next, of course,' he went on, 'I want to thank my best man, Willie Buchanan.' He turned towards Willie, who was standing, feet apart, a glass of champagne in his hand, a yard or two to Alexander's right. Knowing that the eyes of the crowed were all on him, Willie smiled modestly and ran his hand through his thick brown hair.

'Willie,' said Alexander, 'has been my best friend for twenty-two years since we both arrived at our preparatory school in Kent the same term. I certainly don't intend to tell you any stories about Willie aged eight – since I rather fear that's exactly what he intends to tell you about me in his own speech – but I do want to say that, over the years, we've had some great times together, Willie and I. After we left school, we spent eight months travelling together in South America, where we shared some pretty hairy moments. And we went to all our first dances together, where we shared some even hairier moments, and we even worked together at one point in the same stockbroking firm, though Willie has since gone up in the world as a bond dealer. And one of the first things I did when I first met Katie was to introduce her to Willie, because I realised that if my new girlfriend couldn't get along with my best friend then the relationship was going to be doomed from the word go. Fortunately Katie did approve of Willie, and vice versa, so the rest, as they say, is history.'

There was a polite cheer for Willie Buchanan before Alexander continued.

'And lastly – and it really is lastly,' he promised, 'lastly I want to thank my ushers. In particular I want to thank them for coming round to see me two days ago at my flat in London and telling me something that I suppose I ought to have realised myself, but was too blind to see. So I thank my ushers for informing me that my wife' – he turned to look at Katie – 'and my best man, Willie Buchanan' – he shot a single glance of hatred at Buchanan – 'have been having an affair behind my back for the last eight months.'

Then Alexander drew from the inside pocket of his tailcoat a slim folder of travel documents.

'These,' he said, without pausing for breath, 'are two return air tickets to the Maldives, where Katie and I were going to spend our honeymoon. Under the circumstances, Willie, I think it would be more appropriate if you had them' – he thrust the folder into the hands of his paralysed best man – 'and may I say that I wish you and Katie the very greatest happiness in your future lives together.'

And then Alexander Mustoe stepped down from the stage and, walking with the utmost dignity, passed through the stunned crowd which parted before him, up the steps into the Mulhollands' drawing room, through the hall and out through the front door. In all that time not a word was spoken, as the eyes of every person in the tent were transfixed by the shocked, guilt-ridden faces of the bride in her white dress and the sleek best man left on the dais.

And then, outside on the gravel, there was the sound of a car being started, as Alexander Mustoe drove himself away from his wedding reception, followed by the dull clatter of tin cans trailing behind his bumper.

THE PLAYGIRLS
OF NAGALAND

i

Three years ago, almost to the day, I went on holiday to Calcutta. I had at the time a job on a magazine, and the relentless pressure from deadlines made it difficult to get away very often. Consequently I was exhausted. Faced with an article for possible publication, I could not tell whether it was brilliant or thoroughly silly, and the extravagance and pretension of the magazine's fashion editors, which it was part of my job to regulate, had drained me. So we flew to Calcutta, my girlfriend and I, because it is a long way from London, and as different as any city I could think of.

We had one contact in Calcutta, the wife of a Bengali newspaper editor, who immediately volunteered to give a dinner party for us at her house 'to introduce you both into Calcutta society'. The prospect, though kindly meant, was vaguely unwelcome. We had chosen to holiday in Calcutta precisely because we believed there was no Society to be introduced into. The dinner invitation seemed to portend a whole round of cocktail parties and receptions, at the end of which I would be more tired than ever. On the morning of the party a list of the other eight guests was delivered by a driver to our room at the Tollygunge Club, with a short biographical résumé of each person. I was amused that this American habit should also flourish in Calcutta. These three- or four-line biographies are intended, I suppose, to allow you to develop some interesting lines of conversation in advance, or at least to save you from making some momentous gaffe over a fellow guest's status. My heart sank when I read the list. There was to be an Indian newspaper tycoon at the dinner, whose long portfolio of publications was meticulously listed; there was to be an industrialist with cement factories in Dacca; a film producer whose work is shown at the Venice Biennale; and two young princesses of Nagaland, Jaisha and Jenju. In their résumé Devika Prasad had noted, 'They are very cheerful girls and quite gassy.'

Devika's house was in a suburb of west Calcutta, in a part of the city that had been built originally for English clerks of the East India Company. The name of her house was Mon Repos, and its architecture too made you think of a seaside villa in Hastings or Eastbourne. Inside, however, was pure Manhattan. The decoration was entirely in black and white. Every stick of furniture, every last vase and ashtray, was black or white. On the walls were framed black and white photographs by the American photographer Herb Ritts, and the table was set for dinner with white octagonal plates and serving dishes on a black cloth. Our host and hostess were also dressed from top to toe in black and white.

Devika's black hair was arranged in a chignon, which looked marvellously lustrous above her white shawl, and on her bony, indoor fingers were a mass of black onyx rings.

'And this,' she said as she completed her introductions, 'is Jaisha. And this is Jenju. They come from Nagaland actually, but they always winter here in Calcutta. So you are sort of honorary Calcutta residents, aren't you, girls?'

Jaisha and Jenju beamed. 'We feel so much at home in Calcutta,' Jaisha said. 'You know, I think we would die of boredom if we didn't come here. Nagaland is so beautiful, but there's so little to do, and the men are such slugs, you wouldn't believe. So our mother allows us to spend part of the winter in our house here. With a chaperone, of course.'

I wish I could adequately describe Jaisha and Jenju's intonation, because it was unlike anything I'd encountered before. The singsong cadence was Indian, as was their emphasis on particular words, seemingly chosen at random, such as 'The men are *such* slugs, you *wouldn't* believe.' But there were other strands in their accent too. American, certainly, and a suggestion of Parisienne in their vowels, and even a trace of Irish. But it was their appearance that struck you first. They were impossibly beautiful and incongruously smart. Their clothes, as was clear for all to see from their buttons, came from designers in Paris and Milan, and would not have looked too plain at a gala in the White House. In Calcutta, even at Mon Repos, they were startling. Jaisha's Chanel suit jangled with gold chains while Jenju's purple silk cocktail dress rippled with beading. Jaisha, the elder, was broader in the face than her sister, with perfect white teeth and skin that made her look younger than twenty-five. There was something Tibetan about her. Her nose was slightly flattened and her ear lobes, on which were clipped a huge pair of Chanel earrings, were low like a Buddha's. Jenju had a European face. Apart from her colouring, she could have been French. Her bones were delicate and her lips were full and sensitive. Both girls were extraordinarily animated. They exuded enthusiasm. They gave the impression that everything was fresh and exciting to them, and that everyone delighted them.

'We have been looking forward to meeting you so much,' said Jaisha. 'When Devika said you were coming we were thrilled to pieces.'

'Oh *yes*,' said Jenju. 'You see, we have a question we are longing to ask you.'

'You are the one person who is just bound to know the answer,' said Jaisha.

'Of course he will know the answer!' put in Jenju. 'What a silly thing to say. After all, he works on a magazine.'

'I'll certainly try,' I said, 'though I warn you I'm by no means an expert on everything in it.'

'Well,' said Jaisha. 'You know about Karl Lagerfeld?'

I replied that I knew a little, but not everything, about the Parish fashion designer.

'In your opinion,' said Jaisha, 'is he more talented when he is designing for Chanel or for Chloé or when he is designing for his own label, the KL collection?'

The question was surreal. We had flown halfway round the world, changed aeroplanes at Frankfurt and again in Delhi, to escape discussions about fashion designers. And all the time, waiting on our arrival, were Jaisha and Jenju and the dilemma of Karl Lagerfeld.

I gave them my opinion, and said I was impressed that they were so informed about fashion.

'But of course we read all the magazines,' said Jenju. 'We have subscriptions sent to our home.'

'*Vogue* and *Harpers & Queen* and the *Tatler* from England,' said Jaisha. 'And *Elle* from France. And Paris *Vogue* and *Marie Claire*. And some American magazines, actually.'

'You get all those sent to Calcutta?'

'Not to Calcutta, to our home in Nagaland. We have always subscribed to the top magazines. Our mother takes them, and we read them too now, of course.'

The more I talked to Jaisha and Jenju, the more I was fascinated by them. Their knowledge of trivial details of life in London, Paris and New York far exceeded that of anybody living there. Not only did they know the names of the latest fashionable restaurants, but exactly who ate in them. They knew the latest *avant-garde* jewellery designers in Paris and the most faddish new nightclubs in Soho. They were informed about charity balls at the Hyde Park Hotel and charity galas at the Metropolitan Museum in New York. They knew about shoemakers so exclusive that only by word of mouth can you visit them at all, and the newest shops to open branches on Fifth Avenue or Sloane Street. They would say, 'The new Hermès sounds so fantastic with its enlarged display of scarves,' or, 'The Slalom Ball at the Grosvenor House Hotel must have been marvellous this year, with a week's partridge shooting as the prize in the tombola.'

Both girls had a flattering but misplaced belief that, whenever a new restaurant or nightclub opened in London, I would surely be found eating and dancing there all the time.

'I'm ashamed to say I don't know London half as well as you,' I said after a while. 'You'll have to show me around next time you're there.'

'Next time we're there! Oh, Jenju, did you hear what Nicholas said?' Jaisha's broad Tibetan face was suffused with pleasure. 'I'm sorry to tell you that we've *never* been there. Our mother would never allow it. She doesn't approve of us being in Calcutta, actually. I mean, she accepts it, but she is not happy about it. But anywhere else she would never permit.

And certainly not London! Oh no, London we can only read about in magazines.'

ii

We were very much taken with Jaisha and Jenju, so we were pleased when, two or three days later, they sent their driver to the Tollygunge with a message. We were sitting by the stand of the old race course when a small, dark-skinned, rather wild-eyed man in a chauffeur's outfit with riding breeches was escorted over to us with a letter. It was an invitation to dinner that evening. 'It's going to be most informal, a suit only affair,' Jaisha had written on a postcard emblazoned with a coat of arms that involved a cannon and a rampant leopard. 'There'll be lots of crazy people for you to meet. The driver will collect you at seven o'clock.'

Our speculation about the kind of house that these glamorous princesses of Nagaland might keep in Calcutta proved highly inaccurate. It was a concrete and steel building, built in the late fifties, and closely resembled a modern extension to an Oxford college. This, it turned out, had been the intention. The girls' grandfather, when his abdication had compelled him to relocate to Bengal, had commissioned Powell & Moya, the architects that his old college, Christ Church, had chosen to design its Blue Boar quad (which the King had never seen) to put up something similar in Calcutta. The drawing room, with its distressed concrete walls, floor-to-ceiling draylon drapes, and chrome and plastic chairs, seemed to owe its provenance to a rather sad college bar. The family had mixed opinions on their house in Calcutta. The King, right up until the day he died, had stubbornly insisted on being pleased with it. Jaisha and Jenju's parents, having made their peace with the new authorities in Nagaland, had headed home and seldom visited the house. Their daughters, seizing upon it as a means of escaping to Calcutta for the winter, seemed not to notice it at all.

There were several other guests for dinner, none of them fulfilling Jaisha's promise of a 'crazy' crowd. The Indian men

95

looked timid and rather awed and talked humbly among themselves.

'Come on, you dreadful slugs,' we heard Jenju chiding them gaily as we arrived. 'Don't you know you're supposed to *mingle* at a party? Don't just stand there enjoying your men's talk, you must mingle.'

Both girls looked, if anything, more stunning than at Devika Prasad's. Jenju wore another delicately swathed lilac Italian cocktail dress, while Jaisha's dress was white and very short, with sheer black stockings and high-heeled black grosgrain shoes.

'Oh, thank heavens you are here,' said Jaisha. 'This party is going at a snail's pace. But you'll soon change all that, we're relying on you.'

'I'm sure,' Jaisha added flatteringly, 'it will really swing now that *you* are here. It was so perfect your arriving in town like a bolt from the blue, so we just had to make you guests of honour.'

The surprised guests of honour were paraded, like nawabs, through the party. With each new introduction, Jaisha and Jenju's build-up of their other friends became more elaborate.

'Next I want you to meet this very old friend of ours,' they would say. 'Ali is the son of a very prominent industrialist and gives some of the *wildest* parties in Calcutta, don't you, Ali, and this is his very attractive wife, Malavika. Malavika is considered quite a beauty, aren't you, Malavika?'

'I wouldn't say that,' replied the modest Malavika.

'Of course you are,' exclaimed Jenu. 'Everyone is saying so. You are absolutely the toast of the town. Really, Malavika, you shouldn't be so bashful about yourself.'

Although their praise for everybody and everything was just a little indiscriminate, one overlooked it because the girls' high spirits were so delightful and their enthusiasm so genuine.

Entirely through their good humour, the party picked up. The humble Indian men drank more lager and mingled. Naga waiters arranged on the sideboard a huge buffet of Bengali and European dishes, from which people helped themselves to fish curry and potato salad. A record player was set up for dancing.

96

It grew late and the party dwindled until we were the only guests left.

'Don't chicken out yet,' said Jaisha. 'It's so depressing when everyone goes home at once. Let's have a jolly good post mortem about all those people at the party.'

Jaisha settled herself on the end of a plastic sofa. Jenju fetched an ashtray and they both lit up another cigarette.

'Didn't you think the men were so sweet but dull?' Jaisha said.

'Not really. I enjoyed myself.'

'They're not at all the stuff which dreams are made of,' said Jenju. 'Not boyfriend material at all.'

'Not in a month of Sundays,' said Jaisha. 'They're so uninternational.'

'But better than Naga men,' said Jenju flatly, at which they both looked a bit sad.

'And at least we can smoke in front of Indian men,' said Jenju. 'When we are married we won't be able to smoke or drink or even come to Calcutta.'

'I was writing to the boy I was betrothed to for three years,' said Jaisha, 'and the first thing he said when we met was "Put out that cigarette please."'

'Perhaps you could marry a rather dashing Indian man instead,' I suggested.

'An Indian man? Oh no, never,' they both chorused.

'That couldn't happen,' explained Jaisha. 'None of our relations would ever speak to us again. It's impossible.'

'Oh no, we must return and marry a Naga man next year. We have promised our mother to do so.'

'Will you have to marry the non-smoker?' I asked.

'No, fortunately, I've been allowed to turn him down because we didn't hit it off. That's been agreed. But the next husband my mother chooses, I must marry,' said Jaisha. 'And Jenju will be married the year after.'

'But *who* will I marry?' said Jenju pathtically. 'We know all the suitable men already, and they're all so boring. All Naga men do all day long is hunt boar and drink. I'm sure I'd never be satisfied with any of them.'

Already, at the ages of twenty-five and twenty-three, they

were by Naga standards rather old to be unmarried, and Nagaland, I learned later, is an exceptionally conservative place. Geographically it is remote, bordered by Manipur and Assam to the south-west, Burma to the east and Tibet to the north. Under the British administrations, Naga was mostly closed to travellers owing to the ferocity of the native tribes in the Naga Hills; headhunters who wore nothing but necklaces of yellow spirit stones. The adventurer Christoph von Furer-Haimendorf wrote a book about them in the thirties called *The Naked Nagas*, in which he described how he led a raiding party of sepoys into the hills and returned with a tin trunk full of severed headhunters' heads. During the war it was in Nagaland that the British, with native support, halted the Japanese; there was a heroic last stand at the tennis court of the Governor's bungalow at Kohima, the capital, in gratitude for which the British Government presented the natives with a cottage hospital. Under Indian rule Naga has remained a restricted area, because of the sensitivity of the border with Tibet, but matters have lately eased somewhat. Several new chain hotels have opened in Kohima, and coaches of tourists arrive to see the museum of native headdresses. The old royal families and chieftains of Naga have prospered, leasing land to the hotels and setting up craft emporiums. They are intricately intermarried, and herein lay Jaisha and Jenju's problem. Every appropriate husband, they had known since birth. Almost all of them were first or second cousins, and those that weren't were related to them in numerous ways by marriage. Several times a week one or other of the old ruling families gave parties, and at every party the same twenty suitors were present. None had ever excited in Jaisha and Jenju even a glimmer of romance. Molly-coddled and parochial, the young men of Naga knew nothing of dress designers in Milan or nightclubs in Soho. They had travelled nowhere. Few had ever left Kohima except on boar-hunting trips into the Patkoi Hills. Boar-hunting and pig-sticking were their sole pastimes. A dozen of them, with forty beaters, would make camp in the Patkoi for a week at a time, and discuss their exploits – so it seemed to Jaisha and Jenju – for twice that time when they got back. It is the custom in Naga for boys to be educated at home, while girls are sent away to boarding schools in India, and this added to their conviction of their suitors' woeful ignorance.

'You see, we were schooled by Irish nuns,' said Jaisha, 'at a very good boarding school in south India. It was a lot of fun, actually. Every Saturday there was a charity bazaar, a kind of bring-and-buy, with shove-half penny, and pinning the tail on the donkey, blindfolded you know.'

Jenju, who seemed at that moment more acquiescent than her sister, lit another cigarette. 'Oh, maybe we are making too much fuss and bother over this marriage business,' she said. 'Perhaps we should just grit our teeth and get on with it. We don't have any choice in the matter, after all.'

'Wouldn't your family come round to it after a bit, if you married a, um, non-Naga?' I asked.

'Absolutely not,' said Jaisha. 'You don't understand. We'd be ostracised by everyone, all our cousins we see all the time. We could never live in Naga married to a foreigner.'

Jaisha stood up. 'Well, anyway,' she said brightly, 'let's be a little more cheerful. We must get you a glass of some very nice cognac before you go home. And now tell us more about the mad and glamorous social whirl in London.'

iii

I could not have been more surprised, four and a half months later, by a telephone call to my London office.

'Hello, hello? Is that you, Nicholas? It is us. We are here in London.'

It was Jaisha.

'How lovely, and how amazing. What are you doing here? How long are you here for?'

'Eight months,' said Jaisha. 'Our mother has allowed us to come to college in London. In South Kensington. You know the International College of South Kensington?'

'I'm afraid I'm not very well up on schools. What are you studying?'

'Fashion awareness, colour co-ordination, make-up and modelling – you'll be quite shocked how stiff the course is.'

'And your mother has really allowed you to come?' I was

surprised, in the light of our conversation in Calcutta, that she'd given her permission.

'She was highly reluctant, of course. But her misgivings have been completely satisfied by the Dowager Lady Glenaffric. She'd been lodging with us in Naga for the hunting and persuaded our mother to let us come. She assured her she would keep an eye on us. But now she's gone to Scotland, actually. We're staying in her flat while she's away.'

Jenju, whom I could hear prompting her sister in the background, came on the line.

'It is so exciting to be in London,' she said. 'We simply can't wait to visit all the restaurants and clubs. But who on earth is going to escort us?'

I made a plan to take them out to dinner the following evening, and said that I would collect them from their flat in Onslow Square at eight o'clock.

I arrived to find them as dazzling as before, their clothes bought, they said, that very afternoon in Beauchamp Place.

'If only we could give you a drink,' Jenju said, 'but we're all alone in this flat. Lady Glenaffric kindly said we could have drinks, but there's nobody to look after us here.'

A tray of bottles and glasses was conspicuous on a side table, and I suggested that, if anybody wanted them, I would happily pour drinks.

'But we have no ice,' said Jaisha plaintively.

'I could fetch some. There's bound to be an ice tray in the top of the fridge.'

'How can you know all these things?' said Jenju. 'We haven't the first idea how to make ice.'

It became obvious that, on the domestic front, the girls were hopeless. In the four days they'd been alone in Onslow Square they'd eaten nothing but cheese and biscuits. Neither of them had ever boiled a kettle. They would no more have dreamed of touching the oven than of ironing their own shirts. They had bought milk in a carton from a corner shop, but could not open it. Their bedroom floor, they said sadly, had become a jumble of clothes because there was nobody to pick them up for them, and they hated to sleep in a mess. This litany of ineptitudes might give the impression that they were shockingly spoilt, but they did not seem so. The impression they gave was of innocence. In Nagaland and Calcutta the prospect of their needing ever to prepare their own meals was so remote that nobody had troubled to teach them. Perched on Lady Glenaffric's brocade sofa in their fitted Italian suits and diamanté earrings, they were to all intents and purposes incapacitated, and you felt that unless they were taken swiftly out to dinner they would starve to death.

IV

I had to go away for a week after our dinner, but on my return I rang Onslow Square. There was no reply from the flat, nor was there any reply on my next four or five attempts. It crossed my mind that they might have become so weakened on cheese and biscuits that they could not lift the receiver, or else they had sloped home to Nagaland disillusioned. Their disappearance worried me. It seemed important that London, after their years of anticipation, shouldn't utterly disappoint them. I decided that if they were still in the country I would give a party, to which I would invite anyone and everyone who might amuse them. I had also, at the back of my mind, a subversive intention. Jaisha and Jenju's vivaciousness at dinner that evening had made the idea of their returning to an arranged marriage in Nagaland more horrible than ever. It seemed nothing short of cruelty that they should be condemned to forty years of conversation with some oafish husband about boar-hunting and pig-sticking in the Patkoi Hills. Their spirit would quickly be ground down by it all, and I could easily imagine them in ten years' time, listless and dejected, no longer bothering to keep up with the fads and foibles of Paris and London, until they could barely remember what it was that had once so intrigued them. What a waste of their gaiety it would be. In the restaurant, it was impossible not to notice the impression their beauty made when they came into the room. A couple of roguish men I knew only slightly, to nod at, made a pointed detour past our table hoping for an introduction. Their interest reinforced my idea of a party. If Jaisha and Jenju could only be introduced to some compatible men, perhaps their mother and the boar-hunters might be out manoeuvred.

After two more days of trying, I at last got through to Onslow Square at ten o'clock in the morning. Jenju answered the telephone sounding pitiful.

'I've been terribly worried about you,' I said. 'Are you all right? You sound weak.'

'Oh, it's you, Nicholas,' she replied. 'No, just tired. We were out dancing until five a.m. We had such a good time, first in Annabel's and then on to Tramp.'

'Great,' I said. 'I'm sorry I woke you up. You'd better go back to bed.'

'No, I'm awake now. And anyway we must go into college sometime.'

I asked who had taken them dancing.

'Just some friends we met through Lady Glenaffric,' said Jenju. 'She'd asked them to take us out on the town, and they really know how to have a good time, those guys.'

'And what about the other evenings? I've rung your flat several times but got no reply.'

'We've been asked out every single night, can you believe it? People are so generous in London, inviting us for cocktails and dinner, our diaries have been chock-a-block.'

I mentioned my idea for a party. 'It's your turn to be guests of honour.'

Jenju sounded thrilled. 'You really mean it?' she said. 'I must go and wake Jaisha at once and tell her. She's going to be absolutely over the moon about this guest of honour business.'

The party was quite a success. My friends seemed enchanted by Jaisha and Jenju, and there wasn't a moment when they weren't the centre of attention. Their artlessness galvanised even my cynical and peevish friends, and I noticed several of them making a note of the Onslow Square telephone number.

'London,' said Jaisha, 'is exceeding our wildest dreams.' Only two tiny clouds were on their immediate horizon: their school and the size of the monthly allowance given to them by their parents. The International College of South Kensington was clearly a college in name only, being in fact a glorified but half-hearted finishing school for foreign girls; its fees were horrendous, its syllabus paltry, its *raison d'être* scarcely more ambitious than supplying a respectable place for its pupils to sit between noon and half past four. Jaisha and Jenju nevertheless found it exhausting. The work consisted largely of projects, such as cutting out photographs from fashion magazines and gluing them into scrapbooks. 'You should see our bedroom,' they would say. 'The whole place is strewn with pictures from *Elle* and *Marie Claire*. When on earth will we find the time to stick them all in? I'm telling you, this college work is backbreaking.'

The cost of clothes shopping, too, took its toll. Nobody, in the space of a few weeks, could have become more familiar with designer shops in Sloane Street, Bond Street and Beauchamp Place. Each time you saw them they were wearing something new from Valentino or Versace, and a good part of their conversation was taken up with teasing out your honest opinion of their latest purchase. After a while you learnt not to risk admitting you disliked anything, or even preferring one particular outfit to another, because even the mildest, most innocuous comparison drew squeals of horror, and promises that the slighted garment would never be worn again. Clothes shopping never palled for them. For the first time they could see, hanging on the rails, the dresses they had admired from afar in magazines, and they told me that it gave them a thrill every time they entered a boutique. I have an idea that they enjoyed the peripherals of shopping, the fitting rooms and shiny carrier bags, almost as much as the dresses themselves, but the fact is they were hooked. Quite soon they were pleading dire poverty. I have no idea how generous their allowances were. Jaisha once mentioned the irksome formalities involved in getting money out of Nagaland, and said that luckily her family had transferred some, years before, when their grandfather was still king. This now resided in a bank in the Old Brompton Road, along with a large satin-lined purse filled with blue diamonds.

One Monday morning, seven or eight weeks later, Jaisha rang me at my office sounding excited.

'I simply have to tell you,' she said. 'We've just spent the most glamorous weekend in Normandy staying with some very charming men – absolutely genuine French playboys – at the most fabulous château. We insist you come round for a drink this evening, we're bursting to tell you about them. These playboys are just so handsome.'

I dropped in at Onslow Square on my way home, fetched ice, cut up a lemon and generally performed my duties as barman. The girls watched, impatient to describe their weekend. Their account was enthusiastic but tortuous, and they often contradicted themselves and each other.

'We were invited as absolute blind dates,' said Jaisha, 'by some very distant cousins of Lady Glenaffric. It was Louis-Philippe's birthday and about forty people were staying in the house party, all the greatest possible fun, including some other English, though mostly French of course. And the men were so handsome, they made our blood run cold.'

'Yes,' said Jenju seriously. 'When they looked at me with their laughing eyes, I got complete goose pimples.'

'And they're coming over next week, so you must meet them,' said Jaisha. 'Louis-Philippe is coming, and Jean-Marie, who Jenju rather liked, I think.'

'Jaisha! How can you say those things when you know you fell head over heels for Louis-Philippe yourself?' said Jenju.

'What if I did?' said Jaisha. 'So would you if you'd been driven by him at two hundred and fifty kilometres an hour. It sent shivers down my spine.'

Everything I heard about these playboys predisposed me to dislike them intensely, and I asked Jenju exactly what it was that made them so attractive.

'Oh, playboys are just different from other men,' she replied. 'They're so reckless and dashing, and so wild and unpredictable. I can't explain it. All I can say is that when you meet a playboy you know at once he's a playboy. There's no mistaking him.'

'And what did they do all day, these playboys?'

'Nothing special, you know. Just drinking and flirting outrageously with the girls. When we drove into Paris after Louis-Philippe's party, they danced madly well at Castel's.'

'And don't forget what good shots they were,' said Jaisha. 'At the boar hunt on Sunday morning they shot fifteen boar.'

'Even though we'd been dancing at Castel's half the night,' said Jenju. 'Jean-Marie didn't even have time to change. He just slipped on his hunting jacket over his evening shirt.'

The appearance of boar-hunting in the weekend itinerary took me by surprise.

'You must have felt a bit *déjà-vu* about the boar hunt,' I said. 'Didn't it make you feel you were back home with your Nagaland admirers?'

'Oh no, this was completely different. Not so wild, of course, the countryside is much tamer than at home, but watching the playboys shoot is such enormous fun. They're real charmers, those boys, though they can be quite fierce sometimes, telling you off for chattering and smoking when they're trying to concentrate.'

'You should see Louis-Philippe's Maserati too,' said Jaisha. 'He keeps it down at the château, which is actually his elder brother's place. It's a bright red two-seater. I can tell you, any girl is a complete sitting duck to a man with a car like Louis-Philippe's. I just wish he was driving it here next week, but they're flying over for the evening.'

'You're going to be so impressed by these playboys,' Jenju assured me as I said goodbye. 'You're really going to pick up some good tips from them.'

vi

We rather dreaded our evening with the playboys. From Jaisha and Jenju's character reference they sounded smooth and arrogant, and we expected a tiresome dinner with men in gold jewellery and blow-dried hair, trumping each other in their awful flirtatiousness. It was obvious that they were drawn to Jaisha and Jenju for all the wrong reasons, and I was fearful that the girls, in their sweet-natured naiveté, might get badly hurt.

All these reservations disappeared the moment we saw the playboys. We could have laughed out loud as they followed Jaisha and Jenju into the restaurant. They were very small, with tiny feet and hands. Both were dressed in navy blue blazers with brass buttons and silk ties, and they had extremely formal good manners, as French boys do. They were insistent about helping Jaisha and Jenju into their chairs, an ill-advised manoeuvre in a crowded restaurant. They seemed faintly overawed by being in London, and gave the impression that this great adventure of flying over for dinner was not something they had done before. Their English was good, if rather stiff; their conversation consisting mostly of pleasantries about the food and wine.

Louis-Philippe was more reflective than Jean-Marie, who was himself far from gregarious. They had been friends since childhood and were neighbours in the country. Both were twenty-five and younger sons of large châteaux, though Louis-Philippe's was bigger and enabled him to work for the estate. Half his time, he explained, was spent actually working on the farm, and half in the estate office. He made it plain that he preferred his days outdoors. Jean-Marie spent the middle of each week in Paris, where he bought and sold nineteenth-century paintings. He did not strike me as particularly scholarly. Louis-Philippe said that, because Jean-Marie was of *bonne famille*, he was an acceptable middleman for grand old Parisienne women who needed to dispose of something without fuss.

What they both lived for was the weekends when they could shoot and hunt boar. Probably the sole accurate fact about them in Jaisha and Jenju's advance notices was that they were first-class shots. When they talked about it their stiffness melted away, and they were boyishly enthusiastic. They described the damp hides in the Ardennes woods where they waited for their quarry, and their keeper, a character, and the difficulties of enticing modern townspeople to act as beaters. The more they talked, the more they revealed themsleves as polite, solid, country-loving French boys.

There was nothing remotely playboyish about them. Louis-Philippe, to be sure, had a red Maserati, but he clearly drove it with the utmost care. Their dancing expedition to Castel's, they said, was something they did once or twice a year, and they'd been shocked by the size of the bill. Far from being reckless and wild, they struck me as thoroughly prudent. At the end of dinner, explaining that they must catch an early flight back across the Channel to arrive at work on time, they shook hands around the table, kissed the girls fondly on both cheeks, and disappeared to their hotel.

'Well, Nicholas,' said Jaisha after they'd gone. 'What's your verdict?'

'Favourable,' I replied. 'I liked them very much.'

'We knew you would,' said Jenju. 'You can't help being impressed by playboys.'

vii

It was barely three months after the dinner that Jaisha rang me again at my office, this time with an even more sensational bulletin.

'You won't believe this,' she said, 'but we're engaged to be married.'

'Who is?' I asked. 'Not you and Louis-Philippe?'

'And Jenju too,' said Jaisha. 'She is engaged to Jean-Marie, and I to Louis-Philippe. Don't you think it's romantic? They both proposed at the same time at Louis-Philippe's château, and of course we turned them down flat the first time, but then they asked us again later the same evening, and we accepted them.'

I was frankly amazed by this turn of events. I knew the girls had seen a lot of Louis-Philippe and Jean-Marie, and sometimes spent the weekends with them in the Ardennes, but the impossibility of their ever marrying a foreigner was so well established that it never occurred to me that there was more than friendship between them. I wondered whether they had dared tell their mother yet, and if so what her reaction had been. Remembering the family outrage the girls had predicted when I suggested they marry a dashing Indian, I feared the news of their simultaneous engagements to French boys would be cataclysmic.

'Our mother is paying us a flying visit in London next week,' Jaisha said, satisfying my curiosity. 'We are going to break the news to her then.'

'What do you think she'll say?'

'She will utterly forbid it, of course,' said Jaisha, 'and will order us to come straight home with her to Kohima.'

'And you'll refuse?'

'Point blank. We are both determined on that score.'

The day before their mother's arrival, I invited the girls for a drink at my house. I thought that as the hour of reckoning approached, they would begin to lose their nerve, and that they might be grateful for some bolstering up. It was difficult to tell, faced with concerted pressure, whether or not they would cave in. Outwardly, they were as determined as before; but Jenju in particular seemed apprehensive about the confrontation. I guessed she might be vulnerable to a prolonged brow-beating, and that she needed all the moral support I could provide.

'What's your plan of attack?' I asked.

'We're going to tell her our news over lunch in the soda fountain at Fortnum & Mason,' said Jaisha.

'Good idea,' I replied. 'You should wait until halfway through your main course before you broach it. And make sure you all go your separate ways in the afternoon. It will give her time to get over the shock.'

Just then the telephone rang and both girls rushed for the receiver.

'It's got to be Louis-Philippe and Jean-Marie,' said Jaisha. 'I hope you don't mind, we gave them your number.'

Their mother's reaction at lunch the next day was even worse than Jaisha and Jenju had feared. I only have it at second hand, but the exclamations of horror, the threats, accusations, acrimony, weeping and general commotion held the other lunchers in the staid soda fountain spellbound. (I happened to eat there myself a couple of weeks later, and the waitresses were still talking about the pretty 'Indian' girls and the terrible set-to with their mother.) The whole stupid idea of this marriage was out of the question, she said, and only confirmed her worst misgivings about their coming to London in the first place. Her daughters must have gone crazy even to suggest such a thing. Hadn't they considered the shame it would bring on their family? Did they intend to live the rest of their lives as outcasts in Nagaland?

All this and much more besides, I'm sure, was put to them. My idea that they should go their separate ways in the afternoon was defeated by their mother's drastic counter-attack. The girls were told to clear their belongings immediately from Onslow Square and move into a room adjoining her own at the Dorchester. 'If I trusted you alone on the aeroplane I'd put you on a flight home tomorrow,' she said. 'As it is you'll have to remain here another two weeks, but under my supervision.' Their cheque books were confiscated and they were forbidden to use the telephone. When I tried to talk to them myself (having eventually discovered their whereabouts from Lady Glenaffric) my call was intercepted, and I was told they were resting and couldn't be disturbed. Flowers arrived daily from Louis-Philippe and Jean-Marie, but were turned away. For hours on end their mother remonstrated with them. Every possible objection was advanced, every dire sanction imposed. Had the girls not been sharing a bedroom and so been able to renew their determination when they were alone, I'm sure they would swiftly have lost the siege, but twelve miserable days went by, and still they insisted they wanted to marry Louis-Philippe and Jean-Marie, come what may.

On the thirteenth morning their mother had had enough. Such a marriage, she said, was not only unthinkable according to their customs, but could never work on practical grounds. 'French husbands would be fish out of water in Nagaland. Jaisha, you will telephone Louis-Philippe in front of me, and tell him that I wish to see him and his friend tomorrow morning in my suite. I'm going to order them to stop bothering you, and to give up all thoughts of this ridiculous marriage. This nonsense has gone on long enough. Tomorrow evening we are flying home, and you will both marry Naga boys within the month.'

A year after the weddings we were holidaying in the north-eastern frontier states, and took up our open invitation to stay with Jaisha and Jenju in Kohima. They were living in a wing of their parents' palace, the Hathi Bhavan, where two large suites of rooms had been given over to them and their husbands. The palace stood on the edge of the city in a large walled garden, where the lawn was kept perpetually green by a barrage of sprinklers. Relaxing on long chairs in the shade of a banyan tree were Jaisha and Jenju. Jaisha was having her toenails painted by a beautician in a white smock, while Jenju flicked through French *Elle*. Both were wearing the latest American sportswear, and I could see that my prediction that they would quickly become morose in Kohima was badly wrong. Marriage seemed to have enhanced them.

'We've both been so looking forward to your arrival,' said Jenju. 'We are on complete tenterhooks to hear the latest gossip from the mad and glamorous social whirl in London, aren't we, Jaisha?'

'Oh, Jenju!' said Jaisha. 'We should at least give our guests a moment to relax before questioning them. We have two whole days, after all, before our husbands get back from their hunting.'

The men, we were told, were on a ten-day boar hunt in the Patkoi Hills.

'It really is too bad of them not to be here to greet you,' said Jaisha, 'but you know men and their sport.'

'When they come back I'm sure they will tell you all about it,' said Jenju. 'They have such an obsession with hunting, those boys, that they hardly talk about anything else.'

For two days we lazed beneath the banyan tree. For people who hadn't been in London for a year, they remained extraordinarily well informed. They questioned us wistfully about a young hatmaker just out of the Royal College, and were quite shocked when we didn't know the steps of a dance craze apparently sweeping the nightclubs. Jaisha lit a succession of cigarettes, and dispatched her driver several times to buy fresh supplies. They pumped us for news about every single person they'd met in London, however briefly, and made us promise to extend open invitations to stay with them in Kohima to anyone who would come. 'We miss London so much,' said Jaisha, 'our husbands get quite shirty with us, we talk about it so much.'

'Might you ever come back for a holiday?'

'That is highly unlikely at the moment,' said Jaisha. 'Our husbands wouldn't like us to go alone, and they are far too busy with their hunting to accompany us.'

On our third afternoon a convoy of jeeps pulled into the palace courtyard, and the boar hunters had returned. Jaisha stubbed her cigarette into an ashtray and leapt to her feet.

'The men are back,' she said. 'Now we'll have to stop our interesting chatter and listen to their exploits instead.'

Their husbands clumped across the lawn in their hunting boots to join us, kissed their wives, then threw themselves on to long chairs and called for drinks. Their shooting suits, of English cut, were impeccable, and their tiny sun-browned fingers poked through woollen mittens. Soon we were joined by other men from the hunting trip, all cousins of the girls, and they bragged happily together about their adventures on the hill. Later we were joined by Jaisha and Jenju's mother. She was a fearsome woman, and it wasn't difficult to imagine her brow-beating her daughters quite mercilessly for those twelve terrible days at the Dorchester. But with her sons-in-law she was indulgent and benign, and you got the strong impression that she was delighted with her choice.

After dinner on our last evening, Jaisha and Jenju and their husbands were lounging under the banyan tree with a drink.

'Louis-Philippe,' I said, 'I hope you'll forgive me for asking you something that's intrigued me for months. How was it exactly that you and Jean-Marie got round Jaisha's mother at your meeting in the hotel?'

'Oh,' he replied elegantly, 'we just talked to her a little. She is a very charming, very sophisticated woman.'

'You see,' chorused Jaisha and Jenju affectionately, smiling at their husbands, 'playboys are completely different from other men.'

THE SPENDTHRIFT

Mr Leonard, assistant manager of the Purfleet and South Ockendon branch of the National Allied Bank, hovered impatiently outside Mr Clowes's office door. Under his arm was a sheaf of files and a computer print-out from the bank's central terminal in Ipswich. This, knew Mr Clowes, was the weekly statement of his customers' accounts. Every Thursday morning, on the dot of ten, Mr Leonard delivered them to the manager's office to discuss matters arising. He laid the print-out on Mr Clowes's large panelled desk.

'I think you'll find the picture reasonably satisfactory,' said Mr Leonard, indicating the turquoise columns of figures. 'Excepting, of course, the usual anomalies.'

Mr Leonard's lips pursed as he pronounced 'anomalies'. He had a lean face with closely cropped black hair and small suspicious eyes. The effect, thought Mr Clowes, made him resemble a vole. Mr Clowes derived no pleasure from his weekly sessions with Mr Leonard.

'Monitoring the accounts alphabetically,' said Mr Leonard, 'I believe we have nothing to cause us too much concern in the A's at least: Aghassi; Ahir, S.; Ahir, W.; Ahluwalia – £253 overdrawn as of this morning, but he informed us he's installing new dry-cleaning equipment for his shop, so we've granted him temporary overdraft facilities – Ahmad, Nasim; Ainsworth; all satisfactorily in the black . . .'

Purfleet and South Ockendon is not the most profitable branch of the National Allied; few of its accounts are out of credit, so the bank makes little by way of overdraft charges.

The majority of customers are Asian immigrants, prudent to a fault: Indian Muslims with grocery or engineering businesses and religious scruples about borrowing money. Mr Clowes often felt his job was a sinecure. His customers' affairs were so humdrum, and involved so little element of risk, that the post of manager was superfluous. Sometimes he would be asked to lend a few thousand pounds to install a carwash in a garage forecourt, or a deep-freeze unit for some late-night delicatessen, but these loans would be repaid with such promptness and precision that they needed none of his expertise. All, that is, with the exception of account number 631-920-214-32885: the current account of Mr Harry Houghton.

It was this account, Mr Clowes could see, that was once again about to be presented for his consideration. Mr Leonard was weighing the dossier between forefinger and thumb. Harry Houghton's file was by far the fattest in the branch, thick with carbons of letters from the manager.

Mr Clowes scanned the computerised statement for the name Houghton. It was not hard to find: one of the few with the letters DR after the figure. H. B. Houghton – £18,639.40 DR.

'You will observe,' said Mr Leonard, 'that Mr Houghton's overdraft has increased by another £2,600.'

'So I see,' said Mr Clowes, shaking his head balefully. He looked ridiculously small behind his vast office desk, as though his shoulders had shrivelled into the lining of his suit jacket.

'Might I inquire whether you tried telephoning him, sir?' persisted Mr Leonard. 'You said last Thursday that if we didn't hear anything . . .'

'Yes, I did try,' said Mr Clowes. 'I rang the telephone number in the file on Monday morning. Unfortunately it was either out of order or, perhaps, temporarily disconnected.'

'Cut off for non-payment if you ask me,' said Mr Leonard. 'But you know my views on Houghton.'

Mr Clowes knew only too well. Were Mr Leonard manager of Purfleet and South Ockendon, Harry Houghton's name would be referred to the police. 'It's not as if we haven't given him fair warning,' said Mr Leonard. 'You must have written a hundred letters inquiring after further funds, but we haven't had the simple courtesy of a reply. Really, Mr Clowes, this matter is completely out of hand. It's not even as if we held any collateral. The overdraft is completely unsecured. Head Office would be scandalised if they knew.'

'I know, I know all that,' said Mr Clowes. 'The subject is very much on my mind, I do assure you.' Allan Leonard's persistence was maddening, not least because everything he said was true.

'Perhaps you'd be interested,' said Mr Leonard, 'in seeing the cheques Houghton drew on his account this week – all written after you informed him that his overdraft had reached £15,000.'

A pile of cheques, neatly paperclipped and appended to Houghton's statement, was placed in front of Mr Clowes on the mahogany rim of his desk. It was a magnificent piece of furniture, of the kind known as a partner's desk, with swan's neck brass handles and an embossed leather top; far too grand really for the manager of such a small suburban branch, but Mr Clowes had inherited it from his predecessor in Buckhurst Hill, where he had first become a manager so many years before, and it had travelled with him from branch to branch. Mr Clowes was well aware that this desk was an object of ridicule to his staff, and especially to Mr Leonard. The first thing Leonard would do, if ever he inherited the office, would be to replace the desk with a standard-issue teak one and a turret of wire in-trays. Mr Clowes removed the paperclip and examined these latest cheques.

April 12 – the sum of one thousand six hundred and forty pounds only to Sotheby's Ltd.

April 12 – the sum of forty-three pounds only to Langan's Brasserie.

April 12 – the sum of eighteen pounds and fifty pence only to Heywood Hill Booksellers.

April 12 – the sum of eighteen pounds only to Oddbins Wine and Spirits.

April 12 – the sum of twelve pounds only to Europa Stores Ltd.

April 12 – the sum of seventy-eight pounds only to Ziani's
　　　　　　Italian restaurant. (The handwriting on this one
　　　　　　was very unsteady. The signature was barely
　　　　　　legible and there were several amendments: he
　　　　　　had increased the sum from fifty-two to
　　　　　　seventy-eight pounds, presumably paying on a
　　　　　　whim for an extra companion.)
April 12 – the sum of thirty-eight pounds only to the Red
　　　　　　Tapioca Club (Westaway) Ltd.

'You will observe,' said Mr Leonard, who had moved in his
excitement to the manager's side of the desk and now began
fingering the rest of Houghton's file, 'that no funds have been
paid into his account since January 10, when we received two
cheques for ten pounds and fifty pounds respectively.'

Mr Clowes flicked back through the thick wad of
statements.

'Ah yes,' he said, 'ten pounds from a Miss S. Sheldon and,
good heavens, fifty pounds from Sir Gerald Oppenheimer.
Now isn't that remarkable!'

'Is it, sir? I'm not with you.'

'Sir Gerald Oppenheimer. The entrepreneur.'

Mr Leonard continued to look blank.

'Goodness, Leonard, don't you ever read the newspapers?
Gerald Oppenheimer is chairman of Oppenheimer Engineer-
ing and Pharmaceuticals. They bought out Reliant Rubber
and Dodo Books last year and were underbidders for the
Observer. Sir Gerald must be one of the richest men in
Britain.'

'Well, maybe he is,' said Mr Leonard. 'But Houghton
doesn't appear to be on his payroll, and the odd cheque for
fifty quid won't help his overdraft.'

When Mr Leonard had left his office, Mr Clowes hung on to
the Houghton file. It was certainly fat, but the correspondence
was curiously one-sided. The bank had written to Houghton
on average once a fortnight for twelve years, but never
received so much as a postcard in reply. The account had been
opened on Houghton's eighteenth birthday, had moved immediately into the red and stayed there. His address was listed

as 26 Elvaston Mews North. Whether he owned or rented this property wasn't known; certainly he had never applied for a mortgage. Mr Clowes perused the file of old statements. This, too, was very thick: Houghton got through cheque books at the rate of two a week, sometimes writing as many as twenty cheques in a day. Even more puzzling was his source of income. Although nothing had been paid in for several months, there had been deposits in the past, of quite large sums. Last June a cheque had been paid in for £11,320 from the Hon. Mrs Wyatt's Discretionary Trust. At Christmas a cheque had arrived from a John Farquhar drawn on Hoare's Bank for £21,400. There was no indication as to who either of these people might be or the nature of their obligation to Harry Houghton. In the twelve years since the account had been opened, no pattern of revenue had emerged. Sometimes there were dividends from shares, but nothing that could remotely be called regular income.

It surprised Mr Clowes that Houghton should bank at his branch at all. The account had been opened by Mr Clowes's predecessor, shortly before he retired, but nothing in the file explained the customer's choice. No other Houghtons banked at Purfleet and South Ockendon. Houghton had no home in the area. Indeed, Mr Clowes severely doubted whether H. B. Houghton even knew where his branch was. The bank, on the other hand, knew as little about Houghton. Mr Clowes thought that the surname sounded substantial; the sort of name that would sit more comfortably on the cheque books of Messrs Coutts &Co. or Williams & Glyn than the National Allied. Although no snob, Mr Clowes knew that he would not have allowed the same situation to develop with Aghassi or Ahir, S. or Ahluwalia.

At midday, instead of lunching in his usual way at his desk Mr Clowes walked to the public library. In the reference section he found a copy of *Who's Who*. Nine Houghtons were listed in *Who's Who*, none of them Harry, but Mr Clowes had not expected to find him there; he was hoping instead for some clue to the identity of H. B. Houghton's father. He noted that Houghtons as a tribe tended towards academia and the church, though the titular head of the family, Lord Houghton of Sowerby, was a Life Peer who sat on a committee relating to the Inland Revenue and Commonwealth Scholarships. Another Houghton, the Rev. John, was Vice President of the Bible Society, and a third, Professor Garth Houghton, was Director of Gattonside Polytechnic and wrote (with J. B. Hewitt) a textbook entitled *Gravity in Space by Worked Examples*. Sir Cyrus Houghton was Rector of Gloucester University. At the end of each entry Mr Clowes checked to see whether they had sons or daughters, designated in *Who's Who* by a simple *s* or *d*. Some Houghtons did and some Houghtons didn't, and really at the end of his investigation Mr Clowes was forced to concede that he was none the wiser.

That evening Mr Clowes again tried ringing Harry Houghton at home, and once again failed to obtain a ringing tone. The operator declined to confirm whether or not this was due to mechanical failure on the part of British Telecom.

The next morning a typed memo arrived on Mr Clowes's desk signed by Mr Leonard. It said at the top 'For information only'. Appended was a small pile of new H. B. Houghton cheques.

April 19 – the sum of two hundred and seventy-five
              pounds only to Stephen Bartley (Fine Art) Ltd.
April 19 – the sum of forty-two pounds only to Zen
              Central Chinese restaurant.
April 19 – the sum of six pounds only to Odeon Cinemas
              Ltd.
April 19 – the sum of fifty pounds only to Chequepoint,
              the twenty-four-hour *bureau de change*.
April 19 – the sum of one hundred and eleven pounds only
              to the San Lorenzo restaurant.

Mr Leonard had added at the bottom, 'Please note that H. B. Houghton's overdraft has reached £19,123.40.'

Shortly before lunch, and with little prospect of success, Mr Clowes again dialled Elvaston Mews North. His pessimism was fully justified.

At lunchtime Mr Clowes went for a long walk the length of Purfleet High Street. Normally he took great interest in the mortgage rates displayed in the building society windows which line the street, but today he was too preoccupied to notice. Mr Clowes was a worried man. If Houghton's overdraft reached £20,000 then it exceeded his threshold of responsibility and he would be obliged to make a report to the area manager; and at the rate Houghton was spending that could only be a matter of days. He was concerned, too, about Leonard. No doubt he had kept copies of his numerous memos relating to Houghton's account, and would lose no time in submitting them to the inquiry. If Mr Clowes was found guilty of negligence he would find himself in premature retirement. The only solution, he realised, was to speak to Houghton. And if he could not reach him by telephone then he must go and see him in person.

That afternoon Mr Clowes asked that no calls should be put through to his office, and for all Houghton's files to be summoned from the vault. Clearing banks store their customers' old cheques for three years in white plastic sacks before destroying them, and when these were carried into Mr Clowes's office they entirely covered his desk top. Then, fortified only by a mug of minestrone and two Bourbon biscuits, Mr Clowes set to work.

The task he had set himself was daunting and he knew it would mean working far into the night. He rang his wife and warned her he would be late home. Then he unzipped the first of the eight white sacks and began to study every single cheque still in existence. Cheques made out to auction houses and wine shops he ignored, but those made out to restaurants he put to one side. There were several thousand of these, seldom fewer than twelve a week. Mr Clowes noted the names of the restaurants, and the dates when Houghton had patronised them, in a ledger. At first there appeared to be no rhythm to Houghton's spending. Sometimes he had a craze on a particular place for a few months, then ceased going there. There was a Chinese restaurant in Knightsbridge which he used continuously throughout 1988, but had abruptly forsaken; prudently so, thought Mr Clowes, for it was very expensive. Gradually, however, as he sifted the cheques, he began to see repetitions from week to week. On Sunday evenings Houghton was in the habit of eating pizza in the Fulham

Road. For Sunday lunch he favoured the Rib Room of the Carlton Tower Hotel. On Monday or Tuesday evenings he ate Greek food in Camden, and Thursday as often as not he was in the mood for Indian food at the Bombay Brasserie in Baileys Hotel. It fascinated Mr Clowes to retrace Houghton's movements around London. He did not know many restaurants himself, so looked up their addresses in the London telephone book and placed them geographically with the aid of an *A–Z* street atlas. Soon he could re-create whole evenings as Houghton paid for cocktails at Trader Vic's in the Park Lane Hilton, before making his way across Mayfair and Soho to L'Escargot in Greek Street.

The more he learned, the more Mr Clowes became obsessed by Houghton. He felt like a biographer piecing together his subject's life, and grew sympathetic. He knew when Houghton had been ill, because then no cheques were written for several days. He knew when he dined on his own, because on those occasions Houghton paid only for himself. He knew from the size of the bill when Houghton ordered only one course, and wondered whether it was the consequence of one of his own sharp managerial letters. Mr Clowes felt obscurely guilty for depriving Houghton of his pudding.

But above everything Mr Clowes longed to know what Houghton looked like. The clues from the cheques were sketchy. His barber was George Trumper in Curzon Street, which suggested a military cut, and his shirts were made to measure by Turnbull & Asser, an extravagant habit implying abnormal proportions of some kind; it was possible that Harry Houghton had elongated arms.

It struck Mr Clowes that there was no point in challenging Houghton at home until he had carefully observed him. He wanted more than anything to see Houghton in his natural habitat. He wanted to watch him enjoying one of the dinners for which the bank had underwritten him to the tune of almost £20,000.

On Saturday evening Mr Clowes caught the train into Victoria Station. He had told his wife that he had to visit a retired teller from the bank, recently hospitalised, but instead cut across the park in the direction of St James's. It was a light evening and there was a promise of summer in the air. The park was full of tourists scattering popcorn for the ducks, but none of them gave Mr Clowes a second look. His overcoat was buttoned to the neck and upon his head sat a herringbone deerstalker. He couldn't have been taken for anything but the most respectable manager of a small suburban bank. And yet Mr Clowes felt more reckless than at any time in his life.

Frequently as he walked he patted his breast pockets; they were still there, his cheque book and guarantee card. Mr Clowes felt a thrill of anticipation at the amount of money he would have to spend that evening on dinner, if Houghton's bills were anything to go by. When he reached Trafalgar Square he headed left along Pall Mall, past the great white façade of the Athenaeum and the granite portico of the Royal Automobile Club, then turned right up St James's itself. In the pocket of his overcoat was the photocopy he had made of the relevant page from the $A-Z$ and he consulted it freely. Halfway up St James', soon after the Space Age headquarters of Swissbank, he turned left into Park Place. At the end of the street was a curved plate glass window, metallic revolving door and a blue neon sign: Le Tourniquet. Harry Houghton had spend several thousand pounds in this one restaurant alone, and furthermore had booked a table for nine o'clock this evening.

Mr Clowes had prepared his ground carefully. He knew that Houghton ate at Le Tourniquet five Saturdays in six, and had rung to confirm he would be there. 'Yes, that's right,' said the manager at the booking desk. 'Mr Houghton has reserved a table for four persons. You would like a table for one to be placed next door? As a surprise for an old friend. Yes indeed, I think that will be possible to arrange.'

Mr Clowes found the restaurant dazzlingly bright. The restaurateurs of Purfleet and South Ockendon oblige their patrons to eat in semi-darkness, by the light of candles in opaque lanterns, but Le Tourniquet radiated steel-bright light. The floor was white-tiled and gleamed under fierce spotlights. The white tablecloths were crisp with starch. Even the chairs and tables were made of the shiniest aluminium. It seemed to Mr Clowes that he had left the half-light of the real world for the set of some Broadway musical where chorus lines of waiters in top hats and tails shimmied along the bar.

And yet the decor did not disturb Mr Clowes nearly so much as the customers. The first thing he noticed was their clothes: brocade waistcoats, and tailcoats which seemed to be cut from chintz curtains, and red sunglasses, and trousers made of leopard skin, and swirling Aloha beach shirts. Several of the male diners had very long hair, drawn into pony-tails, and the female diners sported Eton crops and peculiarly shapeless shirts apparently tailored from sackcloth. The women wore no make-up. It surprised Mr Clowes that any of these strange people could afford to eat out in the West End.

Mr Clowes was shown to his table and handed a menu. It was a disappointingly small menu, hardly larger than a birthday card, and not a patch on the great parchment bill of fare at the Sombrero Trattoria in Ockendon. Another shock awaited him inside. The prices were astronomical: eight or nine pounds for a starter and twenty pounds for a piece of fish not including the vegetables. Mr Clowes was very glad that the National Allied had not been asked to underwrite an establishment of such folly.

His chair, on the other hand, was perfectly sited; virtually abutting Houghton's table for four. This was for the present unoccupied, and it considerably excited Mr Clowes to know that, within a few minutes, this most notorious spendthrift would be presiding over its gleaming white tablecloth.

Meanwhile he ordered something to eat. The choice was limited, and disliking the sound of both soft-boiled ducks' eggs and goat's cheese with ricotta, Mr Clowes plumped for a bowl of *crudités* – subtitled on the menu as 'a floret of raw vegetables', and consisting, when it arrived, mainly of several mange-touts, slivers of courgette and a baby artichoke upon a glacier of crushed ice.

And then Harry Houghton turned up.

Mr Clowes knew it was him even before he reached the table. He was a tall young man with straight black hair which lapped a couple of inches over his ears. He wore a grey chalkstripe suit (Mr Clowes knew that it had been made by Welsh & Jefferies and cost £880) and a purple paisley tie. In his wake followed another man, smaller and stouter than Houghton, and two girls in unstructured and slightly transparent Japanese blouses.

From his table Mr Clowes had no difficulty in monitoring developments; indeed, only the foot-wide gap between the two tablecloths indicated that they were not all of one party. He had no difficulty, as he nibbled slivers of icy vegetables, in hearing every word that was said.

Houghton was an accomplished conversationalist. He spoke chiefly in anecdotes featuring himself in a good light. He talked authoritatively of the art world, betraying considerable inside knowledge, and especially of the auction houses where, he said, he intended bidding the next week for a pair of terracotta obelisks.

'They're not quite fine enough for the mantelpiece,' said Harry Houghton, 'but amusing as bathroom doorstops.'

He enthused, too, about clothes. 'I was wandering through the Burlington Arcade after lunch and have discovered a brilliant new tie shop. The silk ones are just the right width – half an inch narrower than Jermyn Street. I bought six.'

Mr Clowes, who did not suppose that a silk tie would cost much less than thirty pounds in the Burlington Arcade, flinched as he computed the bill.

Harry Houghton had a predilection too for modern art. He praised a recent exhibition at the Waddington Gallery, regretting that he could not afford to buy a canvass. 'Not at £60,000,' he said, 'I just couldn't justify it.' Mr Clowes was relieved by this parsimony.

But by no means all Harry Houghton's talk was of acquisition. He spoke of Syria. ('Room service at the Damascus Sheraton was shocking') and the privations of Lausanne ('The nightclubs are dead by two in the morning'). Tokyo had been so expensive that he had never paid off his Barclaycard ('just the monthly interest on the two grand'). Several kelims he had ordered from the hotel boutique of the Muscat Inter-Continental were shortly expected to arrive by container ship ('though with any luck the invoices will disappear somewhere in the Red Sea').

One of the girls in Houghton's party was French, and he

went to great trouble to draw upon the tablecloth a list of the most comfortable country house hotels within reach of Stonehenge. He seemed well informed, too, about high finance and told a mildly scandalous story, which Mr Clowes hoped was untrue, involving three schoolgirls and a very senior official of the Bank of England.

The longer he listened, the more Mr Clowes was mesmerised by Harry Houghton. There was something heroic in the scale of consumption. Houghton's every remark opened fresh vistas of debt. Money clearly meant nothing to him. The notion that he might be concerned about his overdraft was comic. Mr Clowes was now certain that, far from ignoring the content of his letters, Houghton had never even opened the brown oblong envelopes with Purfleet and South Ockendon postmarks.

'Could I please borrow your celery salt for a moment?'

Harry Houghton was leaning across the narrow chasm between the tables.

'By all means,' said Mr Clowes, his hand hovering uncertainly over the display of white china.

'The small one with the silver rim,' said Harry Houghton. 'Crucial stuff, celery salt, with gulls' eggs.'

'I don't believe I've ever tasted gulls' eggs,' replied the bank manager. 'Is it legal to eat them?'

'Legal?' Harry Houghton looked at Mr Clowes as though he were mad. 'Certainly it's legal. Though at three pounds an egg one might eventually drift into crime. Take one,' he said, passing a basket across the table. 'We've ordered far too many and they become nauseous after a dozen.'

'Are you sure?' said Mr Clowes, opening his purse and extracting three one-pound coins. 'Well, you must certainly allow me to pay for it.'

'Grief no,' said Harry Houghton, waving away the money. 'I wouldn't hear of it. We'd only leave the egg if you didn't have it. In any case I want to know what you make of gulls' eggs. It isn't every day one meets somebody who has never tried them.'

Mr Clowes carefully picked away the grey-blue shell until the egg was white and naked. It sat on his plate, translucent and wobbling. The yoke was very dark yellow, its texture much richer than a hen's egg. Mr Clowes found it exquisite. He rolled it around his tongue, savouring the novel delicacy. He was thrilled by the notion of gulls' eggs. It distressed him that, fifty-seven years into his life, he had only now discovered them. And he determined to order some more without delay.

'Waiter, waiter,' he called, 'please bring me three – no, make that six – gulls' eggs.'

The waiters at Le Tourniquet think nothing of supplying several first courses to the same customer, and the eggs quickly arrived.

'This is the most positive thing that's happened all week,' said Harry Houghton. 'Discovering a new gulls' egg addict. But what you really need to wash them down is a glass of pink champagne. If I were you, sir, I'd order a bottle immediately. Pink champagne, gulls' eggs and celery salt go so well together.'

'I've never had pink champagne either,' said Mr Clowes. 'You must think me very parochial.'

'Refreshing rather than parochial. These friends of mine here,' said Harry Houghton, indicating the two girls and his stout companion, 'have tried everything. So have I. That's why we have so little to say to each other. But you, sir, are a genuinely unspoilt person. Come and join our table and we'll order a bottle.'

At first Mr Clowes felt some discomfiture but Harry Houghton took pains to put him at his ease. If there was a degree of condescension in his voice, Mr Clowes barely noticed it. The cold wine relaxed him. He felt absurdly light-headed. Life, he saw, had only properly begun this evening in the white glare of Le Tourniquet. A second bottle of champagne arrived, then a third. Mr Clowes's own table was now occupied by a pop star of such celebrity that even Mr Clowes could recognise him. Harry Houghton and his friends seemed perfect companions. Their account of a villa holiday in Cap Ferrat, and how they had defrauded a credit card company of several thousand francs, made Mr Clowes laugh as he had never laughed before.

The restaurant, he noticed with a start, was almost empty.

The cane-backed chairs were being stacked in a corner, and a waiter began sluicing the white-tiled floor with hot water. The time, Mr Clowes saw, was almost two in the morning.

'Looks like they're hounding us out,' said Harry Houghton. 'Perhaps I'd better attract a bill.' He semaphored languidly in the direction of the manager.

The bill, already prepared, arrived promptly on a saucer. The bottom line, Mr Clowes noticed to his horror, read £272.

'Split five ways?' said Houghton's stout friend. 'If we round it up to three hundred for service that's sixty a head.'

'I'll pay for the girls,' said Houghton magnanimously. 'So if you two bung in sixty each that'll be fine. Make the cheques to the restaurant, not to me, because I never remember to send them to my bank.'

With a trembling hand Mr Clowes wrote a cheque for sixty pounds. Sixty pounds for a dinner for one. Mr Clowes felt sick as he added his cheque and guarantee card to the others on the saucer. A waiter bore them away to record the card numbers.

Half a minute later he was back. He coughed apologetically. 'Mr Clowes? I'm very sorry, sir, but we aren't able to accept this cheque. Your card only covers you up to a fifty-pound limit and your cheque is for sixty. Could you possibly settle the difference in cash?'

Mr Clowes felt a rush of panic. He knew he had nothing in his pocket but five one-pound coins and his return railway stub to Purfleet.

'But you've accepted cheques from these other people,' he protested. 'One cheque for far more.'

'Ah, but that was from Mr Houghton, sir. Mr Houghton is a regular customer, so we're permitted to waive the rules a little.'

At this point Harry Houghton, who had been retrieving his overcoat from the cloakroom, reappeared at the table.

'Add this gentleman's whole bill to mine, will you?' he said. 'Just alter the details on my cheque. I'm afraid I've been leading him into extravagant ways, and very amusing it's been too.'

'But I couldn't possibly . . .' began Mr Clowes, raising his hands in dismay. 'I couldn't possibly have my dinner at your expense.'

'Not at *my* expense,' replied Houghton, disappearing through the revolving door. 'At National Allied's. I have this wonderfully docile little bank manager miles out in the suburbs.'

THE CURRY CLUB

Jagan Nand could hear their car doors slamming in the street outside and sporadic raucous singing. And then the glass door of his restaurant was kicked open with a training shoe, letting in a blast of cold air from Balham High Road and a horde of lumbering giants.

'Table for eleven, John, and twenty-two pints of Carling,' the goalkeeper said and then, without waiting to be given any particular table, jostled with the team over to the long corner banquette next to the tank of ornamental fish.

Jagan Nand hurried behind his bar and set to work pouring out the lager. Through the formica Mughul arches he could see the football team spinning the salt and pepper shakers like tops on the table, creating blurry spirographs of mess on the cloth.

'Do us a favour and hurry up, John,' shouted the winger to Jagan Nand. 'We're dying of thirst over here.'

'Yeah, show some commitment, Ron,' shouted the striker.

Jagan Nand dreaded Sunday evenings. For the rest of the week the Mumtaz Mahal Indian restaurant was a sedate place. Its fifteen tables were seldom all occupied at the same time, so Jagan and his wife Shamila ran it together, with their fifteen-year-old daughter Piyali helping her mother in the kitchen. Jagan was front-of-house manager, took the orders and ran the bar. The women prepared the food and acted as waitresses. It was now more than twenty years since the Nands had left Shahpura for England, and ten years since they'd raised the money to buy the Mumtaz Mahal. Most of the loan was paid back, and as soon as it was all cleared Jagan intended to close on Sundays. Not that many people came any more to the restaurant on Sunday evenings, because of the football team.

'Why are we waiting? Why-y are we waiting?' chanted the two centre backs as Jagan loaded the twenty-two pints of lager on to tin trays. And then, as he carried them to the table, they broke into applause, drumming their fists and unzipping their tracksuit tops in anticipation.

'Get eleven more of these standing by, Ron,' the striker ordered, 'and fetch us eleven menus while you're at it.'

How many times had Jagan longed to turn away the football team? But every Sunday night they drank fifty or sixty, sometimes even seventy, pints of lager between them, as well as their curries, cucumber raitas, Bombay aloo and piles of poppadoms. To turn them away was an indulgence Jagan Nand could not afford.

Clapham Athletic was an amateur football team that played on Sunday afternoons. In the summer they met on Clapham Common, but in the winter their fixtures moved to the Elephant and Castle leisure centre, where they played in a gym. Its membership had hardly changed in four years, and it had only two rules. The first was no women supporters at the post-match dinner. Since the club's inception, when they pitched into the Mumtaz Mahal because it was the first place they could find open after the game, the restaurant had become their unofficial lads-only clubhouse. Their other rule largely accounted for their loyalty to the Mumtaz: furnace hot, scalp-shrivelling curry. Nothing appealed to the machismo of Clapham Athletic quite like vindaloo, a weekly affirmation of their masculinity.

'When we say *very hot*, John,' they reminded Jagan Nand every Sunday, 'we don't just mean *hot*. None of your Madras curries. We mean *very, very hot*. One hundred and ten per cent effort. We want to be blinding knackered by this curry, OK, Ron?'

So on Sunday nights Shamila Nand would add extra chillis to her vindaloo, shaking her head sadly as she did so, knowing that all the subtlety of the dish would be overpowered by the capsicums. But however many chillis she added, the team were never satisfied.

'Call this hot!' they bragged to each other as the roofs of their mouths and the tips of their tongues burned like nettle rash. 'Oi, John, my mouth's like a fridge. Can't you even serve up a hot curry in this place?'

'Yer, this curry's rubbish,' shouted the winger, shovelling a huge spoonful of it into his mouth.

As the meal proceeded, the team became drunker and louder, and their arguments about soccer and vindaloo less coherent. Jagan Nand grew accustomed to hearing the same football phrases, loutish and lewd, sailing across the table week after week.

'Del left that fullback for dead,' the striker would say. 'He skinned 'im.'

'Yer, beautiful player,' replied the goalkeeper. 'He won't be walking again, he'll be going home in an army ambulance.'

'Ball of vision,' said the midfield player. 'The lad's got vision.'

'Come off it, he couldn't score in a brothel,' said the goalkeeper.

'That foul I did, that had vision,' proclaimed the fullback.

'Call this curry *hot*?' said the winger. 'This curry's a *virgin*.'

'Oi, John, fetch us over eleven more lagers,' shouted the goalkeeper to Jagan Nand.

Every Sunday their behaviour got worse. Jagan Nand found it difficult to comprehend. When they paid their bill they did so by a variety of cheques and credit cards, and Jagan deduced that during the week they had respectable jobs. Once or twice a player, reeking of aftershave, had brought a girlfriend for supper at the Mumtaz on a weekday, and then their manner had been diffident, even gauche. But in a team, they were appalling.

One night, boisterous with victory, the centre back plunged his hand into the ornamental fish tank and tossed a goldfish, flapping for dear life, on to the table. The goalkeeper dribbled it with his fingers to the edge of the cloth, then flipped it like a Subbuteo ball the width of the table. It was intercepted by the winger, who threw it into the air.

'On the head, on the head,' shouted the keeper. 'Nod it home, Jim.'

The team cheered as he headed the orange slither towards Jagan Nand's illuminated panel of the Taj Mahal. But the keeper dived across the banquette, deflecting it, and the fish was back in play.

'Please, I am asking you, gentlemen, put that fish back in its tank,' pleaded Jagan Nand, 'or I will call the police.'

And so, eventually, they did, but after a few feeble gasps of its gills the goldfish floated belly up on the surface of the tank.

The following Sunday, as they swayed out of the restaurant singing a particularly disgusting song about Tottenham Hotspur, two of the team tugged down their tracksuit trousers and mooned their gross white bottoms against the window-pane where Shamila was clearing dishes.

Then, only a week later, came the incident that turned Jagan Nand's despair into fury, his passive resignation into an urgent desire for revenge.

It happened that it was Piyali's sixteenth birthday, and her parents had given her a splendid turquoise and gold sari. Piyali was delighted and, though the sari was far too good for waitressing, insisted on wearing it all day. When the team arrived they noticed it at once, and wolf-whistled their appreciation. Jagan Nand hovered protectively by his daughter.

'Actually, this sari is her birthday present,' he said.

'Well, fancy that,' said the goalkeeper, eyeing Piyali lasciviously for the amusement of his teammates. 'How old is she, then?'

'Piyali is sixteen years old today,' replied Jagan Nand uneasily.

At this the team emitted a long, low, lecherous growling sound. 'Woar-rr, woar-rr,' it went, 'woar-rr, woar-rr.'

'Sweet sixteen, never been kissed,' leered the keeper, lunging at Piyali's sari. Piyali jumped nervously back behind her father, but the keeper's muddy, thick-fingered hand had caught hold of the gold border, and as she retreated the sari began to unroll.

Obscenely the whole team cheered. 'Pull it off,' they shouted, beating their fists on the table. 'Unwrap the birthday present, let's see what's inside.' At which Piyali yelped, tugged her sari back, and fled to the kitchen in tears.

Shaking with fury, Jagan Nand was drawn between striking the goalkeeper and comforting his daughter. In fact he stood immobile for a moment, clenching and unclenching his fists, before following Piyali into the kitchen, where she was sobbing and shaking and clutching her mother, who was sobbing and shaking too. Outside in the dining room the football team continued their lecherous chanting and hammering.

'This is terrible, Jagan,' said Shamila. 'You see what they do to Piyali. They'll kill us all. You must get the police.'

'No, Shamila,' Jagan said wearily. 'Not the police. If I call them, those drunks will fight and wreck our place.' But as he comforted his wife and daughter an idea occurred to him, an idea that awakened a capacity for calculated revenge that Jagan Nand had almost forgotten was in his blood. 'By Kali, those men will suffer,' he promised his wife. 'The vengeance of Kali will be horrible.'

Much later that night, after the footballers had paid their bill and left, Jagan Nand bolted the door of his restaurant, drew a chair up to the telephone, and dialled his brother in Shahpura. After numerous clicks and silences on the line, the number eventually rang and Nataraj was there, faint but audible, on the other end.

'Nataraj,' said Jagan, 'there is something you must do for me, that you must do today.' He explained to his brother exactly how the package should be wrapped, and how it should be sent express post from the main post office in Shahpura so that it might arrive in Balham with all possible speed. 'You understand exactly what it is that I need?' repeated Jagan. 'None must be more than one inch in length. And as green as emeralds.'

Nataraj reassured his elder brother. He would go to the village straight away. It was early morning in India, and within four or five hours, he promised, the package would be wrapped and delivered to Shahpura post office.

'Good,' said Jagan. 'It is a matter of honour that nothing should go wrong. Family honour is at stake. And the honour of Kali too.'

When he'd replaced the receiver, he sat in his empty restaurant and thought of his home village: fifteen miles along a dirt road from Shahpura, thirty small huts with their mud walls surrounding the clearing where the bus called every second day, and the little shrine in the cave behind the water tank which nobody outside the village must ever see, where the stone lingams and the gruesome statue of Kali were housed. Even in Balham, Jagan Nand could not think of the Kali statue without apprehension. Many statues of Indian gods are extreme to Western eyes, but Kali the destroyer is invariably depicted as the most extreme of all: her hair garlanded with carved skulls, her eight raised arms holding daggers, her teeth sharpened into fangs daubed with red dye, and further necklaces of skulls draped around her neck. The statue in Jagan Nand's village seemed especially revolting because of its association with the cult of thuggee. In the early nineteenth century, when that part of central India, from Jabalpur to Shahpura, was plagued by bands of thuggees who strangled travellers with silken cords as an act of devotion to Kali, it was before this statue that the thuggees later prostrated themselves. And when the British set about suppressing the cult, it was to Jagan Nand's village that the awful statue was brought by Jagan's great-grandfather and hidden in the cave behind the water tank. For the last hundred years it had received only innocuous offerings of marigolds and saucers of ghee, but in the villages around Shahpura, Kali the destroyer remains a more potent deity than anywhere else in India: the goddess of revenge.

The parcel arrived at the Mumtaz Mahal six days later, and Jagan was pleased that his instructions had been followed precisely: the chillis were wrapped in newspaper, to keep them fresh, and none were longer than an inch. They were bright green, exactly as he remembered them as a child. Nataraj had done well; he must have posted the young chillis within an hour or two of picking them from the bush. They were, Jagan had no doubt, the hottest chillis to be found anywhere on earth. He remembered how, aged nine or ten, he had ignored his mother's warnings, and accepted a dare to pluck a tiny chilli from the fearsome bush and pop it into his mouth. The burning in his throat was like the heat from white-hot coals, and tears had streamed down his face for hours. The burning took two days to subside, and he lost his sense of smell for a fortnight.

Jagan Nand tipped the chillis straight from their wrapping, taking care not to touch them, into a Pyrex dish, and set about preparing himself for the task ahead. Like a surgeon he arranged his sharpest black-handled knives on a cloth, put on washing-up gloves, and tied a fine gauze cloth around his face, covering his mouth and nose. From Piyali he borrowed a pair of school swimming goggles to save his eyes. And then, lifting the first Shahpura chilli from the dish, he slit it neatly from end to end and cut out the deadly hot seeds, which he collected in a thick stone bowl.

All Saturday he worked on the chillis until the seeds from several hundred were removed from their green cases. Then he fetched a pestle and began to grind them – it took two hours – until the seeds had entirely disintegrated in a fine paste that he left to dry into powder.

Next he turned his attention to the cases of the chillis, which he cut into horizontal strips so paper-thin that they were virtually transparent. Finally he began preparing his ingredients for the following night's dinner.

When Clapham Athletic arrived at the Mumtaz Mahal there was nothing sheepish about them. If they felt any remorse for their behaviour the previous Sunday, they did not show it. On the contrary, they were in high spirits.

'Table for eleven, John, and twenty-two pints of Carling,' shouted the goalkeeper as they headed for their usual table, 'and don't hang about, OK?'

'You would like hot curry tonight, gentlemen?' Jagan asked as he took their orders. 'Madras curry? Vindaloo curry?'

'Vindaloo for everyone,' replied the captain, 'with Bombay potatoes, poppadoms and raita as usual. And John,' he added sarcastically, 'why not surprise us for once and actually make it hot?'

Jagan Nand returned to the kitchen shaking his head. The punishment he was going to inflict was very grave, but nothing else would avenge the treatment of Piyali. In the kitchen

Shamila looked up from the stove. 'They are here, Jagan?' she asked.

Jagan nodded. 'Eleven vindaloo curries,' he read from his pad.

Anybody who cooks with chillis knows that their heat does not manifest itself with the first mouthful. It is with the third or fourth that the fire assaults the throat. And so it was with the special Shahpura chillis that laced every last particle of the team's food. When Jagan Nand delivered the dishes, and the footballers had slopped the curry on to their plates in huge, messy spoonfuls, there were raucous protests at its lack of heat.

'Come off it, Ron,' shouted the winger, 'what's so hot about this?'

'Yeah, show some vision,' said the midfield player.

But after about five minutes an extraordinary thing happened: the flow of football talk and exchange of obscenities began to falter, and then almost to dry up. Watching from behind the bar, Jagan Nand could see that the team were spooning themselves large dollops of cooling cucumber raita, and yet even the raita seemed to have lost its usual soothing property and was actually adding to the fire in their mouths. One by one the team's faces turned red, then purple and blotchy, and their scalps began to prickle painfully and then break out in a sweat, until their hair lay soaked across their foreheads.

'More curry, everybody?' said the keeper. 'There's loads left.' And since it was the custom at Clapham Athletic to finish every last dish of vindaloo, they manfully took another large spoonful each.

By now their mouths felt as if they'd been skinned; their tongues were scraped raw as though the top layer of flesh had been removed with sandpaper. Their heads were racked by fierce migraines, and their eyes – bloodshot and rheumy – bulged from violet and white sockets. In Hindustani there is a word, *tukkarara*, to describe an elephant going berserk, usually through heat. Jagan Nand looked at the football team and muttered '*Tukkarara*' to himself.

'More raita, gentlemen?' asked Jagan Nand. 'More lager?'

The captain breathlessly nodded his assent.

Jagan Nand poured the drinks and loaded the glasses on to tin trays. Nobody noticed that, before he delivered them, he shook a tiny layer of white powder on to each head of froth. Or that the shallow dishes of yoghurt and cucumber were similarly dusted with the invisible spice.

It took the team two hours to finish the dinner, forcing it into their mouths in an almost hallucinatory heat-induced trance. And all the time Jagan Nand delivered more lagers to the table, which the footballers felt sure must eventually cool their calescent throats. When he brought them their bill, they could barely hold a pen to sign their names on their cheques, and when they stood up to leave they stumbled half-blind towards the door. Jagan Nand watched them go, smiled, and thought that his great-grandfather could not have done better.

Outside in Balham High Road they huddled together for a while, like refugees, summoning the energy to set off home.

'You know,' croaked the goalkeeper, 'I don't think that place is as good as it used to be. I reckon it's gone off.'

'Yeah,' gasped the winger, 'let's not go there again. There's a Chinese across the road over there, look, the Lee Chun Fu. Let's go there next week instead.'

Clapham Athletic had no way of knowing that Lee Chun Fu's great-grandfather was a leading member of a particularly vicious Hong Kong Triad.

THE SWAFFHAM MADONNA

'If we are to believe this map, and frankly I don't, then Certino is the next village.' Hector tossed the *Carta Toscana* into the glove pocket and mopped his brow with his shirt sleeve. 'Christ, this car's a furnace. Typical Italians to rent us one without air-conditioning.'

Lucy looked over Hector's shoulder to the track ahead. It rose steeply towards a grove of cypress trees, beyond which, with numerous lazy loops, she could see it snaking to the summit. The tyres of the Fiat struggled at the gradient, throwing flints against the chassis. Lucy stuck her head out of the window. The warm breeze exhilarated her. It was her first time in Tuscany, and everywhere she looked there were new sights to enchant her: hills which bulged from the landscape like root ginger, abandoned farmhouses and clusters of poppies.

'Somewhere on this ghastly winding road,' said Gerard, looking at the typed directions, 'we've got to take a road signposted Monteriggioni. There should be a church on the corner and a wine shop.'

'Thank God for that,' said Thomas, who was sweltering on the back seat with Lucy. 'I'd give a million lire for a drink.'

'That's virtually what they cost,' said Gerard, who was a banker. 'A million lire's barely ten quid at current exchange rates.'

'All I want is a swim,' said Hector. 'The first thing I'm going to do, the minute we arrive, is strip off and dive into the pool. You don't object to skinny-dipping do you, Lucy?'

'No, I'm sure not,' said Lucy, horrified at the prospect of Hector without his clothes but not wishing appear prudish.

'Of course she doesn't,' said Thomas. 'She's an art student, remember. She must see pictures of pricks all day long.'

There was little in their appearance to differentiate the three Yates brothers. All were tall, with tight furrows of brown hair which ran like plough lines from the crowns of their heads. Their noses were enormous, accentuated by nostrils rampant. The Yates nose. It was part of the topography of west Norfolk. There were tombs in the parish church dating from the Middle Ages, each carved with the recumbent forms of Yateses of Swaffham Manor, with the same camberous profile.

'The villa should be coming up on the left,' said Gerard. 'We're to look out for a wrought iron gate with white horses' heads on the gateposts.'

'Could that be it?' said Lucy, pointing to a house set behind a breezeblock wall.

'Has to be,' said Hector. 'Typical Italians to put ghastly chessmen on the gateposts.'

Il Bagno was more modern than the farmhouses they had passed on the hill. It was built, not of local Tuscan stone, but of fire-blown pebbledash with a girdle of glazed tiles. In front of the house was a patio of concrete slabs, recently laid, which wobbled as they carried their cases in from the car. The hall was dark, tiled and smelt of Paraquat, and when they pulled back the shutters they found a pair of cheaply gilded cherubs dangling from the ceiling. Outside, two spindly trees, enveloped by wire mesh, and the metal frame of a swingball game, its tennis ball hanging bald and forlorn from a length of elastic rope, stood like grissini sticks against the boundary wall.

'I've found the pool,' shouted Thomas from somewhere behind the house. 'It's one of those fibreglass ones, not buried in the ground.' Then they heard a loud splash as he honeypotted into the water, followed by a yelp as he resurfaced. 'Christ, it's cold! It's bloody freezing in here.' Thomas hung over the side of the plunge pool, his hair flattened with water against his scalp. 'No it's not,' he panted, 'it's wonderfully refreshing, it's absolutely lovely. Get in, everybody. Come on, get in.'

Lucy went indoors to change into her bathing costume. The house was chilly after the heat of the garden, and she felt a pang of loneliness. Her room led off the hall, its entrance almost blocked by a mahogany bedhead. Beneath the window stood a chest of drawers covered by a lace runner and two ceramic ashtrays. She carefully moved the ashtrays and arranged her art books on the top instead. She was relieved to have got them to the villa without mishap; she had worried, such was the glossiness of the paper, that they might attract an excess baggage charge which she could not afford. The Courtauld Institute library's imprint stood out of each spine. Some volumes already fluttered with bookmarks, cross-referencing from plate to plate. The sight of Gombrich, Vasari and Berenson reassured and excited her. So many pictures she wanted to see lay within forty miles of the villa. Botticelli, Uccello, Simone Martini, Fra Angelico: she had written essays about them in such detail, and longed to see them *in situ*. The opportunity had arisen in such an unexpected way. Just as she had resigned herself to spending another university vacation in Norfolk, her whole family had been asked to drinks after church at Swaffham Manor. The Yateses and the Estridges were not close friends, the Estridges owing several thousand too few acres of the county for friendship to blossom without inhibition, but the invitation was readily accepted. Few neighbours had been inside Swaffham Manor. The meanness of Sir William, combined with a reluctance to see any but the grandest Norfolk families, made invitations to the manor a rarity. Lucy was particularly pleased to be asked, for it would give her an opportunity to see Fra Cerubino's great *Madonna and Child Visited by the Magi*, the sole example of his work outside Italy. Lucy knew the fresco well in reproduction: the Madonna seated on a simple dais throne, a tender hieratic figure, on her lap a remarkably beautiful Christ-child, one hand raised in blessing, the other holding an orb. The light, as every scholar noted, was at once illogical and wholly satisfactory, the shadows across the dais indicating that it fell from the left, from behind the Magi, while perfectly illuminating the face of the holy infant from above. How the fresco came to be in East Anglia was a mystery. It had been looted from the Monastery of San Marco, near Florence, soon after its completion in the mid-fifteenth century. No sources indicated why this vandalism had been allowed, or how a section of cloister wall had been transported to England and incorporated in a Norfolk manor house. All concurred, however, that it was a sublime painting, and some art historians rated it as one of the ten great masterpieces of the Renaissance. Their high opinion may, of course, have been biased by the fact that so few had actually seen it. The Yateses were notoriously unaccommodating to art historians, and those who had penetrated the manor were so pleased with themselves that they were disinclined to disparage the Fra Cerubino.

When the Estridges arrived at Swaffham Manor, Lucy was disappointed to see that the party was being held, not inside the house, but in the tithe barn designated for shooting lunches: a long, bare room remarkable chiefly for its collection of Edwardian boot-scrapers. Goodness knows what had galvanised Sir William into giving such a party; altruism of some kind, no doubt, for the room was full of farmers, not all of them his tenants. Set between the windows was a plank trestle, supported by Fisons fertiliser bags, on which was displayed gala pie and ready-salted crisps. Next to the buffet, his vast hand dredging the Pyrex depths of the crisp bowl, stood Hector Yates.

It already seemed extraordinary to Lucy, only eight days after this first meeting, that she could ever have liked him. And yet it was so. He had towered above her, stolid and confident, and his arrogance rather impressed her. He had spoken on topics of no conceivable interest to Lucy, and she had found herself fascinated: by the short-sightedness of organic farmers, and how the Swaffham Hunt had met last winter at Dunton Priory, found at noon, then run for an hour and twenty minutes to Helhoughton before killing a vixen in Mrs Colquhoun's rock garden. Hector's corduroy trousers were worn at the crutch and he smelt of saddle soap. When he explained, 'No, sorry, I'm afraid you can't see the Fra Cerubino today, Mother has locked the house against this little lot,'

Lucy was disappointed. But when he said, 'Oh, by the way, Gerard and Thomas and I are going to Italy next Monday, do you happen to know of a fourth person who might like to come along?' Lucy was thrilled.

From her bedroom she could hear horseplay from the pool: violent thrashing punctuated by squeals and yells. Lucy hoped the boys would be wearing bathing trunks; she knew she would be embarrassed if they weren't, and how feeble it was to mind. She had often been told she was too serious, that she should relax more, try to feel things less deeply. She inspected herself in the mirror. Her bikini, borrowed from another neighbour, fitted better than she'd expected; the yellow pattern was bolder than she would have chosen, but it suited her. It was thrilling to be in Italy, so why did she feel uneasy? Of course, she was a puritan. When she began sightseeing she would feel happier. She meant to take field notes of everything she saw. In her notebook she had already listed the sights within a couple of hours' driving distance of Certino: Florence, Siena and San Gimignano, of course, but there were other, lesser towns too if only there was time – Poggibonsi, with the Della Robbia altarpiece in the church of San Lucchese, and Simone Martini's flawed crucifix at San Casciano in Val di Pesa.

Swimming, for the Yates brothers, did not imply swimming in the sense of widths and lengths. Swimming was a euphemism for any activity involving the pool: vaulting over the side through a rubber ring; diving to the bottom with an inflated arm band before releasing it to the surface beneath another swimmer; arranging obstacle courses between people's legs, and timed endurance competitions for keeping your face in water. Lucy was a strong swimmer and could hold her breath for two minutes before exploding. Hector discovered this fact when he gripped her underwater with his knees while she was attempting to swim between them. She struggled from the clinch spluttering and furious.

For four days the routine at Il Bagno was unvaried. The boys rose early and rapped on Lucy's door for help with the breakfast.

'Estridge!' bawled Hector, rattling the handle. 'Get up, you lazy cow, you're the only person who understands the stove. Typical Italians not to have a kettle.'

Fortified by grilled prosciutto and eggs, they made an expedition by car to Certino. Thomas, who was in charge of drink, had ordered six bottles of Pimms from the wine shop, and berated the owner daily about its own-arrival. Gerard meanwhile made similar representations to the newsagent charged with procuring the *Financial Times*. Hector and Lucy toured the supermarket, filling the wire basket with pasta and tomato paste and a cardboard crate with lager. By eleven o'clock they were back at the villa and swimming. At half past eleven they drank gin and tonic; at noon they ate pasta and swam; at dusk they played swingball. Later they ate more pasta and swam.

On the fourth evening Lucy said for the fourth time, 'Shall we drive into Florence tomorrow? It would be fun to do some sightseeing.'

'Sightseeing?' said Hector. 'You mean museums and things? No, thanks.'

'God no,' said Gerard. 'Flogging around museums is the last thing I want to do. Not in this heat.'

'What about you, Thomas?' asked Lucy. 'Will you drive me into Florence? We can see the Uffizi and the Pitti Palace.'

'Art galleries?' replied Thomas, who was busy removing the sprig of basil from his plate of pasta. 'Why on earth should I want to do that? Seeing that Madonna every time one goes into the billiards room at Swaffham is quite enough art, thank you, without actively seeking it out.'

'I thought having the Madonna at home would make you more interested, not less,' said Lucy. 'You do realise Fra Cerubino came from round here? The Monastery of San Marco is entirely frescoed by him. Your section of the cycle really ought to be seen in conjunction with the altarpiece, the *Madonna and Child with Saints and Angels*, though yours is generally thought to be by far the best bit.'

'Exactly!' said Hector. 'You've hit the nail on the head. Ours is the best bit and we don't think much of it, so why write off a whole day seeing these other ones? It's not even as though he's a good artist.'

'Not *good*?' Lucy was aghast. 'He's one of the most amazing artists ever. He completely changed the course of painting, made it much simpler and more direct. Fra Cerubino's influence was immense: you can trace it right through the Renaissance – all the way to Dürer, in fact.'

'Come off it, Lucy, don't let's overstate our case,' said Thomas. 'You're not telling us this Fra Cerubino was actually a *good* artist? He couldn't even get the perspective right. In our picture the Madonna and baby are sitting at the back of the room but are taller than the Three Wise Men in the front. It's an elementary balls-up.'

Lucy could not believe what she was hearing. In her anguish she could do no more than burble, 'Iconography . . . didactic . . . deliberate foreshortening of perspective,' but she knew the glossary of art history meant nothing to the Yateses. She thought of bringing her books from her bedroom and reading aloud from Vasari, or her notes from Dr Dunwoodie's lectures at the Courtauld, but the painstaking tonal comparisons, so persuasive at her weekly tutorials, seemed scant protection against the heathens of Il Bagno.

'His other mistake,' said Thomas, warming to the shortcoming of Fra Cerubino, 'is the ridiculous cannon ball the baby's holding. It looks heavy enough to be chained to a prisoner's foot, and a one-day-old baby is apparently balancing it in one hand. In fact it's even more absurd because the child looks about four, with tufts of curly hair, and yet we know he's only just been born because the Wise Men are still there with their frankincense and myrrh. It's incompetent whichever way you look at it: either he's suggesting that the Three Kings lingered in the stable for four years, or else that the Nativity happened twice, which isn't in the Bible. And that's ridiculous, because wasn't Fra Cerubino meant to have been a monk or something, so he might at least have got his facts right.'

'He was a Dominican friar and a member of the Order of Preachers,' said Lucy. 'And the ball in the Christ-child's hand is an orb.'

'Well, whatever it is, it makes a good target in billiards fives,' said Gerard. 'I don't know whether anyone's explained it to you, but the house rule at Swaffham is four bonus points for potting the baby's halo, two for the cannon ball. You're not actually allowed to aim your ball at the painting, you know, it's just a bonus if it flies off the table.'

'Actually the old man has rather put a stop to it lately,' said Hector, 'even though it was originally his own rule. But the insurance people get shirty when you chip bits of paint off.'

'That frightful man who came down from the valuations department at Sotheby's, he was even shocked we play billiards in the same room,' said Thomas. 'God, what a poof. Do you remember his socks?'

'And his Hush Puppies,' said Gerard. 'Father's face when he turned up in Hush Puppies with a navy blue suit: he went puce.'

'And then expecting to stay for lunch,' said Hector. 'So presumptuous. You see, Lucy, his appointment was for half past twelve, and he finished his job in twenty minutes and then just hung about. Nobody objected to giving the fellow a drink, but he obviously thought if he waited long enough he'd get lunch too. In the end we had to ask him to leave.'

'I think my tutor at the Courtauld tried to see the Madonna once,' said Lucy, 'but something went wrong. There was a muddle over dates and you'd forgotten she was coming.'

'An old bag in tweeds, about fifty?' said Hector. 'God, that was embarrassing – nobody had a clue who she was. She turned up on Saturday morning before the meet, and the last thing anyone had time for was art historians. She made rather a nuisance of herself, saying she'd confirmed with Mummy on the telephone. Father told her to push off. You know her, then?'

'She's wonderful,' said Lucy. 'Very inspiring and very warm. I can lend you her book if you like, it's easily the best thing written in English on the Renaissance. It's a pity you didn't meet her properly. Dr Dunwoodie's terribly knowledgeable about the iconography of your Madonna – her lecture was brilliant.'

'What?' said Thomas. 'She gives lectures about our picture? Bloody cheek. If Father knew, he'd blow a fuse.'

'Or take a cut of her fee,' said Gerard.

'I must say, I'm pretty staggered,' said Hector. 'What if a thief went to this lecture, it might give him ideas. She doesn't give the actual address of our house, does she?'

'I can't remember,' said Lucy. 'Anyway, this is ridiculous, you're in all the art books. It always says "Provenance: Sir William Yates, Swaffham Manor, Norfolk".'

'Christ,' said Hector, looking grave. 'We must put a stop to this at once. If the insurance people found out they'd double the premium. This is serious. The damn thing's insured for three million pounds and the premium's already sky-high without this Dunwoodie woman tipping off every cat burglar in England. She's no business to, it's not her ruddy picture. If you don't mind, Lucy, I'll make a note of her address after the holiday and get our solicitors to fire off a letter.'

Lucy felt trapped. Unable to drive the Fiat herself, she could see no prospect of escaping from Il Bagno. Florence, so close on the map, was now an inaccessible Shangri-la. She seemed condemned to spend the remaining fortnight of her holiday marooned at the end of a rough track, more removed from the treasures of the Renaissance than in the Courtauld library.

But Lucy was resilient. She was also cunning. If the Yateses wouldn't drive her into Florence then she'd find another way of getting there. The next day she suggested they have lunch at a trattoria they'd noticed on the Monteriggioni road, a mile beyond the village. When they arrived, however, she said, 'Actually, I'm not feeling at all hungry, I think I'll skip lunch today. If nobody minds I'm going to try hitchhiking into Florence. I'll stand outside and see what happens.'

The Yateses were indifferent to Lucy's scheme, their attention already drawn by the bistecca on the menu.

'It won't be real beef, of course,' said Hector. 'Typical Italians to pass off some old piece of donkey.'

Lucy positioned herself on the grass verge. Behind her was the trellis wall of the restaurant, through which she could already hear the boys grumbling about the staleness of the bread. She had no experience of hitchhiking, and felt some apprehension, but the prospect of the Duomo and the Ponte Vecchio overrode her fear. She had no idea how long it would take to reach Florence, but if luck was with her, and she didn't have to change lifts too often, she reckoned she could make it in an hour and a half.

But luck was not with her. The Monteriggioni road was deserted. For an hour no traffic passed in either direction, and when Lucy did eventually hear the sound of an engine and excitedly stuck out her thumb, it turned out to be a moped. Later a farm lorry lumbered by, loaded with olives, and a Volkswagen whose driver slowed to the verge, looked her up and down, then sped on. When the Yateses emerged from the trattoria, swaying with Chianti, Lucy was still there. 'Very wise of you to miss lunch,' said Thomas. 'We ate some tough old horse which should have been fed to hounds years ago.'

Lucy's determination strengthened. The next morning, while the boys were inquiring about Pimms, she made inquiries of her own at the post office. A bus, she discovered, left for Florence from the main square every morning at seven o'clock. It took three hours, calling at numerous hill towns on the way, and returned late the same evening. That would allow her a clear five hours' sightseeing in Florence.

Lucy rose at half past five. It was a longish walk from Il Bagno to the village, and the boys had declined to drive her there so early. She slipped noiselessly out of the house with a plastic bag containing her water-bottle, guidebook and Dr Dunwoodie's lecture notes. Dawn is chilly in Tuscany, and she shivered. The walk, however, warmed her, and when the sun sidled out from behind a hill it grew hot. The track, precipitous enough in the Fiat, was perilous on foot; progress was so slow that she fretted about missing the bus, but if she hurried she risked twisting her ankle. Nobody passed her on the track. The only sound was her espadrilles slapping against the flints. By the time she arrived at Certino she was blistered and exhausted.

'Dove autobus?' she asked a woman in the deserted market square. 'Autobus per Firenze?'

The woman shook her head. 'Nessun' autobus. Nessun' autobus Agosto. Autobus Settembre.' There would be no buses into Florence for another three weeks.

Lucy sat down on the steps of the church and wept with frustration. Even her guidebook seemed to taunt her. Flicking through the plates she felt that the frescoes of Fra Cerubino belonged to some distant world, quite separate from the Yates brothers and Il Bagno. She ought never to have come on this holiday. It had done nothing but make her unhappy. The Renaissance was a bait dangled capriciously before her, then snatched away. She knew if she stayed, thwarted, in Italy much longer she would begin to hate the country. And how could she tell Dr Dunwoodie that she'd spent three weeks in Tuscany and seen nothing but a fibreglass swimming pool?

In her wretchedness she wandered into the church. It was a fifteenth-century building, architecturally unremarkable, and dark from the heavy velvet curtains which hung across the door. A smell of damp rose from the nave. It seemed likely that the place was not much used; Lucy had already noticed a new brick church on the edge of the village. Off both transepts lay ante-chapels, gloomier still, and it was more from a desire to bring some light into the place, rather than any aesthetic expectation, which led her to activate the metred spotlight with a hundred-lire coin.

Illuminated before her eyes was a sight so unexpected, so remarkable, that she was rooted to the spot. She stood transfixed for a full three minutes, then reeled outside into the piazza.

'Parp! Parp!' A car was hooting outside the drink shop.

'Over here, you blind bat,' shouted Hector, who was loading the boot with sambucca. 'What on earth are you doing in Certino, Estridge? Miss your bus?'

'It doesn't run in August,' said Lucy, in a daze. 'There are no buses in August.'

Hector laughed. 'No buses in Italy in August. Typical! God, this country's a shambles. So you missed out on your culture.'

'I expect I'll get over it,' said Lucy. 'They're only paintings, after all, and you can see paintings anywhere.'

'Quite right,' said Hector, draping his arm around her shoulders. 'That's the first sensible thing you've said all holiday. Let's go to the hotel and have a drink – you probably need one after your long wait.'

'Do you suppose they've got a telephone?' asked Lucy. 'I

ought to ring England. I promised my mother I'd let her know I'm all right.'

'It's in the back,' said Hector. 'I'll order you a grappa.'

Lucy talked to England for nearly twenty minutes, and had Hector been more observant he would have noticed a preoccupied look in her eyes on her return to the bar. She drank her grappa in a single gulp and ordered another.

'You're on good form today,' said Gerard approvingly. 'If you ask me you didn't want to go to Florence at all. You're much happier drinking with us.'

'Perhaps you're right,' said Lucy. 'All this grappa is turning me into a Philistine.'

'Thank God for that,' said Hector. 'I was beginning to think you were a bohemian or something ghastly.'

For three days Lucy sparkled. It was as though art history was a terrible burden which she had at last managed to lay down. The Yates brothers were delighted with her. She swam four times a day, tugging playfully at their swimming trunk elastic. She organised marathon swingball tournaments which she contrived to lose by a credible margin. She invented a noxious ice cream made from frozen sambucca. But best of all, she did not so much as allude to culture. Her only eccentricity was a fascination with the local church, which she insisted on inspecting for a few minutes every day after finishing the shopping.

On the fourth morning, however, Lucy once again rose at dawn and walked into Certino. This time she felt no exhaustion. In her step there was briskness and resolve. It was breakfast time when she arrived at the hotel. An English-woman, plump and dressed in tweeds, was already seated in the dining room, dunking nubs of fresh bread into her hot chocolate.

'Good morning, dear, come and join me,' she said. 'And incidentally, congratulations. It hasn't been verified officially yet, but on first appraisal I believe that you are right.'

For a week there was more activity in the church than there had been for a hundred years. Strange men arrived in Peugeots from Florence and Rome, and even stranger men in velvet-collared overcoats from London and New York. Photographic lights were borrowed from a film company and power cables laid across the piazza from a mobile generator. A small laboratory was established in a back room of the farmacia, and for the first time in six centuries the Church of Santa Fina was locked and chained at night.

Thomas noticed the disturbance one morning while remonstrating for his Pimms. 'They seem to be making a film in the church,' he said. 'Typical Roman Catholics to rent out God's house for some spaghetti western.'

'Or else it's a conference of mafiosi,' said Hector. 'I've never seen so many shady-looking characters in one place.'

Just then Gerard joined them from the newsagents. His mouth was slobbering with excitement. 'You're not going to believe this,' he said. 'You're never going to believe this, but *look*, a copy of yesterday's *Times*.'

'Remarkable,' said Hector, snatching the outside four pages. 'I want to see what the weather's like in East Anglia. If it's still dry, we'll have to harvest early."

'Racal are up four pence,' read Gerard from the stock exchange prices, 'but BAT have dipped twopence.'

Lucy wasn't listening, however. Her eye had been caught by an article at the bottom of the front page, accompanied by a blurred reproduction of a fresco. The story, by Our Sale Room Correspondent, was headlined: 'Renaissance Fresco Found':

The Swaffham Madonna at Swaffham Manor, Norfolk, formerly valued at £5m and thought to have been the only example of Fra Cerubino's painting in Britain, has been shown to be a fake.

The real fresco, which was removed from the Monastery of St Mark in Florence sometime in the late fifteenth century, has been discovered in the side chapel of the Church of Santa Fina at Certino, a little-visited village thirty miles from Poggibonsi.

The discovery, made by a student at the Courtauld Institute on holiday in the region, was corroborated by Dr Eileen Dunwoodie, Britain's foremost authority on the Renaissance, and by experts of the Italian Accademia del

Oratorio in Rome. There seems to be no doubt that the Certino Madonna is the genuine work.

For four hundred years the discredited *Madonna and Child Visited by the Magi* has formed part of the collection of Sir William Yates at Swaffham Manor. The Fresco has proved something of an enigma to art historians. Swaffham Manor is not open to the public, and the family has been reluctant to accommodate academics.

The Madonna is regarded as one of the artist's most important paintings. Fra Cerubino (1405–71), a Dominican friar, spent seven years completing the cycle, which depicts the life of Christ in a deceptively naive style.

Sir William Yates was yesterday unavailable for comment. A spokeswoman at Swaffham Manor said he had spent the day playing billiards fives.

MISS MACKENZIE

I have only once been on a guided art tour, when I escorted an old aunt on a trip to Helsinki and Leningrad. It was arranged by a firm of specialist travel agents in Knightsbridge, which made a great deal of its exclusive entrée to palaces and museums not normally open to the public. But most people chose Cultura Study Tours for its small, socially integrated groups. Genteel widows and other single people felt reassured because they were put together with like-minded souls, and it was surprising how often they met up with old acquaintances, entirely by accident, on the trip.

Since her husband died, my Aunt Elizabeth had sworn by Cultura Study Tours. In five years she had been on five of their trips, and each time she returned from the Loire Valley or a Nile cruise she was full of praise for their efficiency and her pleasant travelling companions. So when she asked me to accompany her on the palace tour along the Gulf of Finland and into Russia, I was delighted to accept. I expected it to be dull, and full of old women, but the trip was only ten days and, besides, I liked my aunt.

The rest of the group was exactly as I'd predicted. We were only a dozen in number, and I was the youngest by a good forty years. There was a retired doctor and his wife from Cuckfield in Sussex, and a widowed landowner from Herefordshire with his sister, and six other women who had arrived alone. Five widows, and a Miss Mackenzie.

Even before we had left Helsinki airport, Miss Mackenzie had explained her situation in life to every member of the group. She was sixty years old and had spent the last forty years as private secretary to the Duke and Duchess of Arbroath.

'This very pleasant tour of the palaces,' she said in the primmest and most superior Scottish accent I've ever heard, 'is by way of being a thank you present for my first forty years at the castle. Not that I'm set upon retirement yet awhile, I've given His Grace my firm undertaking on that.' Looking at Miss Mackenzie standing square in her neat rusty-green twin set and matching rusty-green hat, you got the firm impression that the Arbroaths had little say about the length of her tenure at Arbroath Castle.

'When I began at Arbroath of course,' she went on, 'the Old Duke – that's the present Duke's father – was still alive, and as a matter of fact this is the first time I've ventured abroad in all that time.'

Miss Mackenzie did not seem remotely anxious about her first exeat from Scotland. She was a naturally commanding woman, and as the group made its way from the arrivals hall to the coach waiting outside, she several times sharply cautioned the porters to take more care with her suitcases.

For five days we were driven along the Finnish coast, visiting a palace or country house every morning and another in the afternoon. And then in the evening we would stop at a small, comfortable hotel in Jaala or Vlämaa where Cultura Study Tours had arranged for fires to be lit in our bedrooms; and after hot baths the group all reassembled downstairs for dinner.

Miss Mackenzie was invariably the first person down, and when we appeared we would find her standing impatiently at the foot of the stairs in a long black wool dress.

'Didn't you think the scenery today was quite breathtaking, Miss Mackenzie?' said Aunt Elizabeth as she ordered her glass of sherry. 'The sunset over the lake was enchanting, was it not?'

'Most atmospheric, to be sure,' replied Miss Mackenzie prissily. 'Though I can't in all conscience pretend I haven't seen better near Arbroath. When you've seen the sunset at Inverkeilor, I'm afraid you're spoiled for anything else.'

The next afternoon we visited a palace that was remarkable on two counts. It was so near the Russian border that from the roof of the orangerie you could see the smoke from the chimneys of Vyborg twenty miles away. And the furniture inside this rather pompous First Empire style palace was exceptional: French rococo as good as anything in the Louvre, the state rooms lined with chinoiserie and ormolu, the bedrooms dotted with cabinets by Charles Cressent and Robert Gaudraux. Of all the palaces along the Gulf of Finland this was the climax; it was a miracle, as everyone remarked, that the Russians had never annexed it.

I found Miss Mackenzie examining an elaborate dining chair with ill-concealed disdain.

'Not your favourite kind of chair, I see, Miss Mackenzie,' I said.

'I'm not saying there's anything wrong with the chair as such,' she replied. 'It's just that when you've seen better on a daily basis for as long as I have, you find yourself wondering why you've come all this way to look at it. In the Great Hall of Arbroath we have a set of twenty-six like this, and I venture to say their condition is better too, though all are in everyday use. We don't think of them as anything special.'

By the time we crossed the Russian frontier for Leningrad, there was a lively but unspoken scramble, each time we got into the coach, to avoid sitting next to Miss Mackenzie. The fact was that she was a bore. Nothing she saw in art or nature impressed her, and the way she patronised the retired doctor's wife from Cuckfield irritated the entire group. 'The steppes must look very impressive to you, coming from Sussex, I do see,' she said loftily. 'But compared with the hills around Forfar they're nothing to write home about.'

When we passed a herd of big-horned Russian cattle grazing by the side of the road, Miss Mackenzie only wished that we could see His Grace's herd of Highland Belted Galloways. When we noticed a wooden peasant's hovel in a clump of trees, she was put in mind of the picturesque ghillie's cottage at the head of the loch where His Grace himself sometimes spent a few days fishing.

In Leningrad we stayed for three nights at the old Hotel Astoria, where Hitler had planned on celebrating his capture of the city, and had even had menus printed for the dinner, so confident was he that the siege would succeed. Each morning we were driven to the Hermitage and shepherded at speed along the wide, polished galleries of Leo von Klenze's treasure house, from collection to collection, remarking to each other how we had had no idea that quite so many Renaissance masterpieces and French Impressionists were hanging in Leningrad.

For Miss Mackenzie, however, the Hermitage was a home from home. A decorative portrait of Charles II by Lely was a simple copy of an earlier portrait in His Grace's dressing room; a small oil by Turner of the Swiss Alps was surely inspired by a view of the Esk from Montrose.

By the third morning I was the only member of the group who was still prepared to walk round with her, and I took perverse pleasure in the tenuous, ingenious means she found for turning the conversation to her ducal employers. And I hoped, too, to find one picture or stick of furniture in the Hermitage so splendid that Miss Mackenzie would pause for a moment, and admire it, with no feeling of *déjà vu*.

At last I found what I was looking for. Hanging above the stairwell in the north wing was an enormous Titian; the largest painting of his career, twenty yards wide and almost as deep, depicting Bacchus and Ariadne with a host of satyrs, fawns and naked, dancing nymphs. Each side of the frame must have taken a whole tree trunk, and several dozen men to lever it on to the wall.

'Now there, Miss Mackenzie,' I said; 'is a painting to reckon with.'

Miss Mackenzie was struck dumb for a moment at the head of the great stone staircase as she gave the Titian a swift appraising glance. Then she sniffed. 'I'm surprised they've put *that* on public view,' she said primly. 'Titian's subject matter can be a trifle indelicate. Her Grace has hung our Titian away in a turret bedroom which only married couples are given the use of.'

A year later I was driving north and found myself within a few miles of Arbroath. There was a painted sign by the side of the road saying that the castle was open to the public that day, and I couldn't resist making a small detour. I was keen to see what the ridiculous Miss Mackenzie's lair was really like.

The outside of the castle was turreted and certainly impressive. I bought a ticket from a fluffy-haired old woman in the hall, and was told that if I hurried along I could easily join a guided tour that had started a minute or two earlier. I caught them up in the Hall of the Lairds, where a huddle of tourists was inspecting the great beamed baronial ceiling. Addressing them was Miss Mackenzie.

'Any questions, anybody,' she was asking, 'before we move on to the Duchess's yellow sitting room?'

An attentive American raised his hand. 'That's an unbelievable hearth you've got there,' he said, pointing to a great armorial stone fireplace that reached almost to the roof. 'I've not seen one so big before. Can you tell us something about it?'

Miss Mackenzie's face lit up with a wintery smile. 'It is indeed a remarkable fireplace,' she said. 'I can understand why you find it impressive, coming from America.' And then she added, in her most superior Scottish way, 'But I know His Grace will forgive me when I tell you that the great fireplaces in Leningrad make this one look very modest by comparison.'

LEGAL TENDER

Joyce Pargette, by her own estimation, looked considerably younger than her fifty-three years.

Her hair was colour-rinsed every six weeks at an expensive salon in Knightsbridge, so she remained the same corn blonde today that she'd been at eighteen. Twice a week, on Tuesday and Friday afternoons, her hair and nails were blown and buffed, and on Thursdays a masseuse came to the house with her portable massage table and ironed out what little tension she could discover in Mrs Pargette's soft, plump neck and shoulders.

Joyce Pargette lived as full a life as could be expected for a woman so delicate and nervy. Her husband had long ago ceased relying on her for anything. It was Mark Pargette who left the money on the table to pay Carmen, the Pargettes' Portuguese maid, to save his wife the short journey to the bank, and it was frequently Mark Pargette too who bought their supper on his way home from work.

If he had chosen to make an issue of it, Mark Pargette could have pointed out that his wife was invariably strong enough to do those things that she really wanted to do, such as attending a charity fashion show or a fitting at her dressmaker, but seldom for anything uncongenial to her. Mark Pargette, however, had no wish to make an issue of anything. He was a decent man, who hated fuss. He had been married to Joyce for thirty-three years, had brought up three children with her – all grown up now – and was resigned to his wife's little weaknesses. He was fifty-eight and in a couple of years he would be retiring. It was well known among his partners that poor Mark had a difficult wife, so they were no longer surprised when Joyce was too tired at the last moment to attend the annual office party, or to help entertain at dinner some important clients from the Bundesbank.

Joyce Pargette soaked herself in a hot bath scented with Bronnley soap and Floris bath essence. It was half past eleven in the morning and soon she really must get dressed to meet a girlfriend for lunch at the Berkeley Hotel. Downstairs she could hear Carmen clattering about in the kitchen, washing up last night's supper things. Joyce had slept badly and felt horribly headachy. Lately she had been waking up in the middle of the night and worrying; always the same recurrent worry, it drained her.

In less than two years' time, went her worry, *Mark will be at home all day long.*

The prospect of her husband retiring horrified her. It would utterly disrupt her life. The weekends were bad enough, but having Mark hanging around in the house seven days a week, month in, month out, would be exasperating. What would he do all day? She was used to him slipping out of bed at seven-fifteen, bringing her up a cup of tea and the newspaper, and disappearing to the office until eight or nine in the evening. Where, moreover, would he sit? Mark Pargette had created for himself a tiny study on a half landing, scarcely large enough for his desk and a chair, but Joyce did not believe he would remain there, silent and occupied, all day long. She imagined him wandering about the house, reading his newspaper in the drawing room, making cups of coffee in the kitchen, using the telephone, watching the afternoon racing on television. And what was worse, Joyce resented the fact that her husband would learn precisely how little she did during the day, and would be silently censorious.

Only one possible solution presented itself. It would, she realised, be exhausting to carry out, and would do terrible things to her nerves, but really she had no choice. She must divorce Mark before it was too late.

Joyce Pargette was a fastidious woman when it came to shopping. Whenever she wished to reupholster an armchair, or have a bathroom retiled, or order herself a new winter coat, she made appointments with every leading decorator and dressmaker. She loved to choose between different schemes and estimates.

'I'm sorry, darling, but I just can't come out with your German friends tonight after all,' she would simper to her husband when he arrived home to find her limp and listless in bed, 'but I've spent literally *all day* making decisions over that beastly armchair, and I'm half dead.'

Once she'd decided that she needed a divorce, Joyce Pargette brought the same fastidiousness she lavished on her search for the perfect chintz to her search for the perfect solicitor. Time spent on reconnaissance, she knew, was seldom wasted, so two or three times a week when she lunched with friends, she slyly broached the topic of divorce. Who, she asked, were the really brilliant solicitors of the day? Who were the Nicky Haslams and Nina Campbells of divorce litigation? And within a couple of months a dozen or more suggestions had been made to her, among which the same four names came up again and again.

Meanwhile she spent the remainder of her days in preparing her affairs for the proceedings. Had Mark Pargette been able to see his wife after he'd set off for the office, he would scarcely have recognised her. No sooner had he shut the front door behind him, than Joyce leapt out of bed. By eight o'clock she was bathed and dressed and sitting at Mark's desk on the half landing going through his papers. It was important, she knew, to find out precisely how much money they had, so that she could secure her whole rightful share. There are so many stories, her friends had told her, of wives who, after years of marriage, end up with next to nothing because they don't know what they're entitled to. The minute they file for divorce, their husbands are up to every trick in the book to minimise their assets. Shares disappear, and houses are put into trust; the deviousness of men in this situation cannot be overestimated. Joyce Pargette had no intention of falling into that particular trap, or of experiencing any decline in her present standard of living.

Mark Pargette kept his papers in good order, so at the end

of a fortnight his wife felt she had a fair idea of their financial set-up. Invested in the stock market they had a little over £300,000, in easy-to-sell blue chip equities. Mark's pension from work, which he had topped up with several private pension schemes, was better than Joyce had supposed, and she added the £140,000 lump sum to her list of liquid assets. The mortgage on their house in Markham Street had been paid off several years before, around the time the children left home, so it was an easy matter for her to summon an estate agent from John D. Wood around the corner to value the property at £550,000.

Once she'd dealt with their capital assets, Joyce Pargette began on the household items. A helpful young man from Phillips in Bond Street came round and made a detailed inventory of their furniture, everything from the set of eight dining room chairs Mark had inherited from his godfather to the prints hanging up the stairs. It was remarkable, and encouraging, to learn how much everything was worth. Joyce would never have guessed that the mahogany chest of drawers in Mark's dressing room and the gloomy old grandfather clock she'd wanted to throw out would apparently fetch several thousand pounds each. By the time Phillips had completed their report, Joyce was able to add another £80,000 to her tally.

The only items the young man from Phillips did not value were Mark's diamond cufflinks, evening-dress studs and ivory hairbrushes. These Joyce bundled into a bag and took to Spinks, who said that they hesitated to give a valuation off the top of their heads, but they thought £700 or thereabouts was a pretty sound estimate. All in all, including their three-year-old Rover, Mark's suits and some odd silver, the Pargettes seemed to be worth £1.1 million.

Joyce Pargette wrote out a clear list of all their assets (excluding, it must be said, her own clothes) and then made four telephone calls. When she had finished she had appointments for the beginning of the next week to see the four best divorce lawyers in London; all of them, as it happened, with rooms in New Square at Lincoln's Inn. Joyce would see one of them each morning and another each afternoon. By Tuesday evening she hoped to have made her choice. It is by no means normal practice for clients to subject divorce lawyers to taking part in a 'beauty contest' for their instructions, but Joyce Pargette was a highly pragmatic women. She would never have chosen the caterers for a cocktail party without comparing their finger buffet with several other firms; no more would she choose her lawyers without a searching interview.

The Pargettes' weekend followed its usual course. Mark was given no clue whatever that his wife was committed to so clinical a divorce. On Saturday morning he did the weekend shopping and staggered home with several heavy carrier bags. These he unpacked while the kettle boiled, and then he took a cup of tea, an apple and two slices of toast up to Joyce on a tray, and drew back her curtains. After lunch, which he also prepared, he delivered a skirt of Joyce's which needed hemming to the invisible menders, and then drove on to his regular Saturday afternoon squash match at Hurlingham, before taking Joyce out to dinner at the Brasserie St Quentin. Her mood, he was relieved to see, was less tense than usual, and their evening was almost convivial. She had once been very charming, which was why Mark had married her, and even now, especially when they were with strangers, her charm could still flicker fitfully into life. Nobody looking at them across the restaurant would have guessed that the corn blonde dining with her tall, attentive husband wanted nothing in the world so badly as a swift decree nisi.

On Sunday, as he'd done for years, Mark left Markham Street straight after breakfast and headed for his golf club. Joyce complained freely about his weekend sports, as she'd done for years, though she knew she'd be more put out if he capitulated and hung about all day at home.

The rooms of all four solicitors were remarkably similar. All were housed in Georgian buildings with wide, clattery stone staircases and lists of the partners painted on wooden boards at the door. Each set had a small, panelled ante-room with hard leather chairs and a carriage clock, where Joyce had to wait until the solicitor was ready to see her. And then she was ushered into a high-ceilinged, not always enormous office, dominated by an enormous partner's desk covered with stacks of paper wrapped like parcels with pink cloth ribbon. And the numerous legal volumes, some ancient and leather-bound, some newer and cloth-bound, imbued Joyce with the same feeling of confidence that weighty pattern and sample books gave her at an interior decorator's.

What annoyed her, however, was the solicitors' apparent lack of enthusiasm to take up her case. Joyce was used to stepping into shops where every last assistant was intent on selling her something.

'You know you have a duty to make sure that the marriage is truly finished,' said the first solicitor, a bald-headed patrician in a three-piece dark suit. 'May I ask whether you have consulted a marriage counsellor?'

Not knowing that the question about counselling is statutory, Joyce Pargette took a dim view of the bald-headed patrician and his efforts to repair her marriage. Fancy, she thought, going to your dressmaker and being told you have a duty to make sure your old dress is truly worn out.

The patrician solicitor, for his part, had never encountered anyone quite like Mrs Mark Pargette. The clients who came to seek his advice were normally sombre, confused or despondent. Often they had no real wish to proceed with a divorce, and then he would advise them against it. Once he had explained the expense, and the complexities of the division of property and the emotional stress that divorce brings, as often as not they would return home, thoughtful and sanguine, with renewed determination to make their marriage work.

He was confused, too, by Mrs Pargette's apparent lack of grounds.

'There's nothing *wrong* with Mark,' she said, 'nothing wrong with him at all. He's absolutely fine. I just want to be on my own.'

'Your husband doesn't ill-treat you, Mrs Pargette?'

'Oh no, nothing like that.'

'And what about your children? Have you taken into consideration their feelings about your possible divorce?'

'Oh no, there's no problem with the children either. They're all grown up and have flown the nest now. Julia, our youngest, is twenty-two.'

'I see,' said the solicitor, making notes in pencil on his large lined pad. 'And what about money? Do you have any idea of what your expectations might be?' So few wives, he knew from experience, even today, have any detailed knowledge of their financial position, even of their husband's income.

'Oh yes,' replied Joyce. 'Let me give you this. I've made out a list.'

The solicitor read it and raised his eyebrows. On two sheets of writing paper, set out in fountain pen with turquoise ink, was the detailed synopsis of Mark Pargette's estate, with its grand total of £1,130,500.

'And what, Mrs Pargette, do you want me to do with this?' asked the solicitor at last.

'Tell me how much of it I can expect,' replied Joyce.

'Well, that rather depends on a number of factors,' he said steadily. 'The grounds for the divorce, for one thing. You may not be aware of this, but in this country you can't just snap your fingers and, hey presto, you're divorced. It takes a little time and you have to come up with some reasons.'

Joyce nodded with every pretence of attention, but really this was all too tiresome. She'd asked this man to sort out a divorce for her and he was weighing her down with details. All she wanted was a figure, surely not impossible when she'd furnished him with the facts.

'As you may know, Mrs Pargette, there are five grounds under English law for irretrievable breakdown,' he went on. 'These are cruelty, which you have already discounted; adultery, which again seems not to be the case; desertion – I assume that Mr Pargette still resides with you at, er' – he consulted his notes – 'at Markham Street in Chelsea?'

'Yes, of course he does,' replied Joyce, 'which is the whole point of my coming to see you.'

'Otherwise,' continued the solicitor, ignoring the slight tartness in her voice, 'you are left with a two-year mutually agreed separation; or in the event of the other partner being unwilling to consent to a divorce, a five-year separation, which is, er, unilateral.'

'Five years!' exclaimed Joyce. '*Five years?* But Mark will be retired long before that, and then what would I do?'

'That I couldn't say, Mrs Pargette. But should you decide to proceed with this divorce I can only advise you to ensure that your husband concurs with it.'

'He will – oh, he will,' said Joyce. 'I've always been able to wind him round my little finger when I want to.'

'Most gratifying,' replied the solicitor dryly.

'And now, about the money,' said Joyce. 'You've seen the figures. How much, if you were running my case, do you think you could get me?'

The solicitor raised his eyebrows again disdainfully at this vulgarity, then glanced down at the columns of figures again before replying.

'The old rule of thumb,' he said, 'is one-third of the couple's joint income going to the wife – always assuming, of course' – he chuckled – 'that the husband's income is the larger. Do you happen to have any income yourself, Mrs Pargette?'

'No,' she replied firmly, 'I've never had enough spare time to take on a job.'

'Quite so. Now on the subject of capital, the division is normally so organised that the wife suffers no substantial change in her quality of life.'

Joyce nodded her corn-blonde head contentedly at this piece of news. For the first time the man was making sense.

'Looking at the figures here, and assuming they are correct, I would suggest to you that a severance in the region of £350,000 would be appropriate. I recommend the clean break since you have pointed out that Mr Pargette is shortly to retire, so his income will diminish. If you prefer, of course, we could go for a smaller cash severance of, say, £300,000, plus a proportion, perhaps a third, of your husband's pension.'

At this, Joyce Pargette rose graciously but decisively to her feet and bid the solicitor goodbye. 'I'll let you know what I think of your scheme. If I choose you I'll be in touch,' she said.

But she knew that she wouldn't be. Three hundred thousand pounds indeed! She had never heard of anything so mingy. For one thing she had already spotted, in the window of a local estate agents, the prettiest little two-bedroom flat at the top end of Dovehouse Street with an asking price of £265,000. By the time she'd decorated it there would be nothing left at all. No, what she needed, she reckoned, the very minimum she could get by on, was half, or just over half, of their joint estate: £600,000 was the sort of figure Joyce Pargette had in mind. With that she could buy her little flat and make it comfortable, and still have £300,000 left over to put in the bank for an income. That solicitor in his buttoned-up three-piece suit was clearly not the man of enterprise she needed on her side. But she had three more appointments, and she felt confident that one solicitor at least would show more initiative.

As it turned out, both her next two candidates were more encouraging. A much younger solicitor, barely forty, with a copy of *Private Eye* lying open on his desk, thought it worth going for £480,000, with the figure of £450,000 as their realistic target. Mrs Pargette's third visit to New Court, on Tuesday morning, took her to the chambers of a celebrated maverick who was known to enjoy pushing the spirit of the law to its limits. He gave Mrs Pargette a tumbler of dry sherry, asked her a dozen questions about her private life that Joyce could hardly see were pertinent, and then said he'd have a damn good crack at getting her half a million.

'Not that you deserve it, mind,' he said, 'but I'm not averse to a bit of mischief to rattle the hencoop. Who are your husband's solicitors, incidentally?'

'I'm not absolutely certain,' said Joyce. 'Would it be the same people who drew up his will?'

'Could be. But presumably he's informed you who's acting for him?'

'Oh no,' replied Joyce. 'Mark has no idea yet that we're getting a divorce. I don't want him to find out until I've chosen the best solicitor in town.'

Joyce Pargette had lunch alone for the second day running at a modest Italian place in Chancery Lane, and at one minute to three was waiting outside the chambers of Miss Kathleen Glaser.

By nature, Joyce was mildly prejudiced against female

professionals of any kind. She would no sooner have consulted a woman doctor or dentist than allowed a woman to advise her on the colour of her dining room walls. But Miss Glaser had been so often and so warmly recommended by divorcee friends that she was prepared to allow her the benefit of the doubt. Kathleen Glaser had a reputation as a man-hater. Although from time to time she did actually represent the husband in a divorce case, this happened very rarely. On numerous occasions she had been instrumental in securing huge settlements for her clients against all the odds; male solicitors everywhere felt apprehensive when they learnt that Kathleen Glaser was representing their client's spouse.

Miss Glaser was a formidable figure in every way. Physically she was enormous, with broad, athletic shoulders that she accentuated with a tailored Prince of Wales check suit. She wore no make-up, and held her dark hair back from her face with a plain tortoiseshell clip.

'I'm sure she's a dyke,' Joyce's divorcee friends had said, 'just look at her hands'; which Joyce could barely bring herself to do, so alien were Kathleen Glaser's short, unpainted finger-nails to a woman whose cuticles were so lovingly groomed.

What impressed Joyce Pargette, however, was the solicitor's resolve. The minute she sat down in Miss Glaser's chambers and introduced herself, Kathleen Glaser gave her a sharp appraising smile then began making notes on a large sheet of foolscap. No time was wasted inquiring whether or not she'd consulted a marriage counsellor; the interview was brisk and businesslike, and within minutes the lawyer seemed to have completely grasped the spirit of the Pargettes' marriage.

'As I see it, Mrs Pargette,' said Kathleen Glaser, 'you have been married in good faith for thirty-three years, during which time you have discharged your duties and obligations as a wife to perfection. You have brought up three happy children and have created for your husband a comfortable home, the perfect backdrop for his successful career in the City. You have on occasions even helped him up the ladder in his work by entertaining English and foreign business clients over dinner, people in whom you had no earthly interest beyond that of helping Mr Pargette. You have lavished your un-divided care and attention on your house, have denied your-self the chance of a rewarding and satisfying career, and in every possible way have been a cheerful and willing helpmate – ghastly expression – am I right?'

Joyce beamed with pleasure. Half the sacrifices she had made on Mark's behalf hadn't even occurred to her until Miss Glaser put it all into perspective. 'That's exactly it,' she replied happily. 'Exactly it.'

'Good,' said Kathleen Glaser, laying her square hands flat on the desk. 'And as I understand it, you've simply had enough. You've done your bit, and now you deserve a little peace and quiet. You don't want to be housekeeper-cum-chief-bottlewasher for the next twenty years as well, am I right?'

'That's exactly it,' replied Joyce.

'Good,' said Kathleen Glaser. 'Then all we need to work out is the financial side of things. Any idea what your husband is worth?'

Joyce passed her the two sheets of writing paper.

'Oh, this is excellent, excellent stuff,' said Miss Glaser as she read it. 'You've got it all down here. If only every wife seeking her freedom was as sensible and prudent as you've been, my job would be a lot easier, and the job of the courts too, I might add.'

Then Miss Glaser made a number of calculations on her pad, something like a mathematical equation, and arrived at a figure that Joyce couldn't read upside down.

'How much are you after?' asked Miss Glaser.

'Well, I'd hoped for £600,000. But I saw a couple of other solicitors and they said I was being optimistic.'

'Men, I suppose? Male solicitors.'

Joyce nodded.

'Pay no attention to them,' said Miss Glaser dismissively. 'If they had their way you'd finish up with half a crown and a Christmas turkey. In my opinion you're not being in the least bit optimistic, rather the reverse if anything.' She referred again to the equation on her notepad and to the two sheets of writing paper. 'No,' she said firmly, 'the figure I'd advise you to go for, if you chose to retain me as your solicitor in this matters, is £900,000. I don't think we'd have much trouble getting you that.'

'But that's marvellous,' said Joyce. 'Are you quite sure?'

'As good as certain,' said Miss Glaser. 'And I'll tell you why. Your husband, you tell me, is proposing to give up work at the unusually early age of sixty. Unless he is physically unfit, I can see no reason why he shouldn't continue working for another five years at his present salary. That will be plenty for him to live on, and we are also allowing him in excess of £200,000 from your capital to buy him a small flat. So the court will accept that he's been well taken care of.'

'You mentioned the court,' said Joyce. 'Will this have to go to court? I thought divorces were more or less tied up by the solicitors between them.'

'That's only if you're prepared to accept a low settlement,' said Miss Glaser. 'You can be sure your husband's solicitors will do everything possible to convince you to come to an amicable agreement without the bother of going to court. It's their job, of course, to sell you short. What I'll advise you to do, if you become my client, is to remain resolute until you've got what you deserve – am I right?'

'Oh yes,' said Joyce contentedly, her corn-blonde head full of bedbacks and valances for Dovehouse Street, and the vague, happy prospect of round-the-world cruises. 'I would so much like you to be my solicitor.'

'Good,' said Miss Glaser, 'I'd be delighted to act for you. And if I might make a suggestion, the first thing you need to do is inform Mr Pargette of your intentions. Not tonight – dinner is the worst meal for breaking that kind of news because it's open-ended – but tell him at breakfast tomorrow morning. No need to explain why, simply tell him, "I want a divorce, and my solicitors will shortly be making contact." Then make sure he goes to work as usual, because I'm going to have a letter drawn up this afternoon that will be hand-delivered to him at his office tomorrow at ten o'clock. That will set the wheels in motion. The only other thing you have to think about right now is where you're going to live. Obviously you can't continue living together under the same roof, and since you are initiating the proceedings it is really for you to move out.'

Joyce looked apprehensive at this, fearing that she might be expected to move in with her sister and brother-in-law in Barnes.

'I suggest,' continued Kathleen Glaser, 'that you contact an estate agent with a good letting department and instruct them to rent you somewhere immediately. You should certainly be installed by the end of the week. Choose somewhere, preferably a flat, costing £1,200 to £1,600 a month: not less, or it will count against you when we establish your standard of living; not too much more though, or your husband's solicitors will try and make out you're extravagant. All the bills for the flat you will of course forward to Mr Pargette.'

After her new client had gone, Kathleen Glaser picked up the telephone and made one call.

Joyce, meanwhile, sat in the taxi taking her home, exhausted but energised by her visit to Kathleen Glaser. The figure of £900,000 echoed sweetly in her head. And yet there was so much to do, so much to absorb, quite apart from the imminent strain of telling Mark. When she got back to Markham Street she rang half a dozen letting agencies, who promised to send her details by first-class post; there were plenty of charming flats, decorated and equipped to the highest standards, they said. And then, drooping from her harrowing day, Joyce retired to bed. When Mark got home at nine o'clock he found his wife stretched out like a corpse under her eiderdown, her arms resting limply on the bedcover.

'Have you had any supper, darling?' he asked.

'No,' she replied in a thin, pitiful voice. 'You see, I've spent *all day* making decisions, and I'm half dead.'

'Poor Joyce,' said Mark evenly. 'Would it make you happy if I got us some eggs and smoked salmon at the late-night grocer?'

'Oh, would you, Mark?' said Joyce weakly. 'You know how much I love smoked salmon with scrambled eggs, and I didn't have a second to shop today.'

The following morning Mark Pargette was surprised, as he stood waiting for the kettle to boil, by the arrival of his wife in the chilly kitchen. Such an occurrence had not happened, at so early an hour, for fifteen years.

'Joyce!' he exclaimed. 'What brings you down here? I was just about to bring your tea up to you.'

'There's something I need to tell you.'

'Marvellous, what is it? Piece of toast?'

'No,' said Joyce. 'No, listen, Mark, what I'm about to say is serious. I want a divorce. I don't want to discuss it, and my mind's quite made up. There isn't anybody else – I just want to live on my own. So now you know. My solicitor will be in touch with you later today. Now I'm going back upstairs to bed.'

With that she left the kitchen.

A few minutes later Mark came gingerly into their bedroom with Joyce's cup of tea.

'Listen, darling,' he said. 'I can see you're upset, and I want you to rest. But when I come home this evening, if you're feeling more yourself, let's go out somewhere and have a good dinner. You've been overtiring yourself lately.'

'For God's sake, Mark,' snapped Joyce. 'Of course we can't go out to dinner tonight. Didn't you listen to a word I said downstairs? I said I want a divorce and that's final. Now leave me alone and go off to your office.'

'But Joyce, Joyce,' said Mark, 'you can't go off and live on your own. You need someone to look after you.'

'I do not,' said Joyce. 'If I just had a bit of peace and quiet I'd be perfectly happy. Is it so much to ask for, a bit of peace and quiet?'

Seeing that there was nothing further to be gained by remonstrating with his wife at the foot of their bed, Mark Pargette set off for work. Within an hour of arriving he had been served with a terse notice of divorce proceedings from a firm of solicitors in Lincoln's Inn. And within the next hour he had a conversation with his own solicitor, and faxed him a copy of the letter he'd received from Joyce's firm.

Meanwhile in Markham Street Joyce was reawakened by the telephone.

'Mrs Pargette? This is Kathleen Glaser speaking. You went through with it all right?'

'Yes, yes I did.'

'Good girl. That's the worst bit over. All you need to do now is find yourself a flat. The rest you can leave to me. And incidentally, if ever you need to speak to me, about anything at all, however trivial, you can ring me here at chambers. Don't hesitate. It's all part of my job.'

'Thank you, Miss Glaser.'

'Do please call me Kathleen,' replied her solicitor. 'We'll be spending considerable time together over the next eight months or so.'

And so it proved. Joyce had had no idea how complicated and laborious are the machinations of divorce. Once she had removed herself from Markham Street into a warm mansion block flat barely a quarter of a mile away, she found her life dominated by the proceedings. Mark, through his solicitors, made several attempts to settle, offering first £450,000 as a clean-break settlement, and some months later half a million pounds. These offers were made during a series of meetings between the solicitors at Miss Glaser's chambers in New Court, or at Mark's lawyer's off the Strand, but there was never much prospect of an out-of-court agreement.

'They're still carrying on as though we lived in Victorian England,' Kathleen Glaser told her client over one of their regular campaign lunches. 'I've told your husband's solicitors that £900,000 is our figure and we're not budging from it, so I can't think why they're shilly-shallying around in this lunatic fashion. Have another glass of wine, Joyce, and cheer up, we'll be in court this side of Christmas.'

One chilly autumn afternoon Miss Glaser took Joyce to meet the barrister who would represent her in court. 'We're not going to settle this,' she'd said, 'so we'd better get a good barrister aboard.' So they walked together across Fleet Street to the Middle Temple to the chambers of John Havelock in Pump Court. Havelock turned out to be a bachelor in his late fifties; small, scruffy, keen to please, pink-faced, overweight, and clearly only just returned from lunch. 'I'm afraid I haven't yet had a chance to read, note and inwardly digest everything that Kathleen sent over to me,' he apoligised, breathing clouds of vaporised claret into the cold room, 'but I regard it as a high honour to represent so charming a lady.' At which compliment he fell back into his chair, knocking a saucer full of cigarette butts on to the floor with the sleeve of his jacket.

From then on Miss Glaser took the lead in their conversation, neatly encapsulating the points to be brought out in court, and alerting John Havelock to those details, detrimental to her client's husband, that could be worked up to their advantage. Havelock listened glassy-eyed, and from time to time nodded his head vigorously.

As Joyce Pargette clattered down the stairs of Pump Court in her sling-back shoes, she hissed doubtfully to Kathleen, 'Are you sure that man's up to it? He seemed half drunk to me.'

'They all are,' replied Kathleen. 'All the male barristers drink like newts. But don't worry about Havelock. He's brilliant on his feet. In court there's no one to match him.'

It was two years, almost to the day, after Joyce Pargette's declaration to her husband in the kitchen of Markham Street, that their petition for a ruling over the division of their assets was brought before the bench. It was a freezing November day, and there was ice on the pavements all over London. Joyce took a taxi to Kathleen's chambers, collected her, and then they rode on together to the Law Courts opposite St Clement Danes church. Inside they found that fourteen different courts were in session that day in the Family Division, and waiting uncomfortably all along the corridors were little huddles of nearly unmarried wives and husbands with their respective retinues of sisters, parents, lovers, solicitors and barristers. There were even children hanging about at their mother's or father's side outside some courtroom doors, and Joyce was relieved that her own three would not be coming to watch the proceedings today. She knew they did not approve of their parents parting, but she would make it up to them at Christmas. With her £900,000 she would buy them the best Christmas presents she could find.

They reached the waiting areas outside the court designated for Pargette v. Pargette, and Joyce saw that Mark had already arrived. He was talking to two men Joyce didn't recognise, presumably his solicitor and barrister, and Robin Maxwell-Slack, his oldest friend. When Mark caught sight of her, he smiled ruefully in her direction and seemed to mouth the words 'Good luck'. Then they were ushered into court and the clerk called out 'All rise,' and the judge in his red robes and nougat-coloured wig entered and took his place on the bench. Joyce was given a chair next to Kathleen, who was positioned immediately behind John Havelock in case barrister and solicitor needed to confer. Joyce was pleased that Havelock appeared to be sober, and had his stack of papers relating to the case in good order.

The entire proceedings lasted less than fifty minutes.

John Havelock, as counsel for the petitioner, spoke first. 'M'lud,' he said, 'I act for Joyce Pargette in this case. The amounts of money involved are not contested. Valuations have been agreed between the lawyers, and the sole question for resolution today for your lordship's attention is the proportion in which these assets should be split.'

After the judge had read the relevant figures – virtually a typed-up version of Joyce's own handwritten inventory – John Havelock launched into his case.

'Quite frankly, m'lud, my client simply got bored with her husband. It is not our intention today to show that Mr Parquette behaved cruelly to his wife in any way, but only that he bored her and did not always behave with total consideration towards her. I have three specific examples of this lack of consideration to bring before the court today. On one occasion, m'lud, Mr Pargette asked his wife to come home with him from a dinner party at half past twelve at night, on the grounds that he had a six a.m. aeroplane to catch to Abu Dhabi the next morning for a business trip.'

Joyce, sitting beside her solicitor, was surprised that this story that she'd told to Kathleen one day over lunch had been brought up in court, but Kathleen squeezed her arm reassuringly and whispered, 'Don't worry, it's going well.'

'Three years ago, m'lud, Mr Pargette's wife had gone to considerable trouble to have an armchair reupholstered and had narrowed her choice of fabric down to three patterns.

When she asked her husband to meet her at an interior decorating establishment at lunchtime, he refused, claiming a boardroom luncheon with First Boston Crédit Suisse as his excuse.'

'And was there such a luncheon?' interjected the judge.

'I understand there was, m'lud,' replied Havelock, 'but that was not material to my client in her disappointment.'

'On the third occasion,' he went on, 'my client had asked her husband to collect during his lunch hour an evening dress for her from a dress shop in Beauchamp Place in Knightsbridge and to deliver it to their house in Markham Street. Once again Mr Pargette declined to help her, claiming a long-standing business commitment, when he knew well that his wife was already tied up with appointments at her manicurist and hairdressers.'

'I find it slightly strange,' broke in the judge for the second time, 'that a business appointment in the City of London should not take precedence over collecting a dress from the other side of town in the middle of the day, especially when your client, you say, was merely having her hair done.'

'It may seem so to you, m'lud, but not to my client.' On which note John Havelock rested his case and conceded the floor to Mark Pargete's barrister. Joyce, meanwhile, felt a creeping unease, and she twittered nervously into Kathleen Glaser's ear. But her solicitor remained stoic and confident. 'Just wait until you hear what your husband's lot have to say for themselves. Right is all on our side. They'll be hard pressed to come up with anything,' she said.

Mark Pargette's case was put quietly, succinctly and entirely without histrionics. His barrister was on his feet for barely five minutes.

'My lord, I put it to you that there is no case to bring before your lordship today. My client is an upstanding man without a stain on his character, who finds the entire proceedings deeply distasteful. He is a member of Brooks's, a sidesman at St Luke's Church, plays golf for his firm, in his younger days opened the bowling for his school, and has done everything possible to avoid detaining your lordship today. He has always allowed his wife full access to their joint bank account, including during the time of their separation, and has cherished Mrs Pargette in every way. As her counsel has already stated, my client has never been cruel to his wife. Indeed, for thirty years he has brought her breakfast in bed, and frequently prepares their evening meal on his return from the City. My client has already made his wife an offer of £500,000 through her solicitors, which has been turned down. As you will see from the papers set before you, my lord, the offer was more than proper, and my client is at a loss to know what more he could have done to accommodate the plaintiff. I rest my case.'

At this the judge, consulting the watch that he had earlier unbuckled from his wrist and laid before him on the bench, said, 'I see that it is twelve-forty-five. I will give judgment at two o'clock.' And then the court all rose as he departed for lunch in the judges' dining room, and Mark and Joyce and their retinues set out across an icy Fleet Street to the Cock Tavern and George pub respectively.

Ignorant as she was of legal matters, Joyce Pargette could not but feel that her case had been poorly stated. 'I'm a bit surprised, Kathleen,' she said, 'that Mr Havelock didn't mention my devotion to the children, and the dinners I attended with Mark's business contacts. I thought we'd agreed on that.'

'Oh, all the wives do that,' said Kathleen Glaser. 'They all have children with mumps and business dinners to tag along to. That wouldn't impress the judge. Don't worry, Joyce, I could tell he was on your side, it'll all work out fine.' And then Miss Glaser led Joyce and John Havelook over to the carvery and bought them all lunch of cold tongue and potato salad.

The judge's summing-up and judgment on the stroke of two o'clock was swift, stern and caustic. No sooner had he taken his place at the bench then he launched into his homily. 'I find this entire case misguided,' he began. 'It astonishes me that the plaintiff should ever have brought her outrageous demands for £900,000 before the court, and that the matter wasn't resolved at some much earlier time between the solicitors acting for both parties. I find the plaintiff's husband entirely blameless, and I share his deep distaste that his wife should have persisted so unreasonably in her claims. As a cricket player, a churchman, a golfer and a member of Brooks's, it must have caused him particular distress. Mrs Pargette throughout these unfortunate proceedings has impressed me as a spoilt, shallow and greedy woman, entirely selfish in her intentions. She was made a proper offer in settlement which she turned down, in the misguided belief that she would obtain more. I award her the sum of £50,000.'

All over the court there was a perceptible indrawing of breath, followed by a dull, pathetic sobbing from Joyce as she brushed away Miss Glaser's steadying arm.

Mark Pargette's barrister was already back up on his feet. 'You are aware from the papers, my lord, that at an early stage of these unhappy proceedings, my client – overgenerously, as matters turned out – agreed to pay £500,000 to the plaintiff. And as your lordship has seen fit to make an award of an understandably lower nature, I feel that my client must be entitled to his costs.'

'Granted,' replied the judge.

Joyce emitted another piercing sob. 'That doesn't mean they come out of my £50,000, does it?' she almost shrieked at Kathleen Glaser.

'I'm afraid it does. And I feel bound to tell you that after my costs and the cost of the other side there won't be very much left.'

The following day, which was a Saturday, Joyce Pargette sat alone at the window of her warm mansion flat, looking balefully out over the Duke of York's playing fields. She knew that she could not afford to continue living there, and wondered where she would go next. The next morning she woke early but stayed in bed, delaying the hour when she must ring her sister in Barnes. It was Sunday and Mark would be playing golf, and now there was not even anything left to complain about.

Mark sank his putt on the ninth and broke for lunch. His regular golfing partner was playing well and was a couple of holes up on him. It was a perfect crisp winter's day and they were both in high spirits. Mark slipped his arm round her and gently kissed her soft, unpainted lips. She kissed him back, laughed and patted his face affectionately.

'You know, I could get struck off for this,' she said as they wheeled their trolleys towards the clubhouse.

'It wouldn't matter, Kathleen, you know we have plenty of money.'

Then they laughed again and linked arms as they reached the clubhouse steps.

Mark Pargette smiled contentedly. He was proud of Kathleen, and would never underestimate his formidable next wife. His knowledge of her professional reputation, however, and his intimate observation of her character over the last eight years, prevented him from telling her about the $600,000 he had on deposit in Grand Cayman.

Nor, since he hated fuss, did he mention his regular Saturday afternoon squash partner.

EXHIBITION SATURDAY

'Milne! Here come your parents. A grey Volvo estate.'

'Orme! Quickly, Orme, your father's coming up the drive in your new Rover.'

Orme and Milne ran out into the top of the drive and made flagging-down signals, so they could ride triumphant in the back of their cars for the last few yards to the school.

'Johnson, I think this might be your parents,' said Scobie doubtfully. 'In a yellow Ford Fiesta?'

'Oh, that's only my mother's car,' said Johnson hurriedly. 'She uses it for shopping and taking my sister riding. Our proper car's a Mercedes. I don't know why they've come in my mother's car. Probably the Mercedes is being serviced or something.'

And Johnson thought to himself: 'Thank God it's only Exhibition Saturday and not Sports Day they've come in the Fiesta.'

There were now fewer than ten boys waiting on the bench by the clump of rhododendrons at the school gates; their grey mackintoshes firmly belted against the grey spring drizzle. Stephen Merton knew his mother would be one of the last to arrive but it didn't worry him. The later the better, he thought, because the later she comes the fewer people will notice.

'Merton! Isn't that your mother walking up the drive with that man?'

Stephen saw at once that it was, but he stared for a bit through screwed-up eyes, pretending he couldn't quite tell at that distance.

'I think so,' he said at last. 'She must have come down by train this time.'

'Your mother *always* comes by train,' said Scobie. 'Haven't you got a car?'

'Yes. Actually,' said Stephen, 'it's just that my father drives it.'

'Well get another then, stupid,' said Scobie. And then he said: '*Some people!*'

Stephen Merton had a special dream. He could see it all so clearly, and he'd prayed for it, but it never happened. The dream was: his mother and father were married to each other again and they arrived together for Sports Day in a huge, gleaming bottle-green Daimler. And when they were halfway up the drive, Milne and Orme and Scobie suddenly noticed and said, 'God, Merton, isn't that the new-style Daimler Double-Six? How come you've got one of those, there's only about three in the whole country.' And his mother in the dream was still his mother, of course, but she was quite different in every way. For instance, her annoying laugh didn't exist anymore, and her shoes were those low-heeled sort with a gold chain like Mrs Orme had, and she was wearing a nice blue coat. And when his parents got to the clump of rho-dodendrons they stopped the car and whizzed down the electric windows and said, 'Jump in, Stephen. And would any of your friends like a ride to the school too?' And everybody said, 'Wow, yes please, Mrs Merton,' and there was a wonder-ful smell of new leather as they clambered into the back seat.

Now that his mother and Edmondo were only twenty yards from the gate, Stephen ran towards them, ostensibly to greet them but actually to head them off before they reached the other boys. Whenever his mother came down to Westleigh House he behaved like a sheepdog, circling and weaving around her, intent on keeping her away from other people. The fewer boys and staff that met her, the better. For several nights before Exhibition Saturday and Sports Day, Stephen had nightmares of possible confrontations: his mother talking to Scobie, his mother with matron, his mother and the head-master. In all these scenes she was laughing her annoying laugh and smiling, and he was standing next to her, ashamed, willing her to shut up, but she wouldn't shut up, just going on and on laughing her annoying laugh and smiling.

'Darling, I'm sorry we're so late,' said Mrs Merton, and she stooped and kissed him on the cheek. 'The train stopped at every little station in the whole of Kent.'

'A very slow train journey,' said Edmondo the art dealer, who had been seeing Serena Merton for the last six months. 'Your mother was worried we'd be the last to arrive.'

Stephen thought: I wouldn't have minded if you had been. But he said, 'Can we go straight out to lunch now? I'm starving.'

'Of course, if you'd like to,' said Serena Merton. 'But I must sit down for just a second before we walk back down the drive again.' And before Stephen could stop her, she was heading towards the bench where Scobie and the other boys with late parents were waiting. Two of them stood up to make room for her.

'Thank you so much,' said Mrs Merton. 'I'm quite exhausted by the walk from the station. I'm Stevie's mother, by the way. Are you all friends of his?' Stephen felt a great red wave of shame sweep over him. How could she call him Stevie! And he dreaded their reply to his mother's question. 'Are you all friends of his?' How could she ask that? He hardly dared look at Scobie. He knew already what he was going to say. 'Friends with Merton? You kidding? He's the most unpopular boy in our class.'

'Yes,' Scobie was replying politely. 'I'm in the same dormitory as Stephen and in the same class too, except he's always at the top of the form and I'm near the bottom.'

Mrs Merton smiled at Scobie and laughed her annoying laugh. Oh *no*, please no, prayed Stephen. Please, please, dear God, don't let her laugh like that.

'I hope nobody will mind if I slip off my shoes for a minute,' said Serena Merton, easing off her purple suede pumps with their little curvy heels, and gently massaging her instep.

Stephen's knuckles, inside the pockets of his grey corduroy trousers, went white from being clenched. He felt he could smell his mother's feet from where he stood. Everyone must be able to smell them. The smell must be coming through her thin pale stockings and drifting all over the grounds. You could probably smell them right down on the First XI pitch.

Then Edmondo said, 'That's the last time we come by train, Serena. Next time I'll bring you down on the back of the motorbike.'

Oh, God, *please no*, thought Stephen, please don't say anything about the motorbike.

'Do you ride a motorbike then?' asked Scobie.

'I have a Motoguzzi,' replied Edmondo. 'Serena and I use it a lot in London. But I think on your Sports Day we'll ride down here on it. If it's nice weather.'

'Please, Mummy, please can we go to lunch now,' pleaded Stephen, desperate to interrupt this conversation. 'I really am starving.'

Unless you had a car, there was only one place to eat within range of Westleigh House. Westleigh village – conurbation really – consisted of several estates of mock-Lutyens mansions arranged around a golf course, and at the apex of several private roads was the Thistledene Hotel, open to non-residents for lunch, tea and day-membership of the health spa.

Stephen Merton and his mother and her lover were walking back down the school drive towards the Thistledene Hotel when a dark blue Rover pulled up next to them.

'Need a lift?' shouted Mr Orme, and Stephen could see Orme sitting beside his father in the front seat, and his pigtailed sister and their dog in the back.

Say no, thought Stephen. We're quite OK walking.

'That would be lovely,' said Mrs Merton smiling. 'How kind you are. Hurry up and jump in, Stephen. We're only going to the Thistledene.'

'Nothing easier,' said Mr Orme. 'Not a great day to be walking is it?'

'I was saying earlier,' said Edmondo, 'that if the weather is better on Sports Day I'll drive Serena down on my motorbike.'

'A jolly good idea,' said Mr Orme. 'You won't get snarled up in the traffic out of London either.'

Before lunch they had drinks in a little beamed bar called the Tudor Snug, where the fireplace was decorated with horse brasses and snaffles and you got a saucer of cheese footballs free with your ginger ale.

'Are you really coming to the Sports on the motorbike?' asked Stephen.

'If it's sunny,' said his mother.

'Wouldn't it be better to borrow a car?'

'More fun on Edmondo's wonderful bike, don't you think? And here's the waiter to take our orders. Have you decided, Stephen? Knowing you you'll have the roast beef.' Mrs Merton laughed her laugh at the waiter, drawing him into the great joke that Stephen always chose roast beef off the trolley at the Thistledene Hotel.

They went into the dining room and the waiter handed Edmondo a wine list with blood red tassels dangling from it and Edmondo, being Italian, and wanting to get along with Stephen for Serena's sake, said: 'Which colour would you prefer then, Stephen? A glass of claret to go with your beef?' Stephen replied, 'No, just another ginger ale.' But he was thinking furiously: *He always makes that joke about me drinking wine.*

Their table was next to some french windows outside which were a paved patio and some tables with umbrellas, furled because of the rain, and beyond them Stephen could see the boundary of the school grounds. The Second XI goal posts just showed above the bushes, and then the out-of-bounds scrubland with the old air-raid shelters left over from the war. Nobody knew much about the air-raid shelters. There was a school rumour that, during the bombing of Dover, the whole school had once spent the night sleeping in the shelters with football jerseys on top of their pyjamas, but nobody knew that for certain, it was just a rumour.

Stephen wished he was inside this secret air-raid shelter now. It was the only place at Westleigh House where he felt perfectly safe and knew he'd be left alone. The roofs of the reinforced concrete shelters had become unsafe, people said, which was why they were out of bounds, and anyway the bit of scrubland they were on didn't really belong to the school but to a local farmer, so they were doubly out of bounds, and when Stephen found a way to get into one of them during one of his solitary half-holiday walks, he realised he had disco-vered a refuge. To get inside the shelter you first went down into a little hollow like a golf bunker, all overgrown with long grass, and then there were some concrete steps down to a wooden door. The door was padlocked but it had broken, so the farmer had leant a millwheel against the entrance – like the great stone rolled before the Holy Sepulchre – which Stephen had prised back a few feet with a bit of metal railing, just far enough to crawl in. During the Christmas and Easter terms he often sat inside the shelter all afternoon in the musty darkness, while outside he could just hear the cheers of the supporters on the touchline watching games. But in the summer he generally lay outside the entrance to the shelter, in the long grass of the hollow, with the sun beating down on to his face and the drone of bees buzzing around his motionless body.

'Now what are we all going to do this afternoon?' his mother was asking him. 'Have you got anything in any of the lovely exhibitions this year?'

Stephen shook his head. What he would like to have done is not go back to the school at all in the afternoon, but hang around the hotel until it was time to be dropped back at seven o'clock.

'What, nothing at all? Really, darling, you must have painted one good picture or something in the art room. You're good at art.'

Stephen shrugged.

'The art is so marvellous at Westleigh,' his mother was telling Edmondo. 'Some of the twelve-year-olds' paintings are almost professional.'

'Perhaps I should sign up some of the young artists for my gallery,' laughed Edmondo. 'You must point out the rising stars for me, Stephen. I am serious, to sign up a young Clemente or Schnabel now could be very profitable.' And then he laughed again in his shallow, flirtatious, Italian way and Stephen's mother laughed back, and Stephen looked at her thinking: *How can this terrible woman be my mother?*

When they arrived back, the school was already full of parents being dragged from exhibition to exhibition. Many of the classrooms had been turned into display areas for Airfix

Spitfires and Stukkas hung on lengths of cotton, or clay animals baked in the kiln, or collections of British and Commonwealth postage stamps. In each new room Serena Merton said to the master-in-charge, 'What a talented lot of boys you do have in your class!' And the master would look down at Stephen to see who this glamorous mother belonged to, and Stephen coloured with embarrassment because he knew the master was feeling sorry for him having such a terrible mother.

Half of Exhibition Saturday was held outdoors where the sculpture show and various demonstration sports like throwing-the-cricket-ball and fencing were going on. Outdoors was also where Orme and Scobie and Milne were most likely to be, and as he walked across the playing fields to see the fencing, Stephen was watchful. When he spotted Milne and Mr and Mrs Milne heading towards them, he tugged at his mother's arm, urging her towards the cricket pavilion in the opposite direction. And when matron loomed on the horizon with a tray of strawberries he wheeled them round and started walking faster and faster towards the school boundary.

When they reached the fence that separated the playing fields from the scrubland, Mrs Merton said, 'I don't think this looks very nice, Stevie. I think we should all head back to the school for some strawberries.'

But Stephen, seized by a sudden urge to show her his secret place, said, 'But you must come on for a few more minutes. I want you to see my camp.'

'I didn't know you had a camp,' said Mrs Merton.

'It's a secret. You've got to come, I made it with a few other boys.'

Stephen didn't say that nobody except he even knew about the air-raid shelter, because his mother liked to hear he had friends, it made her happy.

Edmondo held down the lower strand of barbed wire with his foot, and held up the top one so Serena could climb through. And then Edmondo and Stephen followed her, and Stephen led them across the broken scrubland, past the other overgrown air-raid shelters until they reached his one.

'Do you really play down there?' asked Serena Merton. 'It looks awfully dirty and claustrophobic to me.'

Stephen, looking at the hollow of flattened grass, briefly saw his refuge through his mother's eyes, and felt ashamed. And then he felt angry with her for making him feel ashamed, because it was she who had chosen to send him to Westleigh House.

'You've got to look inside,' said Stephen.

Serena Merton peered doubtfully at the gap between the wall and millstone. 'No, darling, not in my best clothes. I can't crawl in there, it's filthy dirty.'

'But you *must*,' implored Stephen. 'You both must. We've made it all nice inside, it's decorated and everything.'

Serena Merton still looked unconvinced, but Edmondo said, 'Come on, Serena, Stephen wants us to see his camp and we mustn't disappoint him.' Then he said to Stephen, 'This is very exciting, just like the cavemen, no?'

Edmondo went down on his hands and knees and crawled through the narrow crevice. Stephen watched the heels of his shoes disappear inside, and then his mother called, 'Is it all right in there?' and Edmondo replied, 'Perfectly, darling, just try not to touch the wall with your sleeve as you come in, that's all.'

Serena Merton crawled gingerly into the shelter. 'It's awfully dark in here,' she said as the curvy little heels of her purple suede pumps disappeared from sight.

'It is what you call cosy,' Stephen could hear Edmondo saying. 'I don't know what activities we could get up to together in here.'

'You, Edmondo, are quite incorrigible,' replied his mother, and then she laughed her annoying laugh, which through the distortion of the air-raid shelter sounded more terrible to Stephen than it ever had before. 'My incorrigible darling,' she repeated all lovey-dovey, and another ghastly, grating peal of laughter defiled his secret camp.

It took one kick to dislodge the metal railing and send the millstone rolling across the entrance. And he had only run a few yards from the shelter before his mother's muffled cries were entirely inaudible.

For the remainder of the afternoon Stephen felt absurdly lightheaded. On the school lawn he ate a bowl of strawberries, and when Milne and his parents came to say hello he hardly minded at all.

'Didn't I see your pretty mother earlier on?' asked Mr Milne.

'Yes,' replied Stephen. 'But she's gone back to London now with her boyfriend.'

And at seven o'clock Stephen went upstairs to his dormitory and changed into his pyjamas and leant on his elbows reading while the other boys got ready for bed. Just before the lights were turned off, Orme came back from the washroom carrying his toothbrush in an orange plastic toothmug.

'How's your Motoguzzi mother then, Merton?' he asked. 'Is she really coming to the Sports on her motorbike?'

Stephen shrugged, and turned over in his bed to face the wallpaper, for ever oblivious of the admiration in Orme's voice.

THE SPYING EYE

Not since the Cuban missile crisis has the world come so close to war as when the United States was caught red-handed spying on the People's Republic of North Korea. They claimed, of course, that their spy satellite, K-16, which crashed into the North Korean capital of Pyongyang killing sixteen hundred people, was a weather satellite, but nobody much believed them, and a motion of censure was carried at the United Nations by an unprecedently large majority. Even in the free nations of the West, you were hard pressed to find anyone to give America the benefit of the doubt. One man who could have done so was Gregg Cooper. But he was half a world away, doing a dull job in Western Australia, and was not in a position to give an opinion on anything at all.

Beyond the perimeter fence, Gregg could see the Broome to Port Hedland highway and then a sliver of sandy scrub and beyond that the sea. And rising from it in a massive arc, the biggest sky in Western Australia: cloudless nineteen days out of twenty, and translucent as oxygen, and boring as hell, which was why the boys at Cape Canaveral had chosen Broome from all the dozens of possible livelier sites in Western Australia, Gregg reckoned.

He had been station controller for three and a half years and it felt like fifteen.

'K-16 velocity and trajectory constant, Mr Cooper. Count-down to overflight one hour fifteen.'

'Thanks, Mel,' said Gregg lugubriously, as he did thirty-two times a shift, to Melanie, who watched the digital clock and counted the quarters. Aside from security at the gate, and the two foot patrol thugs whose route inside the compound was random, Gregg and Melanie were alone in the satellite tracking station, as they were every day between twelve hundred and twenty hundred hours, when Frank Kosta, Gregg's weasel-faced deputy, came on to the next shift.

From the control panel Gregg could see K-16 was on course for Fiji, which was the last receiving station before Broome. In sixty-five minutes she'd enter his airspace – though why they called it airspace when there wasn't any air, Gregg had never fathomed – and then he'd lock the satellite on beam from the giant white dish and track her for another sixty-five minutes before signing her over to the next receiving station on the American base in Singapore.

If there was a more routine job than his, Gregg Cooper couldn't think of it.

He was a tall, ambling man with lank ginger hair and a lank ginger moustache, and everything about him gave an impression of resignation. The sleeveless white shirt and white ducks of his uniform drooped, and were flecked with cigarette ash which he did not trouble to brush away. Much of his day he spent playing cards for matchsticks with Melanie, a pursuit from which neither derived much pleasure – their game was plodding, mechanical and served only to kill time – and the surface of his desk was littered with little broken matchheads. The remainder of his shift he sat by himself, worrying gently and ineffectually about the hairline crack on the ceiling of the office and the slight pain in his chest, and the hairline crack on the state of his marriage to Val, which seemed never to widen nor to bond from month to month, but remained a cause of unease and reproach.

Since her furtive launch into space three and a half long years earlier, sleek, sinister K-16 – the most expensive and sophisticated spy satellite the world had ever seen (or rather not seen, since its design and capability were concealed even from those senators who lobbied for its hundred-million-dollar funding) – had circled the planet a dozen times a day, in fixed orbit, so that as the earth turned on its axis K-16's course divided it into neat vertical segments like a grapefruit. And on the cusp of each segment was a receiving station which tracked the satellite's progress. (There were stations in Florida, Hawaii, Fiji, Manila and Singapore, a station in Antarctica and another in the Arctic, stations on the Turkish–Soviet border just north of Kars and at Basingstoke, England, and others on the island of Koje off South Korea, and at Karachi and Cairo and Frankfurt, and his own at Broome in Western Australia.) They were all identical in design, with their cluster of prefabricated cabins and white-painted dishes, thirty feet across, all individually capable of altering the height and even the course of K-16 if required.

What was thrilling about K-16 was her incredibly powerful magnifying telescopes. Gregg knew that they revolutionised spying. The images she beamed down from space – formed of pixels, a mass of tiny dots like newspaper photographs – were clear and detailed. Spy satellites were not, of course, anything new in themselves. Gregg Cooper had worked with K-16's three predecessors, K-13 to K-15, and seen the dark, blurry photographs they produced: so indistinct that you could scarcely distinguish a column of tanks from bank holiday traffic, or a convoy of nuclear warheads from an arcade of candy stores. But results from K-16, by all accounts, were dramatic. Each pixel, instead of representing a ten-foot square such as Sino-Soviet satellites still achieved, had been boosted to cover a single square centimetre. So as K-16 spun over Vladivostok, or Azerbaijan or Tehran, she beamed back black and white pictures in which you could clearly see two Soviet soldiers sharing a sly cigarette outside their barracks, or 'President Rafsanjani of Iran walking across his courtyard to the john', as Gregg's boss in Albany, Oregon, put it.

All this, however, so far as Gregg Cooper was concerned, was hearsay. The greatest of the several frustrations of his posting to Broome was that, with all the capability of K-16, nobody at all needed him to spy in Australasia. Of all the receiving stations, Broome excited the smallest curiosity in his bosses. Gregg knew from colleagues on station in Karachi and Koje that they received priority surveillance requests several times a week, in addition to routine monitoring of troop movements in Afghanistan and the naval shipyards in North Korea. But for Broome, indifference. The governments of Australia and New Zealand, if not technically allies, were considered broadly friendly to United States policy, and there was no pressing reason to spy on them. No threatening Soviet or Chinese naval manoeuvres took place within six hundred miles of the Australasian coast. So the gleaming decoder, which created photographs from the grid of light-sensitive dots from outer space, taunted Gregg in his idleness, and the computer that enabled him to alter the angle of K-16's telescope, or to drop her height through space for a clearer picture, had lain untouched since the post-launch trials. On several occasions Gregg had sought to excite his bosses with rumours of anti-nuclear demonstrations by environmental pressure groups in Auckland and suchlike, but every time their response was the same: they were unconvinced that they'd learn anything from satellite reconnaissance that couldn't be discovered by conventional intelligence gathering at ground level, or even from the local newspapers. So the Broome receiving station continued its humdrum tracking task, and prepared itself for K-16's overflight now little more than an hour ahead.

That day Gregg was even more morose than usual. At the weekend he and Val had been invited over to Frank and Ann Kosta's house for a steak and shrimp barbecue, and in the course of the evening Ann showed them all an aerial photograph of their house. Frank had asked a pilot mate of his to fly over the place, and the picture from a thousand feet gave a great view; the roof of the house, the roof of the garage, the fibreglass swimming pool, the patio where they were sitting right now, you could see it all. Val was impressed, and all the way home in the car she cajoled Gregg to get a similar one taken of their own house. 'It would make a lovely souvenir,' she said sarcastically, 'and if ever you're moved on to somewhere more exciting than Broome, it'd be something to remember it by.'

Val Cooper was as bored by Broome as her husband was, and she passed up no opportunity for self-pity. She was a small, vain woman who wore cork wedged sandals to disguise her lack of height, and too much make-up because she thought it gave her face character. When Gregg first met her she'd been living in Orlando, Florida, a town she loved to contrast with Broome for its sophistication and fine living. When Val Cooper described Orlando's nightlife and shopping malls, she made it sound like *fin-de-siècle* Paris.

The Coopers had no children and, with no job to go to, time weighed heavy for her. The idea of an aeroplane overflying the house, specially to take a picture of the roof, was exciting. 'Such a smart idea of Frank's,' she had said. 'Why don't we have fun like that?'

Then Gregg had a brainwave that was a lot more exciting than that. So ingenious was it that it banished his moroseness at once. If Val wanted a photograph, why didn't he fix her one from a hundred thousand feet courtesy of K-16? This was strictly against regulations, but who was to know? Only Mel was around, and he could send her off on some errand while he programmed the computer to focus the telescope and beam the pictures back to base. The whole operation would be over in five or ten minutes. He could print it out later when K-16 was well out of their area.

'K-16 velocity and trajectory constant, Mr Cooper. Fiji receiving station are handing over to Broome in fifteen minutes.'

'Thanks, Mel,' said Gregg.

To take a picture on an overflight was not a difficult business. All Gregg needed to do was log in the longitude and latitude of his house, which was easily obtained from computerised station ordnance, and K-16 did the rest. An hour later he asked Mel if she wouldn't mind taking the station wagon down to the gas station at the Sandfire Flat Roadhouse to fetch him some cigarettes, which he knew would occupy her for forty minutes, driving fast. Then, feeling excited and conspiratorial, he sat down at the computer and programmed it to print out his photograph. When the pixel dots unscrambled into a ten-by-eight-inch photograph, Gregg was well pleased with the result: their house and backyard and parking lot exactly filled the picture. The image was still a little blurred, which was to be expected from that height, but Gregg could see their metal drying frame behind the house with the laundry flapping gently out in the sun, and the long garden chairs on the lawn, and his car parked right in front of the garage doors.

It took Gregg Cooper another five seconds to remember that his car wasn't at home; it was parked outside the window, here in the research station car park.

Val must have invited a friend over to the house for the afternoon, he said to himself. He was glad she had some company for a change.

That evening, with the satellite photograph safely in his briefcase to surprise her, Gregg settled himself in one of the garden chairs. 'Good day, Val?' he asked.

'What do you think in Broome?' she said, rounding on him. 'In a town where I hardly know a living soul, stuck out here in this glorified truck stop. In the morning I did some household shopping at the general store where the goods are so terrible, and then I came home and carried in the brown bags, and fixed myself a sandwich, and haven't seen a human face until you came home. That was my day.'

'And you didn't ask some girlfriend over for coffee this afternoon?'

'No,' replied Val quickly, 'I was alone all afternoon.'

There was something about his wife's tone that made Gregg quit the subject at once, and keep the satellite photograph of the strange car firmly shut away in his briefcase.

The next afternoon, as soon as K-16 entered his airspace, Gregg Cooper sent Mel back to the gas station for more cigarettes. Then he ordered up a second photograph, and even as the picture began to form he could see the car was back in his driveway. Once again the image was a little foggy, so, on an impulse, he determined to make his surveillance more penetrating. He would drop K-16 a few thousand feet through space and snatch a larger, clearer picture.

This, Gregg knew, breached all regulations. No receiving station was permitted to lower K-16's orbit without authority. It was an expensive and dangerous procedure. Swooping the satellite involved firing her nuclear-powered rockets, and the lower it came, the greater the risk. This is because lower space has more air molecules, which bump and rasp against the fragile skin of the satellite like a light bulb inside a bag full of marbles. If this friction continues for too long K-16 could be thrown off her orbit or even break up.

But none of this deterred Gregg as he watched the altitude on the panel tumble by five, then ten thousand feet and he ordered up a third photograph, before boosting K-16 back up to her regular orbit.

The new photograph justified his risk. It was so pin-sharp that he could see the top of Val's head – she was sitting on a long garden chair – and, right alongside her, he was looking down on to the semi-bald patch of a man in his mid-forties.

There was something about the way the man was sitting, so intimate and relaxed, his legs stretched out in front of him, and one sandalled foot crossed over the other, that enraged Gregg. And glinting on the lawn next to the chair – this made Gregg angrier still – he was sure he could see a cool beer poured into one of his favourite highball glasses that were too good for everyday use.

He scanned the photograph obsessively for other clues. The car, he could now see, had a roofrack on it, but then dozens of cars in Western Australia had fixed roofracks for surfboards and scuba equipment. The aerial view didn't enable him to see the number plate, but he felt he'd seen quite enough already.

His first impulse was to storm home and confront Val with the compromising photograph. He was aware that his posting to Broome had deepened the level of gloom in his marriage, but it had never occurred to him that Val might take a lover. The idea made him rigid with jealousy. As he drove home along the great shimmering coastal highway, the brilliant blue sea appeared to Gregg to have an unnaturally hard glitter, and the fierce evening sun, which normally cheered him after his day inside the receiving station, irritated him with its brightness. There was nothing sinister in itself about his wife inviting a man to sit with her in the backyard. Val was guilty as hell – Gregg knew that – but he had to admit his evidence was circumstantial. He wanted harder evidence before confronting her, such as the man's name and exactly what they got up to together.

'Good day, Val?' he asked as casually as he could manage when he got home.

'Lonely,' replied Val, patting her hair. 'Are you so surprised in a town like Broome?'

The Coopers usually sat outside for a while when Gregg arrived home, and drank a beer or two together, before going indoors to the kitchen for supper. Gregg had never been more observant as he slumped into a garden chair – *the visitor's chair* – and scrutinised his wife for evidence of infidelity. Outwardly at least there was nothing to incriminate her. Her complaints about the boredom of Broome, her frustration with Gregg for failing to secure a new posting, her low opinion of the food and culture of Australians in general, were so routine that Gregg would ordinarily have switched off immediately had he not been monitoring her speech for tell-tale novelty. But when they went inside to eat, Gregg had a notion that the supper was more skimpy and tasteless than usual, as though Val had had less time to give to it than her long, empty day would suggest. As he ate the chumpburger and big green frozen peas on the plate in front of him, Gregg was comforted by the relentless orbit of K-16 – by now, he reckoned, somewhere over Hawaii – that would swoop low over Broome again the next afternoon. The existence of the sleek, white satellite, and his control over its orbit, gave him a feeling of almost godlike power. Through its telescope he could sit in perpetual judgement over the wickedness on earth. As a child, his grandmother had said to him, 'Clear away your toys, Gregg, Jesus doesn't like looking down into untidy bedrooms,' and Gregg had felt the all-seeing eyes of Christ on the back of his neck as he cleared his baseball bat and sneakers away into his closet. Now, with exactly the same precision as Jesus in the heavens, Gregg could look down into his own fallen backyard. He was omniscient.

As soon as K-16 next entered his control, Gregg sent Mel once again to the Sandfire Flat gas station. She looked at him strangely but drove off without comment. Then he dipped the satellite by ten thousand feet, and kept her in lower space with the camera programmed to beam photographs every three seconds. As the sequence began to emerge he saw the balding man was back on his lawn, glass of beer in hand, being entertained by his wife. Val was wearing her bikini. From space, it was still difficult to see the man's face, but Gregg was in no doubt about their intentions.

For eight consecutive pictures the two figures sat talking. Then the man got up, and crossed the lawn to Val's long chair, and lay down alongside her, and the couple began to caress and kiss each other. Gregg waited, godlike, in the silent receiving station for each new photograph to emerge. He laid them in time-dated sequence along the top of his desk: twelve aerial views of the heaving garden chairs, and only the progress of the man's hand along his wife's leg to prove the photographs were not identical. At any moment he expected him to turn his face towards the sun – to look him in the eye – but he didn't, and the half-familiar balding head remained buried in Val's bosom.

As photograph after photograph emerged inconclusively, Gregg's fury made him embark on a final, reckless course. There was nothing else for it but to drop K-16 by a further ten thousand feet. That surely would do it. The man's guilty face was only a simple reprogramming away. The altitude dial in front of him showed K-16 was now orbiting twenty thousand feet below her norm, and the moment he had his picture Gregg would boost her back up again.

And then, in such quick succession that they were almost simultaneous, several things happened. The machine produced a photograph so clear and compromised of Frank Kosta's weasel face that it resembled a 'Wanted' poster, and every light on the control panel flared up for an instant, and a dozen alarms activated themselves, and four telephones began to ring, and the open line to Albany, Oregon, made a noise like a siren that would blare louder and louder until it was answered. It took Gregg Cooper several seconds to realise that K-16 had fallen out of her orbit and was spinning uncontrollably through black space and the blue vault of heaven, and back into the imperfect atmosphere of the earth. And before he had worked out where the wreckage would fall, splinters of blackened aluminium fuselage were already embedding themselves over several square miles of Pyongyang.

LUCKY BEGGARS

'You can call me anything you like,' said John Partington, 'but you can't call me mean. Prudent, yes. Parsimonious if you must, but mean – never. Not when I take my whole family abroad every spring, which is no laughing matter, and I speak as a man in possession of five APEX return tickets from Gatwick to Colombo.'

I had noticed John Partington the minute he arrived at the hotel. His red, fleshy face looked extremely harassed as he backed his hire car into the hotel forecourt. His green herring-bone jacket was several pounds too heavy for Sri Lanka in July, and he sweated profusely. He was a bad driver. The more valiant the bell captain's semaphored instructions for backing and left-wheeling, the more irascible and inept John Partington became; when he searched for reverse, the gear refused to respond and locked in first; when he found reverse, the car stalled, and the three little Partington girls in the back moaned, 'Oh, Daddee,' and rolled their eyes facetiously.

Now we were in the Ocean Lounge, the long thatched cocktail bar overlooking Nilaveli Beach, where Partington at once identified me as a fellow Englishman and had no hesitation in introducing himself. 'Never have daughters,' he said, without first troubling to establish whether I had. 'Their expectations kill you. Three girls between six and eleven, and their standard of living is way above mine. Every year they want holidays abroad, and I don't just mean Crete or Corfu. It's got to be the Caribbean at the very least, somewhere with a twelve-hour flight and palm trees, so they can show off to their nasty little friends at school.' John Partington heaved his big, sloppy bottom on to a bar stool and called for two beers.

'Imported beer, mister?' asked the barman.

'Lord no, just the local rubbish. Heaven knows, I've got to draw the line somewhere. All right is it, Pilsner Three Crowns?' he asked me.

'Yes,' I said. 'It's made up in the hills near Kandy.'

But John Partington had no interest in brewing.

'Then, if you please, after I'd flown them all the way to Ceylon they're still not satisfied. The girls tell me three to a room is too many, and they ought to have a bedroom each. Have you ever heard of a six-year-old having her own twin-bedded bedroom? Neither have I. But their mother won't put her foot down, oh no, implies that it's Daddy being mean. So then I say, "OK, girls, we'll compromise," and I take three rooms — one for Muriel and myself, one for Samantha the oldest, one for the other two, Clare and Tara. But are they grateful? Oh no. All three girls want a bedroom for themselves, or they're jealous of the one who does, so blow me if Muriel hasn't agreed to share with Samantha, to make it fair, leaving me all on my own.'

Just then the three Partington girls skipped into the bar. Each had long fair hair parted in the middle, and wore denim hot-pants with white T-shirts. They had rather vain little faces, but were pink and clean and smelt strongly of lemon shampoo. 'Mummy sent us down here for a Coke,' said Samantha Partington. 'She's unpacking and says we're underfoot.'

'But you've only just had a Coke each, from the mini-bars in your rooms,' said John Partington.

'Oh, come on, Daddee, they're only two rupees, which is 5p in England.'

'That's not the point, it's the principle of the thing.'

'OK then, we'll buy them with our own pocket money. Where's our holiday money, Daddee? You said three pounds each, which is ninety rupees. Pay up, come on, pay up.'

The reason I was staying at Nilaveli was that I was waiting for a friend who was making a documentary in which I had a marginal advisory role. I had chosen the Ocean Hotel because it was cheap and virtually empty; the Tamil terrorist war, now in its eighth year had long ago deterred package tourists from this part of the island and the management had been obliged to lower their rates.

Trincomalee, the old Dutch seaport, was barely four miles from Nilaveli and considered a hotbed of insurgency, so I guessed this hotel would guarantee a bit of peace from tourists. I was right. I had been there for a week and made good progress with my report. I kept to a strict routine and there were few distractions; in the morning I worked on my balcony; at noon I swam two lengths of the swimming pool and ate a club sandwich; in the afternoon I slept; at four o'clock I resumed work for another hour, sorted my notes, and then swam in the sea. The current on the east coast of Sri Lanka is strong, with an unexpected undertow, so the exercise was bracing. In the evening I chatted to the barman about a trip he had made several years before to Enfield, and then I had dinner on my own. It was a solitary existence, but I did not much mind; I had come here to work and would meet up with the film crew in a few days. And yet I must have been bored, because I was oddly cheered by the arrival of the Partingtons. There was something reassuringly normal about John Partington and his billowing khaki shorts, loping along the beach with Muriel in her flowery cotton sundress, and the three Partington girls, immaculate in mini-bikinis, massaging coconut oil into each other's flat chests. From my balcony I had a view of the whole sweep of the beach and I studied them between paragraphs. There was not much to do and I was worried that their holiday was not being a success. John Partington had a defensive look about him. His daughters complained unceasingly.

'Why are there no pedalos, Daddee?'

'Because there aren't, that's why.'

'But *why*, Daddee? There were pedalos in St Lucia.'

'And in Tobago.'

'Can't you ask if there are pedalos on another beach, Daddee?'

'I already have actually, Samantha, and they've never heard of pedalos in Ceylon. Can't you swim instead?'

'Oh, Daddee, it's no fun just *swimming*, we need a lilo or a dinghy or something to swim *from*.'

'You must see the children's point,' said Muriel Partington. 'This isn't really a very suitable beach. There's a ridiculous shortage of umbrellas, and where on earth is that waiter who took our drinks order, it's been half an hour since I asked for a Campari and bitter lemon.'

I often found myself having lunch with them next to the pool; I sensed that John Partington valued my presence to keep the peace and forestall mutiny. Our lunches were humdrum and pleasant. He was a partner in one of the larger estate agents specialising in country properties, and they lived in an old malthouse somewhere outside Tunbridge Wells. Muriel was a dull conversationalist but an attentive mother; a rather ordinary woman who minded little where they went on holiday providing the beach mattresses were well upholstered. One morning I asked her, mischievously, whether she wasn't nervous to be holidaying in a war zone.

'A war zone? John, you never told me there was a war going on here.'

'There isn't really one, dear, just a little local disagreement, nothing to worry about.'

'I do hope not,' said Muriel Partington. 'I suppose I ought to read the newspapers more,' she explained, 'but I haven't the time, what with this lot to tidy up behind and the school run.'

At the far end of the beach – the Kuchchevili end where the fishermen dragged their boats on to the sand – there was a small enclave of native hawkers. These were barred by the hotel from entering the private beach, but the few residents wandered along in due course to inspect their wares. There were children selling king coconuts and sun hats made out of palm leaves, and foreign stamps glued to scraps of cardboard, and splinters of coral. But the principal trade was in shells: cowrie shells of every imaginable local variety, displayed on towels and bits of coconut matting. Some of the shells were very beautiful, with fierce labial teeth and strange dorsal spots of brown and aquamarine, though the prices they asked for them were ridiculous, and it would be foolish to make a purchase without first bartering. It amused me to walk along the beach to the enclave every evening after my swim. I was bargaining in a desultory way for a giant cowrie the size of a human fist; not because I particularly wanted it, or had any intention of displaying it once I got home, but it gave some purpose to my walks, and I was already pleased to have watched the price halve from seventy to thirty-five rupees. I had told the shell boy that I would buy his cowrie when it fell to twenty-five rupees and not before, though I knew I would be disappointed when the deal was eventually struck.

One evening, about four days after they arrived, I found the three Partington girls waiting for me when I emerged from my evening swim in the sea.

'Will you take us to the little shops?' asked Tara.

'Please do, please do,' said Clare.

'We want to look at the shells,' said Samantha, 'but Daddy won't take us. He says it's too far along the beach and he doesn't approve of buying things from beggars.'

'They're not beggars,' I said, 'though they are very poor. Of course I'll take you, but I warn you, you mustn't buy anything for the first price they suggest. You have to bargain in a country like Sri Lanka.'

We walked along the tide line, where the ripples broke over our bare toes, and I found myself warming to the Partington girls. If they were spoilt, they were also affectionate; Tara held my hand as we walked, and they chatted about nothing in a cheerful manner, sometimes running ahead to avoid the waves, sometimes stamping deep footprints in the wet sand and watching them dissolve under the next ripple.

'Are they *very* poor, these shell people?' asked Tara.

'Pretty poor,' I said.

'How poor?'

'I don't know exactly, but I doubt they earn more than five rupees a day.'

'*Five rupees?* But that's only about 12p. That's less than our holiday money,' said Samantha. 'How do they buy things?'

'Well, it's cheaper out here than in London, but I don't expect they buy much. No toys or anything.'

As we neared the end of the beach the hawkers began to hail us, sedulously commending their own display of shells with cat-calls and the sharp hissing sounds of Tamil tradesmen. The girls wandered from stall to stall, at first slightly nervously, then brazenly, inspecting the quality of each shell and holding it against their ear in the hope of hearing the sea. I saw then how the girls would be at forty; testing the quality of linen sheets between finger and thumb in department stores, and looking at new stockings against the light for any sign of an incipient snag. Sometimes Samantha would study a shell for a full five minutes, cradling it in her palm and tracing its brittle spine with her finger, before returning it to its place and moving along. It began to get late, and I felt some responsibility for returning the children to the hotel, but they were reluctant to leave.

'Just five more minutes, just five,' they cried. 'We've narrowed our choices down to only the final few.'

Now they weighed the deep red of one cowrie against the corkscrew strudel shape of another, carrying the shells from one stall to the next to compare them, all the time trailed by a crowd of competing vendors. At last they made their decision and asked me to tender for prices.

'Please, will you ask how much they are, we're not used to bargaining, but you are.'

So I bartered a little with the boys until I achieved what seemed reasonable terms, and we agreed to return the next evening with the money. Fifteen or twenty rupees, I think, was the price set.

I did not see the Partingtons again that evening, because they drove into Trincomalee for dinner. And the following morning, anxious to complete my report, I broke my routine and worked through lunch. When I went down to the beach at five o'clock I was in splendid form; I felt that I had wrapped it up rather succinctly and now I keenly looked forward to the arrival of the film crew. After dinner I would place a call to Air Lanka in Colombo and confirm their arrival time. Meanwhile I would reward myself with a long beer.

I saw at once that something was wrong with the Partingtons. They were festering gloomily under an umbrella. John Partington, tight-lipped, pretended to read Jeffrey Archer. Muriel looked pinched and upset. The girls were belligerent.

Tara, who appeared to have been crying, made vicious slashes in the sand with the heel of her foot. When they saw me, the girls got up and wandered despondently over.

'Daddy says we can't buy those shells,' said Samantha.

'Why's that?' I asked. 'I hope you haven't been naughty.'

'Oh no,' said Clare. 'He just won't let us buy anything from beggars.'

'Ah well,' I said, not quite knowing what to say, 'he's your father, and if he says no then it looks like no.'

'Can't you do something to persuade him?' asked Samantha. 'Go on, I know that if you spoke to him he'd change his mind.'

I did not relish the idea of interfering between father and daughters, but at the same time it seemed ridiculous that they should be denied the shells and that the native hawkers should be dismissed as beggars. Furthermore I felt some responsibility for the deal. Of course, I could easily go and buy the shells with my own money, it was a small amount, but that could be interpreted as a direct snub to John Partington – who might, I supposed, have some good, if obscure, other reason for refusing his daughters.

'I'll tell you what I'll do, girls,' I said at last. 'I'm going for a swim now, but later this evening I'll have a word with your father, and find out what it's all about, and if I am able to I'll try and change his mind. OK?'

'Oh, thank you,' said the girls, cheering up. 'Thank you very much, we knew you'd be on our side.'

That afternoon I went for a longer swim than usual. For the first hundred yards from the shore the water was shallow, and it was almost always possible to stand, but after that the sea bed fell rapidly away and the waves, which had rolled unbroken across the Bay of Bengal from Malaysia, broke with surprising force over your head. On the beach I could see John and Muriel, still huddled over their paperbacks, but the girls seemed ridiculously happy, in that way that children have of altering their mood in seconds, and were organising running races with handicaps based upon age divided by height. Clearly I must speak to John Partington. It was a task I would rather have avoided. There was a latent stubbornness about him, and it was possible that he would be angry with me for interfering. I resolved to broach the topic, not on the beach, but later that evening in the bar when he had put away a couple of local beers before the descent of his family. By the time I swam back to the beach the current had carried me several hundred yards towards the rocks; it was strenuous exercise, and I felt quite relieved to be back on dry land.

John Partington was in the Ocean Lounge on his usual bar stool. He had caught the sun, and the bridge of his large nose was peeling.

'Beer?' said John Partington. 'Barman, two beers – yes, yes, the local beer will do fine.'

I did not prevaricate. 'John,' I said, striking an intentionally pompous tone to soften him up, 'I hope you don't think I'm trespassing on your paternal prerogative, but I seem to have got myself embroiled with your daughters in buying some sea shells. Have they mentioned it to you?'

'They have indeed,' said John Partington, 'and I put my foot down straight away. And let me apologise to you, too, for their wasting your time. They'd no business to. I expressly forbade them to buy anything on the beach, and they flagrantly tried to disobey me.'

'Is there any particular reason,' I asked lamely, 'why they shouldn't buy a shell each? I don't mean to interfere, of course.'

'Yes, there is actually, a damn good reason. I don't mind how the children waste their money – *my* money – but I won't have them giving it away to beggars.'

'Since you mention it, these people aren't actually beggars,' I said. 'They're hawkers. They certainly don't beg for money. They have little stalls selling shells and coconuts. There's nothing reprehensible about it, I assure you.'

'Aha,' said John Partington, 'that's what you say. And you're not the first chap to be taken in by them either – no reflection on you at all, easily done. But you take it from me, the difference between these beach boys and beggars is the difference between Harare and Salisbury, Rhodesia: a simple question of semantics. If you want to identify a beggar, you apply two simple criteria. One, does this man pay income tax?

Beggars don't. And is the stuff this chap's selling worth what he's asking? If it's not, it's charity and you're dealing with a beggar. Now Samantha tells me that for one shell they want fifteen rupees. Well, that's fifty pence, ten shillings in the old money. For something you can pick up yourself on the beach. Now if that isn't begging, I don't know what is.'

'I take your point,' I said, 'but really fifteen rupees for a cowrie isn't extortionate. They're becoming quite rare in Sri Lanka. You only find them on the outlying islands, and most of those have to be dived for. In the hotel shop they're sixty rupees at least.'

'Then Samantha can buy one there. If she want to spend all her holiday money on a shell that's her lookout; I don't want to stop her learning from her mistakes. At least the hotel pays income tax and the whole thing's above board. I'm not an unreasonable man, but I've seen beggars all over the world, and a bigger bunch of scallywags you can't conceive: maiming themselves, amputating fingers, pretending they're blind when they're better sighted than you or I. I'll bet you've never met a blind beggar who can't see a bank note when it's offered to him. Oh yes,' went on John Partington, pausing only to draw deeply on his Pilsner. 'You ever heard the phrase "lucky beggars"? You want to see them in Pakistan. It's not unknown, when a beggar dies, for the family to order the largest headstone in the cemetery; thousands they've stashed away during their lifetime, and never a penny of it paid in tax. I've got a chum posted in Peshawar and he tells me all about it. Some of the beggars commute, you know, by aeroplane from one city to another, following the tourists. you'll see a poor chap one morning in Karachi and maybe give him a shilling for good luck, and in the afternoon you see him again in Quetta. It happens all the time.'

At this point the Partington women descended from their baths. Muriel was wearing a plastic nose shield, because she had caught the sun terribly, but tomorrow was reverting to protection factor eight with her Ambre Solaire. Samantha, Clare and Tara were smothered in soothing calamine lotion which stood out pink on their foreheads, but all their interest,

I could see, was in the outcome of my petition. My long face must have told the story. Samantha at once assumed a mealy scowl, and Tara butted the legs of a stool. I tried to exchange pleasantries with Muriel, but we made a sorry party. The girls said nothing and sucked noisily at their Cokes through straws. Their father seemed exhausted by his thesis on international beggary and stared into his beer. I wished that I had made some plan to eat out that evening, but without a car of my own I was trapped, and the prospect of joining the Partingtons for dinner – an awful certainty unless one of us could come up with an excuse – filled me with gloom.

But I had forgotten it was Thursday night: the hotel barbecue, a weekly treat conveniently coinciding with the waiters' night off. Instead of dinner in the dining room, tables had been shifted outside on to the verandah lit by candles in jam jars, and a discotheque set up in a kiosk so that guests could dance between courses. The swimming pool boy installed himself behind a charcoal grill, with platters of steak and half lobster, and the lunchtime barman, normally sober in a maroon jacket, was got up in a straw hat and was tinkering with the sound system. It was cool on the verandah, for there was a breeze from the beach that was whipping up the tops of the waves. The noise as they retreated was like a metal chain dragged across gravel. The weather would soon turn, for we were approaching the midsummer monsoon, and I was doubly pleased to be leaving the hotel in a day or two. And yet this change in the atmosphere enlivened our party. The children enjoyed queuing for lobster at the barbecue, and were delighted by the native band. 'But I still remember when we used to sit in the Government Square in Trenchtown,' sang the band leader, who had never left Trincomalee. John Partington relaxed and spoke of property prices on the island; for the cost of a medium-sized farm in Hertfordshire, he said, you could buy several villages in Sri Lanka, and coconut plantations large enough to support you for life. 'Quite a thought,' he said, prising the last morsel of lobster from a claw, 'with winters like ours.' Then he said, 'The good life,' and toasted me in Three Crowns lager.

At the end of dinner a collection was made for the band and

I noticed John Partington drop twenty rupees into the tambourine: not lavish, but more than he need have given.

'I'm glad you don't regard the band as beggars anyway,' I joked. 'Though I'm pretty sceptical whether they pay much tax.'

Partington laughed. 'You and your beggars,' he said. 'Damned if I know what you see in them.' Still chuckling, he said, 'Girls, I've got something to tell you, and if I were you I'd listen carefully. Your friend here, very much against my better judgement, has persuaded me to give your beggar friends a reprieve. Tomorrow afternoon I will come with you to see them, and will examine the shells myself. And if I'm satisfied that they're worth the exorbitant prices, then I'll allow you to buy one shell each. How does that sound?' The faces of the three Partington girls showed that it sounded very good indeed.

I did not accompany the expedition the following afternoon. I was waiting for a call that I'd placed to London, already delayed by several hours, and which I was loathe to miss. So I sat on my balcony and watched the Partingtons walk the length of the beach: John Partington striding purposefully ahead with the air of a man intent on springing his virgin daughter from a flat full of drug addicts; the girls skipping happily behind. At their approach I saw the hawkers rise to greet them, crawling out from their palm frond shelters and hunting for the çowries we'd reserved. I saw Tara run ahead to identify them, beckoning her father to admire the colours and the sharp teeth, and John Partington's dignified progress from stall to stall. At each one he halted – his stomach bulging above the leather belt of his shorts – leant forward to examine the shell, then moved on. It was difficult to tell how he was reacting, but I got the impression as the tour progressed that all was not well. There was an ominous tautness about John Partington's shoulders. He moved stiffly. I saw him gesture dismissively at one of the hawkers who was trailing behind him. And then Partington lost his temper. He stamped his foot angrily on the sand. He waved his arms about him. He shook his fist. He seemed to be explaining something of immense complexity, at the top of his voice, while the hawkers brandished starfish and cowries beneath his nose. The hawkers were delighted with Partington. They grinned from ear to ear. They made fabulous concessions. The cowries, already secured for twenty rupees, fell to ten. And still John Partington berated them, sometimes retreating a few yards in his fury, sometimes marching imperiously forward. His contempt for the hawkers was terrifying. He towered above them. It seemed likely that he would hit somebody, and I saw his daughters cower from his rage. And still the hawkers revelled in his anger; lowering the prices still further, committing their families to extended penury in their desire to close this sale. At last Partington could stand it no more. He turned on his heel and strode back along the beach. His daughters followed him in tears, the hawkers shouting final derisory offers. I had no doubt that, by this time, they would gladly have paid him to take their shells away. Even at such a distance the sweat glistened on Partington's forehead. The ankle socks he wore with his sandals made him look absurd. The girls sniffled at his heels, and he shooed them away. Then he removed his jacket and shirt, folded them carefully inside out and laid them on the beach, kicked off his sandals and socks and wandered into the sea.

It took a ridiculously long time to reach deep water. The shallow sea shelf meant that, even after a hundred yards, Partington was only submerged to his calves, and the hawkers took it as an elaborate bargaining posture. Fearful of the sea themselves they did not follow him, but ran along the beach, cowries borne aloft, awaiting his return. Partington snarled furiously and shook his fist. The hawkers waved happily back; never had they met such a man as this. At last the sea was deep enough for Partington to submerge. He swam towards the hotel with measured breaststrokes. The hawkers kept pace with him on the sand. To outwit them, Partington turned and swam in the opposite direction. The hawkers followed suit. Even from the balcony I sensed Partington's frustration. He headed further out to sea pretending to ignore them, but still they kept parallel, clacking the shells together like castanets. And all the time Partington swam deeper into the strait.

Only gradually did it occur to me that he was no longer in

control. The waves were so strong that it was difficult to focus on him, or to tell in which direction he was heading. Only every half-minute did his head bob above the waves, and he shook his arms vigorously. The hawkers waved benignly back. By the time I realised he was drowning it was already too late.

I raced down to the beach and into the sea. There was no sign of Partington and it was difficult to know where to begin. The undertow was considerable and dragged strongly towards the rocks. There was no prospect of rescuing him. Eventually I returned to the beach.

The hawkers were waiting for me. Their faces registered neither panic nor concern. It was not even clear whether they realised Partington had drowned. As I stumbled out of the shallows they beckoned me, and I saw my giant cowrie being dusted of sand.

'King cowrie, mister,' shouted my friend from the enclave. 'King cowrie. Best price, friend price: twenty-five rupees.'

A Selected List of Fiction Available from Mandarin

While every effort is made to keep prices low, it is sometimes necessary to increase prices at short notice. Mandarin Paperbacks reserves the right to show new retail prices on covers which may differ from those previously advertised in the text or elsewhere.

The prices shown below were correct at the time of going to press.

☐ 7493 0576 2	**Tandia**		Bryce Courtenay	£4.99
☐ 7493 0122 8	**Power of One**		Bryce Courtenay	£4.99
☐ 7493 0581 9	**Daddy's Girls**		Zoe Fairbairns	£4.99
☐ 7493 0942 3	**Silence of the Lambs**		Thomas Harris	£4.99
☐ 7493 0530 4	**Armalite Maiden**		Jonathan Kebbe	£4.99
☐ 7493 0134 1	**To Kill a Mockingbird**		Harper Lee	£3.99
☐ 7493 1017 0	**War in 2020**		Ralph Peters	£4.99
☐ 7493 0946 6	**Godfather**		Mario Puzo	£4.99
☐ 7493 0381 6	**Loves & Journeys of Revolving Jones**		Leslie Thomas	£4.99
☐ 7493 0381 6	**Rush**		Kim Wozencraft	£4.99

All these books are available at your bookshop or newsagent, or can be ordered direct from the publisher. Just tick the titles you want and fill in the form below.

Mandarin Paperbacks, Cash Sales Department, PO Box 11, Falmouth, Cornwall TR10 9EN.

Please send cheque or postal order, no currency, for purchase price quoted and allow the following for postage and packing:

UK including BFPO
£1.00 for the first book, 50p for the second and 30p for each additional book ordered to a maximum charge of £3.00.

Overseas including Eire
£2 for the first book, £1.00 for the second and 50p for each additional book thereafter.

NAME (Block letters) ....

ADDRESS...

....

☐ I enclose my remittance for ....

☐ I wish to pay by Access/Visa Card Number ☐☐☐☐☐☐☐☐☐☐☐☐☐☐☐☐

Expiry Date ☐☐☐☐